PORPHYRIA

ANTHONY ERGO

Copyright © 2017 by Anthony Ergo

All rights reserved. No part of this publication may be reproduced, distributed, or transmitted in any form or by any means, including photocopying, recording, or other electronic or mechanical methods, without the prior written permission of the author, except in the case of brief quotations embodied in critical reviews and certain other non-commercial uses permitted by copyright law.

Distributed by Lone Robot Books.

Printed in the United Kingdom.

Find Anthony Ergo on Twitter and Instagram @AnthonyErgo

www.AnthonyErgo.com

Prologue

Three Years Earlier

Ashleigh Hunter

Blake stands tall at the helm as he steers the boat across a rough midday sea. We chartered a vessel at the docks of Salem Sound and are now headed to the site of our current investigation, a place known as Misery Island. I'm one of only two passengers on board – the other person met us at the airport when we landed in Boston a few hours ago. My eyes catch hers as I glance across the boat, and she smiles at me. When I was introduced to the young woman with the dyed-red hair she told me her name was Katalina.

The cold wind and sea spray forces me to zip my jacket up to my chin and thrust my hands into my pockets. I feel for the comfort of my Athame and frown when I remember that it's not there. Blake told me to leave it at The Agency headquarters, suggesting that it would be difficult to get it through customs. *You won't need it anyway*, he reassured me. I've always felt exposed without my Athame and I dearly wish I had it with me now. Instead, I reach for the pendant which hangs from a chain around my neck. The opal gem is my daughter's birthstone and I kiss it for luck before tucking it away.

The bow of the boat slides onto the beach and Blake leaps out, his expensive leather shoes crunching on the shale. He always seems inappropriately dressed for field visits, like style is more important than function to him. When I compare him to Lou, I can't believe that I ever had a thing for him. It was a long time ago and our relationship is strictly business now, much to his apparent regret. I sometimes wonder if he'll ever move on from what was the briefest of romances.

Blake offers his hand, first to Katalina and then to me. I disregard his gesture and jump out of the boat with ease.

'So are you finally going to tell me what we're doing here?' I ask him impatiently.

'All in good time,' he replies. 'Soon enough, you'll know everything.'

Blake seems to revel in his position of power, and I don't like it. It's a mystery why he asked me to join him on this assignment. For some reason, he insisted that the details remain a secret until we arrived on location. I thought the whole point of The Agency's international network was to have local Agents for investigations such as this. I can't understand why he needs *me* in particular to be here. Surely it's got nothing to do with our fleeting romance. We were both much younger, not long after our graduation and barely out of our teens. Besides, I've moved on and married while Blake has climbed the career ladder.

Curiosity nags persistently at the back of my mind: Why me? Why here? Strangely, Katalina hasn't once asked what we're doing at this place. This can only mean one of two things: either she doesn't care, or she already knows.

I follow Blake as he guides us along a forest trail towards the heart of the island. It's a beautiful place, the lush greens of trees and shrubbery providing a pleasant contrast to the miles of cloudless blue sky. It feels more like a holiday resort than its name suggests and I know that Lou and Sasha would love it here. Blake marches ahead, using a cane to push himself up the mild slope. Katalina treks alongside me, matching my steps stride for stride. Since we were first introduced to each other we've hardly exchanged words. I decide to make some polite conversation in an effort to break the iciness.

'Director Blake told me that you're an Agent based in Romania.'

'That's correct,' she replies, surprising me with her perfect English.

I lower my voice a little, trying to keep the conversation out of Blake's earshot.

'All this seems a little unusual, don't you think?' She stares straight ahead but her eyes narrow ever so slightly. 'Why are two British Agents and a Romanian Agent on an assignment in America?'

Katalina rolls her eyes sideways without turning to face me.

'I'm sure it will all make perfect sense, Agent Hunter.'

If find it interesting the way she kills the conversation. Nobody can be that relaxed, unless she's safe in the knowledge of something. With every step I become more suspicious and feel less comfortable about being here.

We eventually arrive at a clearing in the midst of the forest where several cabins are clustered around the wood's edge. A stone well sits in the middle of the abandoned structures, its wooden water bucket cast aside on the ground.

'We're here,' announces Blake, stretching his arms out wide and turning in a slow circle.

If he expects me to be impressed, I'm not.

'Good,' I reply, with my eyes fixed on the fiery well. 'Now how about you talk me through this assignment?'

'Of course, allow me to educate you.' He really does have a natural ability to patronise sometimes. 'You must be intrigued as to why you're here with me. It's quite simple, really. I need the special skills you possess, Ashleigh.'

I don't like it when he uses my first name. Blake pauses for dramatic effect, planting the spike of his cane into the earth so it remains standing upright on its own. His air of mystery is beginning to grate on me.

'I've come a long way and left my family for this,' I mutter in a mixture of irritation and edginess. 'I'd appreciate it if you could get to the point.'

Blake casts a glance to Katalina before clearing his throat to speak.

'This place is an ancient ritual site which belongs to a coven of Black Witches.'

His last two words send a shock wave through my system. A Black Witch is about as dangerous as it gets. A whole coven of them is a nightmare. I wasn't ready for his revelation.

'You can't be serious.'

I take several paces back, and that's when I notice the five-pointed pentagram – the emblem of the Witch – carved into the ground around the well. My eyes focus on the squat brick structure: the well appears to be on fire, with an orange glow illuminating the interior brickwork and sparks flying from the opening.

'I'm afraid so,' replies Blake in a coldly casual way. 'The Hatchet sisters are native to this area but over the last few decades their coven has become depleted.'

Either he doesn't understand the danger, or he doesn't care.

'We can't handle this on our own, Blake. We have to go.'

He tilts his head and smiles.

'I'm afraid you've misunderstood me. You see, I have assisted the coven in replenishing their numbers. I need one more witch. *I need you*, Ashleigh.'

His words are hard to digest in the few seconds that I have at my disposal. It seems impossible that Blake could have turned to the darker side of the paranormal underworld: from leader of The Agency to orchestrator of the undead. The fact that he has stopped referring to me by my Agent title seems to support this theory.

'But . . . you wouldn't have brought me here without my Athame if that was the case.'

He smiles in a way that is anything but reassuring.

'I'm sorry, Ashleigh, but I couldn't risk you getting all *defensive*.'

I can sense that Katalina has positioned herself behind me.

'You know I won't help you,' I retort, peering warily over my shoulder.

Blake walks in a slow circle around the circumference of the stone well, warming his hands over the fire that burns below.

'Are you rejecting me, *again*? Surely you know that my ambition is greater than this Agency. I am a Necromancer and my abilities are wasted in simply banishing paranormal entities. My entire life has been dominated by one question: if I can control a single spirit, can I control an entire horde of them?'

My horror at his words is only eclipsed by the twelve women that appear from the doors of the wooden cabins. Some are in their early youth while others are old and decrepit. All of them have one thing in common: the distinctive foul stench of a Black Witch.

As I scan the faces, I recognise two of the younger Witches from my research: the Hatchet sisters, Eliza and Romona. It's no coincidence that Blake brought me here on this day. Today is Friday the Thirteenth: a date of heightened powers within the spirit world.

'Behold the most powerful congregation of Black Witches in centuries,' he announces with a misplaced sense of pride. 'I have summoned them here from all over the world, including the revered Elder Witch.'

The oldest woman steps forward, her wrinkled face shadowed by a hooded cloak. I fix on her grinning expression, my mind jolting back ten years. The last time I came into contact with the Elder Witch was back in England, during an assignment to locate her. Even then I knew of her sickening legend: she harnesses her powers by stealing the souls of children. When she confronted Sasha, somehow my three-year-old daughter managed to resist the most powerful of all Black Witches. I suddenly feel thankful for the thousands of miles that separate this wretched creature from my family.

'We are one Witch short of a full coven,' continues Blake, a hungry glee in his eyes. '*Now* do you understand why you're here, Ashleigh?'

I shake my head slowly, as disgusted by his betrayal as I am at the monsters encircling me.

'You want to form a Gathering,' I say numbly as the horrendous realisation sets in. 'Surely you must know that I'll never—'

A digitised tune interrupts my words. The Elder Witch tilts her head at the sound of my mobile phone ringing out. I pull it out of my pocket slowly as Blake and Katalina take a step towards me.

'Lou,' I say, reading the name on the caller display.

Blake pushes his lip out, more amused than fazed.

'Then answer it,' he says. 'Tell him everything is fine, and be convincing. I anticipated your refusal to participate and you should know that Ludvig is waiting on standby in London. If you fail to comply, you know very well what will happen to your husband and daughter.'

I look down at the screen of my mobile and at the face of my husband above his number. A lump forms in my throat when I accept what I must do in order to keep him and Sasha safe.

It must end here.

I answer the call and lift the mobile to my ear with a trembling hand.

'Hi, Lou.' I try my best to hide my anguish. 'Sorry that I didn't call you when I landed.'

'That's okay, love.' His voice is warm and close. 'I'm just glad you arrived safely.'

Tears form in the corner of my eyes and I try to blink them away. My brain can't rationalise this most normal of conversations with the vision before me. Blake puts his index fingers in the side of his mouth and forces it up into a false smile, encouraging me to play along.

'I'm with Blake now,' I say, forcing the words out. 'We're about to commence our assignment.'

My eyes move from Blake to the Elder Witch, her wispy grey hair framing a face of pure evil. Her ashen lips curl back to form a grin, revealing a set of crooked, yellow teeth.

'Just be careful, Ashleigh,' says Lou. 'I don't want you to take any risks.'

I only wish that we didn't have the barrier of such distance so he could use his Clairist senses to feel my emotions.

The Black Witches move in closer, joining Blake and Katalina hand in hand to form a closed circle around me. They begin a low chant, spoken in Latin. The fire in the well starts to grow as though stoked by an invisible force.

'Don't worry, Lou,' I tell him. 'Blake has explained everything. I know what I need to do.'

Lou pleaded with me to refuse the assignment and not to go with Blake to America. He was right.

'I never wanted you to do this in the first place,' he says. 'You'll call me as soon as it's done, right? Sasha misses you—'

His voice trails off as I pull the mobile away from my ear. In one rapid movement, I lunge forward and hammer my phone into the face of the Elder Witch. Shards of glass and plastic fall to the ground as the mobile shatters. The Witch howls as she staggers backward, clutching her bloodied eyes.

I know that I have only a matter of seconds left to act. If I can destroy the Elder Witch, I can break the power of the coven and prevent a Gathering from forming.

An arm wraps around me and a strand of red hair rests on my shoulder. Katalina is inhumanly strong and I immediately understand her presence: she's not an Agent, *she's an entity*. I shift to one side and thrust my elbow powerfully into her stomach, forcing her to release her grip. I can't hope to defeat all twelve Black Witches but I know that I can take at least one out, even without my Athame.

Charging forward, I grab Blake's cane and pull it from the ground. The Elder Witch staggers blindly near the well, her hands clawing desperately at her eyes. I take advantage of her vulnerability and thrust the cane into the centre of her chest. The force of the blow sends her reeling backwards, toppling over the edge of the well and into the fiery pit below. Eliza dashes to the edge of the stone wall, thrusting her arm over the side to try and save her leader. She lets out an agonising scream as she retracts her right hand. I wince at the sight of her fingers, stripped of their skin from the intensity of the heat. Eliza pulls out a large knife and rests her charred hand against the turret of the well. I watch in horror as she cuts off the remains of her mangled hand.

A chorus of screams ring out through the forest as the coven react to the destruction of the most powerful of their kind. Suddenly, a column of black flames shoots from the well and into the sky. It's like nothing I've ever witnessed before. Daytime turns to night as blackness descends on the world in an instant. The screams continue, and in the chaos of the darkness, I make my escape.

Scrambling on all fours, I brush past the young Witch girl clutching a cloth doll. Without any clear sense of direction my only thought is to get as far away as I can.

Find a way back to the boat.

Get away from here.
Survive to expose Blake for what he is.
Make it home.

'Stop her!' roars Blake, his voice barely audible above the howls and shrieks.

I feel thorns cut into my legs and nettles stinging my hands as I desperately palm my way through the undergrowth. When I look back, I notice that the column of purple-black flames has started to retract. As it slips back inside the well, daylight returns once more. The effect of casting the Elder Witch into the fire seems to have created some kind of supernatural chain-reaction. For a matter of seconds, the power of the underworld broke through and consumed the sky. Whatever happened, it was better than what could have occurred had The Gathering succeeded.

As I turn to run, Katalina is standing in my path.

'You just destroyed the Elder Witch,' she says with a tut. 'That wasn't a wise thing to do.'

Before I can react, the knuckles of her fist connect with my temple and I collapse to the ground. Black dots cluster around the edge of my vision. In my semi-conscious state I hear footsteps approach.

'She just annihilated my Gathering,' says Blake. I feel the air pushed from my body as his leather shoe connects with my ribs. 'This was years in the planning. Ashleigh Hunter was meant to be the thirteenth Witch!'

'Do you want me to dispose of her?' asks Katalina.

'Not yet,' replies Blake. 'Take her with you while I decide our next course of action.'

I can't move, but if I could, I'd smile.

My vision goes first, and their words trail off as I sink closer to unconsciousness. My last thought is of my daughter. I only hope that my actions have kept Sasha safe.

Chapter 1

Present Day

Sasha

I wake up screaming his name.

Dad.

For three consecutive nights I've experienced the recurring nightmare of watching my father die in my arms. I lift my hand to wipe away the tears and notice that I'm still clutching his handkerchief. Our initials are embroidered next to each other, the bottom of my 'S' intertwining with his 'L'. For years we were so distant but I'm grateful to have at least grown closer in the weeks leading up to his death.

His murder.

I pull back the covers of my bed which are soaked through with sweat. The air is cool inside the third floor London office that has become our temporary home. It calms me as I recover from the bad dreams that haunt me each night. Whenever I think of my father, the next thought that follows is always her.

Katalina.

My eyes burn crimson as I recall how she destroyed The Agency by torching the mansion and killing every Agent there, including my father. If it wasn't for Zara's intervention at the Tower of London, she'd have killed me too. While Kat's betrayal shattered my trust, my father carefully glued those pieces back together in the months that followed. I try not to dwell on the fact that she posed as our housekeeper and my friend following the disappearance of my mother.

Mum.

She's been missing from my life since my thirteenth birthday, on Dystopia Day. For years I knew nothing about her fate. Menzies Blake revealed only a partial truth of what happened; how she sacrificed herself to prevent a Gathering of paranormal entities. It was Aaron's recent discovery that provided the biggest revelation about her. *My mother's life didn't end on Dystopia Day.* Her Agency ID card was found at Kat's ancestral castle in Romania, providing enough evidence to give me a glimmer of hope. With the knowledge of her existence, my grief has been replaced by a desire to find her. If Katalina has harmed a hair on her head, I'll make her pay.

As I lie in bed, summoning the energy to get up, my mobile vibrates and flashes. It's an email from Dexter. Several months have passed since I left him in America but I'm still grateful for his help at The Academy. The fact that he's the son of Menzies Blake no longer matters. He's a good friend and someone I can trust. We've kept in touch and it always cheers me up to hear from him.

I open his email and begin to read.

Hey there Badass,

I've got some good news. Axel has fully recovered and we're about to board a plane to London. It took me a while to find someone who could provide a fake ID. It cost me a fortune! I'm hoping that it will all prove to be time and money well spent. I want to visit my father and make my peace with him. I was wondering if you guys had enough floor space for a hippy and his dog?

I hope you're coping okay. You seemed pretty down in your last email. Say hi to Gym-boy and Blondie from me.
Dexter

His words leap out of the screen and make me smile. I'm glad that I confided in Dexter over the loss of my father. I knew he'd be able to relate to what I'm going through, having lost his own mother not long before joining The Academy. It's been easier for me to write my feelings down in an email than voice them out loud. Dexter seems to understand my rambling essays and I'm looking forward to seeing him again. We have a connection which is closer than friendship without threatening to be anything more; he's like family to me. I'm sure Zara and Aaron will have no problem with him crashing over after everything he did for us.

I hear a gentle knock on the door. Aaron enters what has become my make-shift bedroom. His hair is wet and he's shirtless, with a towel draped around his neck. I'm not sure I'll ever get used to seeing his bare, muscled chest, even though we live in such close proximity these days. It's a welcome distraction from the constant heaviness within me.

I blush and he smiles, handing me a mug as he perches on the side of the bed.

'Drink up,' he says, guiding the cup to my lips. 'It will make you feel better.'

I taste the strong coffee which has an overwhelming sweetness.

'Zara made it,' he chuckles. 'A bit sugary, huh?'

I smile, briefly. None of my smiles ever seem to last long these days. I place the cup on my bedside table, alongside the Athame. My fingers stroke its blunt edge as my mind wanders to my mother. It fascinates me to think about how she would have used it when it belonged to her. I wish I had inherited her White Witch powers. I shove the Athame in a drawer when I realise that Aaron is silently observing me, drawing out my emotions.

'You know, I don't think any less of you . . .'

I turn my head so that he won't say the rest out loud. The result of The Academy test, which confirmed that I have no inherited powers, was devastating news to me. Aaron and Zara were just as shocked when I told them. I thought they'd be angry or disappointed, but it was quite the opposite. If anything, Aaron was even more impressed by how I'd graduated as an Agent and defeated the Hatchet sisters. Zara insists that there's something unique about me which I'm yet to truly discover. It was nice of her to say so, even if I can't bring myself to believe it. Grief hasn't allowed me the room to consider much else, lately.

My eyes fall from Aaron's face and onto his shoulder, resting on his gunshot wound. I'll never forget the time he took a bullet for me when we barely knew each other. It's the only blemish on his perfectly sculpted body. I reach out, tracing my finger over the scar.

'It doesn't hurt anymore,' he mumbles softly, watching my fingers caress his skin. 'All wounds heal with time.'

I want to believe his words. My wounds are all inside and my scars can't be seen, yet I know they'll exist forever. I move closer towards Aaron, allowing his Empath senses to feel the full force of my emotions. He places his warm hand on mine.

'I once read that when you break a bone it repairs stronger,' he says. 'Just like scarred skin becomes thicker. Scars are good; they show that we're stronger than the thing that tried to hurt us.'

'I like that theory,' I reply, hoping that it applies to mental as well as physical wounds.

I could never have got through the last few months without the support of Aaron. He always knows what to say or do to make me feel better.

'I've got something for you.' He produces a small, square package from his back pocket which is crudely wrapped with brown paper and sticky tape. 'Sorry about the wrapping.'

I smile as I take it from his outstretched hand and carefully open it.

'I salvaged it from your bedroom at The Agency mansion,' he explains. 'It was badly damaged in the fire, but I managed to have it restored and reframed.'

I look down at the photograph of my mother and father, taken before I was born. Holding it to my chest, I bite my lip to keep myself from crying.

'Thank you. It . . . means a lot.'

My voice is thick with emotion, choking me up so that my words struggle to come out. He places his hand on the side of my cheek, wiping away a tear before it's able to form fully.

'I miss your father too, Sasha. He was like the father I never had.'

We sit in silence, drawing comfort from each other's presence.

A knock on the door brings us back to the cold reality of our office-turned-apartment. Zara appears, leaning halfway into the room.

'You should both come out when you're ready,' she says. 'Someone is here to see us.'

She disappears before I'm able to ask who it could possibly be.

'A visitor?' says Aaron, pushing his bottom lip out. 'At this time of day? I need to get dressed!'

He squeezes my hand and then quickly slips out of the room.

A visitor. Since we moved into this office space we've not had a single person drop by. The three of us share the common misfortune of decimated families and our bond is all the stronger for it. I place the photograph on my bedside table, resting my father's handkerchief over the corner of the frame. I'm touched by Aaron's thoughtful gift; it's worth more to me than anything money could ever buy.

I pull on one of Aaron's sweatshirts and tie my hair back into a hurried pony-tail. My bare feet are stung by the cold, tiled floor as

I dash from my room to the main office area. I find Aaron and Zara talking to a large man wearing an overcoat and a trilby hat. He turns to face me, removing his hat to reveal a bald head and a black beard.

'Hello, Sasha,' says Edgar Levi. 'It's good to see you again. I'm so sorry for your loss.'

He makes a small bow and lifts my hand into his paw-like grip. I make an awkward smile to acknowledge him. Something tells me he hasn't come all this way just to offer his sympathies.

'Please join us,' he says, inviting me to sit. 'I have some important news for all of you.'

I look to Zara, the one person whose judgement I trust above all others. Edgar's early visit must have surprised her as she's still dressed in her gym-wear. The dark scratch-marks from her duel with Kat are visible across the tops of her arms. When she meets my eyes and nods, she's able to reassure me without uttering a single word.

Edgar loosens the scarf which is all but hidden beneath his thick beard.

'I have just returned from The Agency's international headquarters in Geneva. Your unauthorised assignment in America was one of the topics discussed. The last time we allowed Agents to work abroad freely, it resulted in the Dystopia Day blackout. Your covert operation was in direct contravention of The Agency's rules.'

I share a worried glance with Aaron.

'You can relax,' says Edgar, rolling an unlit cigar between his chunky fingers. 'I managed to convince the leaders of the merits of your work. In fact, they accepted my recommendation that Agent Gordon be installed as leader of the UK Agency.'

If Zara is pleased with the promotion, you'd never be able to tell. Her eyes remain stoic beneath her designer glasses. Maybe it's because she's taking over the job of my deceased father. My *murdered* father.

Edgar twists in his seat to face her.

'Congratulations Agent Gordon. You are now responsible for rebuilding The Agency here in the UK. In time, we will recruit more Agents. I have also transferred funds into your account so that you can upgrade your premises. You'll have everything you need to move things forward.'

Everything except my father.

'That's pretty cool,' says Aaron. 'At last we can get out of this cold, dingy place.'

Zara looks less than excited by the prospect.

'We didn't plan on staying here much longer anyway,' she says. 'I have some unfinished business abroad that I need to see to.'

Edgar holds up a hand, stopping her in her tracks.

'I am fully aware of the situation with the Metamorph and how it has affected each of you. However, The Agency leaders have revoked your travel access with immediate effect. You are all forbidden from pursuing Katalina. Simply put, The Agency cannot risk losing any more Agents.'

I watch as Zara bites her lip and intertwines her fingers over her kneecap, clenching them together so tightly that her knuckles turn white. I know her well enough to realise that she won't take kindly to being told what to do, especially when it's something she feels so strongly about. For the last few months I've observed Zara while she researched, planned and prepared her act of vengeance. Promoting Zara was a clever move by Edgar; he has put her in a position of responsibility and to go against him would be career-suicide.

'There's one more thing you should all know,' continues Edgar, standing up and fastening the buttons of his coat. 'The Agency leadership has decided on a new approach for recruiting Agents. Extreme times require extreme measures. We will now use sentient paranormal entities to combat hostile targets such as Metamorphs.'

I have to repeat his words in my head to try and make sense of them.

'No way!' says Aaron, jumping to his feet. 'Are you seriously suggesting that we work alongside the very things we've been trained to destroy?'

If Edgar's words made little sense, Aaron's reaction is crystal clear.

'The world is changing, Agent Hart,' replies Edgar coolly. 'One Metamorph single-handedly destroyed an entire branch of The Agency. We can no longer rely on the rare abilities of humans alone. The threat level has increased and so must our response.'

'It would have been nice to have been consulted,' says Zara. 'Considering my more senior position.'

Edgar smiles, acknowledging her valid point.

'And so you shall be, moving forwards. But I'm afraid this decision has already been made, and it is final.'

The thought of working alongside paranormal beings is a grim prospect. I struggle to imagine supernatural Agents working against other entities for the good of human society. When Kat burned down the mansion, she didn't completely destroy The Agency but she may well have changed the face of it.

Edgar dons his trilby hat and strides towards the door, leaving Aaron stunned and motionless. Zara remains composed enough to see him out, shaking Edgar's hand as he leaves.

'I trust we can rely on your cooperation, Agent Gordon?'

'Of course,' she replies. 'It's a promise.'

When Edgar leaves and the door is closed, Zara removes a bent arm from behind her back. She holds up her crossed fingers for us all to see.

'The Agency can shove my promotion where the sun doesn't shine,' she says defiantly. 'Tomorrow, I leave for Romania.'

'Hey, slow down a minute,' says Aaron, sensing her rising fury. 'I know we've all been thinking about this but are you sure we're ready?'

'Ready or not, it no longer matters,' replies Zara. 'We're out of time. I need to make arrangements fast, before The Agency locks us down completely. I want you two to take care of things here while I'm gone.'

Aaron scoffs at her request.

'Not a chance. You might be our new boss but that's one order I refuse to accept. If you're going, then so are we.'

He looks to me for support, although he needn't have. For the last three months we've each harboured the sole motivation to exact revenge on Katalina.

'How will we locate Kat without access to The Agency resources?' I ask.

'We'll find her,' says Zara confidently. 'There is someone who knows exactly where the Metamorph is located . . . Menzies Blake.'

I'm immediately repulsed by the thought of having to deal with him. When he was taken away from The Tower of London and remanded in the local mental hospital, I felt like a weight was lifted from me. Now that same weight has come crashing back down. I want there to be another way of tracking down Kat but he is the only living connection to her.

'Blake a complete loony,' says Aaron, twisting a finger at his temple. 'Even if we could get any sense out of him, how on earth do we get inside Cane Hill Asylum?'

The room falls silent as our plan hits the biggest of hurdles.

'They only allow immediate family to visit,' says Zara. 'Maybe I could get to him under the guise of visiting my mother? It will be tricky, but it's our only option.'

I toy with my mobile, my eyes settling on Dexter's email which remains on the screen.

'I know someone who can help us gain access to Blake.'

Chapter 2

Sasha

Despite the decline in international travel since Dystopia Day, London Heathrow remains one of the busiest airports in the world. Dexter told me to wait for him in the arrivals lounge but I'm far from confident that we'll find each other easily. I check my mobile for the twentieth time, hoping for a text message or email to pop up. His flight from Washington landed almost an hour ago and I'm starting to feel anxious, particularly as he travelled using fake identification. I try to reassure myself that security delays are perfectly normal these days. It doesn't help that Dexter is a fugitive who is wanted by Edgar Levi and The Agency. If they catch him, they'll force him to undergo the memory wipe process, just like those students who failed to graduate as an Agent. I've come to learn that The Agency is influential at the highest levels of society, way beyond airport security or the police. I'll never understand how Dexter can be so casual about being on their radar.

I watch as the latest group of arrivals walk into the lobby to be warmly greeted by families and loved ones. Being here reminds me of when I left my father to travel to America. I often ask myself whether things would have been different if I'd stayed. Deep down

I know that if I had, I'd be dead now too. A dozen Agents couldn't prevent the attack by Kat; I'd have been another one of her victims. Sometimes I wonder whether she planned it so that I'd have to live with the grief of having lost both of my parents. It feels like the kind of sick thing she would do. I don't know how we'll locate her, and I'm less sure about how to defeat her. But I'm determined to find a way.

My mobile vibrates in my palm and I answer the call.

'Hey Badass.'

'Where are you, Dexter? I've been worried sick.'

'I'm right behind you.'

I spin on my heels, scanning the arrival lounge as I try to spot him through the crowd of people.

'I can't see you.'

'Look towards the coffee shop on your right. Do you see the suave-looking guy sipping an espresso?'

I follow his instructions and my eyes fix on a young man in a suit sitting alone at a table. His hair is short, with a neat side-part, and he's wearing rimless glasses.

'I still don't see you.'

The young man lowers the mobile from his ear and makes a small wave.

'You're looking right at me!'

I can't believe *that's* Dexter. He looks totally different from the last time I saw him. His long hair and unkempt stubble is gone, replaced with an image more fitting of a city businessman than a fugitive. I break out into a smile and start to make my way over to him, weaving through the crowd.

'Stop,' says Dexter. 'Don't come any closer. You're being watched.'

I freeze on the spot, trusting Dexter's instincts. Until lately, I'd have dismissed this as a crazy response. Recent events have proven otherwise.

'Where?' I ask.

'He's at the magazine stand. Tall, blond hair, dark coat.'

I move my eyes slowly to the right, focussing on the people gathered outside a newsagent store. Sure enough, a blond man dips his head into a magazine the second I turn in his direction. I suddenly feel vulnerable and wish that Aaron and Zara were with me.

'What should I do?' I ask Dexter.

'Walk outside and wait in the taxi queue. I'll meet you there.'

The call ends abruptly. When I turn back to the coffee shop Dexter has already disappeared.

I do as instructed and head out of the airport, joining the long queue for the taxis. The line moves slowly forwards but my heartbeat quickens. I glance back to notice that the blond man has joined the queue at the back. He's pretending to read a magazine while occasionally fiddling with something in his ear. I don't know whether he's with the police, the government or The Agency, and I hope I don't get to find out. As I approach the front of the queue, Dexter is nowhere to be seen. I look around anxiously as the next taxi rolls up and the driver lowers his window.

'Are you getting in?' he asks, impatiently.

The people waiting in line behind me start to grumble at my hesitancy.

'Excuse me, Miss.'

The voice is accompanied by a strong hand which grips my elbow. I try to break free, fully expecting it to be the blond man. When I turn to face him, it's the grinning face of Dexter before me.

'Shall we?' he asks, opening the door and ushering me into the cab.

I peer back to notice the blond man pushing his way through the queue towards us. Dexter slides onto the back seat alongside me as I rush to give the driver our destination.

'Take us to Gordon's Wine Bar in the city, and please hurry!'

The driver grunts and pulls away.

'A wine bar, eh?' says Dexter, smoothing his collar. 'I like your style.'

When I turn to look out of the back window, I notice the blond man staring at us from the roadside. Whoever he was, we've lost him, for now.

As we merge into London's heavy rush hour traffic, I finally allow myself to relax. Dexter seems completely unfazed by our close call as he whips off his glasses, unfastens his top button and loosens his tie. When he ruffles his hair out of its crisp parting, he starts to look more like the boy I know.

'It's good to see you,' I say, hugging him.

'I have a bad habit of attracting the wrong type of attention. Luckily for me, I'm a fast moving target. The blond guy didn't bother me but I thought for one second *you* were going to hit *me*!'

'I don't like being grabbed,' I reply.

'Of course,' says Dexter. 'Aaron told me about the painful lesson he learned on that particular issue.'

As we crawl through the traffic, it feels like something is missing.

'Wait, where's Axel?' I ask.

Dexter is never without his canine companion with whom he shares a special psychic connection.

'Don't worry, he's fine. He's got to have some injections and go through quarantine before I can collect him tomorrow. Hopefully by then he'll have forgiven me for replacing his microchip.'

'Poor doggie, I hope it didn't hurt too much.'

Dexter chuckles to himself.

'That's not the only reason he's in a mood. We both had to obtain new IDs to get here. Axel is officially now called Princess.'

I can't help but laugh. It feels good to do that after the last few months. Our light-hearted moment doesn't last long before the reality of the current situation creeps back into my mind.

'You took a risk in travelling here, Dexter. Edgar came to visit us this morning and I'm sure he's still looking for you.'

Dexter shrugs, like the threat of having his memory erased is no big deal.

'I hope he handles disappointment well, because I'm kind of slippery.' He runs his fingers down the lapels of his suit jacket. 'Good thing I dressed for a wine bar. Since when did you start drinking?'

'I don't. It was Zara's idea to meet there. Gordon's is owned by one of her relatives. She said it's a safe place for us to meet.'

Dexter nods in approval.

'Good old Blondie, always thinking.'

I can't deny that it's great to have Dexter around once more, even if he does bring an added element of danger. As we catch up on life, a concern niggles at me and won't let me fully relax. When we get to the wine bar, we'll need to have a very difficult conversation with Dexter about his father. I hope that he's more understanding than the last time we approached that subject.

+ + +

Gordon's is the oldest wine bar in London, situated in the popular tourist area between Trafalgar Square and the River Thames walk. From the outside, it looks like a building that has stood unaltered since it was built a century ago. The bar is buried deep beneath the streets, with only a small doorway and a subtle sign revealing its location.

We descend a wood-panelled staircase, its walls fashionably plastered with old newspaper cuttings and dusty wine bottles. The stairs eventually lead into a dark, vaulted room. The bar is built into the cellar of the building, with a bare rock ceiling supported by stone arches. The long, candlelit tables are occupied by local workers who have stopped by after a hard day at the office.

'Nice,' says Dexter, whistling in appreciation.

I approach the bartender and lean across the bar to ask for Zara.

'Miss Gordon is in our VIP area,' he confirms in an Australian accent. 'Follow me.'

We're shown to the far end of the room, where Zara and Aaron are sitting at a private booth. They stand to greet us, giving Dexter a warm welcome.

'Nice suit,' says Aaron. 'And you got a haircut too. That's a shame, I can't call you Hippie-Boy anymore.'

Zara motions for us to take a seat, casting her eyes around the room cautiously.

'Should we turn off our mobiles?' I ask.

After being followed at the airport I'm worried about the prospect of being tracked.

'No need,' says Zara. 'The walls and ceiling are three foot thick and made of solid stone. We're in a cellular-free zone.'

Now I understand why she suggested we meet here. I never fail to be impressed by Zara's attention to detail.

Dexter slings his jacket over the back of a chair and picks up the wine list.

'It's great to have the gang back together, isn't it? The drinks are on me!'

Aaron dips his head slightly, and Dexter realises his mistake immediately.

'Sorry, Aaron. I didn't mean to—'

'It's fine,' he says, brushing it off. 'Just because I'm in a bar doesn't mean I feel compelled to have a drink. I can handle it, Dexter. No need to apologise.'

I take Aaron's hand in mine. I'm proud of how he's dealt with his problems with alcohol, even if he relapsed briefly following the death of my father.

'We're not staying long,' says Zara. 'Allow me to update you, Dexter.'

I'm thankful for Zara taking the initiative. She has a way with words, a natural ability to command attention and disseminate information concisely. I listen as she explains her plan to hunt down Kat in her home land of Romania and follow the trail that may lead to my mother. Dexter's eyes grow as he learns that we'll soon be joining him as fugitives on The Agency's wanted list.

'Sounds dangerous,' he says. 'I'm totally in.'

Aaron coughs to clear his throat, eyeing Zara by way of a reminder.

'That's great news, but there's one more thing we need to run past you.'

This is the tricky part and I feel a responsibility to be the one who says it. I shuffle in my seat, unable to find a comfortable position.

'Dexter, there's only one person alive who knows Katalina's exact whereabouts: your father. We need you to convince him to help us.'

I see the excitement fade in his eyes, like he's just been offered a prize that has a catch written in the small print. The table falls silent, and we allow him a moment to process his thoughts. His eyes become fixed on the candle in the centre of the table top, its flame dancing and flickering.

'I travelled here to visit my father. It's been years since he sent me away. I told him I never wanted to see him again, but when my mother died my feelings changed. Maybe I matured, or maybe time helped to heal some of my wounds. I know he's done terrible things but I feel a need to face him, to show him the man I've become. I want him to see that I'm not like him.' My heart wrenches when he lifts his head, the emotion showing in the strain on his face. 'If I can convince my father to help you, then maybe it can heal some of the pain he's caused.'

Aaron reaches out and places a hand on Dexter's shoulder in a show of support.

'You're doing the right thing.'

Zara nods in agreement.

'I know this won't be easy for you,' she says. 'Your father is possessed by the Hangman Ghost and I can't guarantee that his condition can be reversed. The good news is that I think we've found a way to extract the Poltergeist and return him to some form of sanity. We can bring him back to his senses, but we'll need you to convince him to provide the information we need.'

Dexter inhales a deep breath and purses his lips.

'I'm ready for this.'

I place my hand on his arm in a silent thank-you.

'Good man,' says Aaron, slapping him on the back. 'Then let's go to Cane Hill Mental Asylum.'

Chapter 3

Sasha

Zara wastes no time in driving us to the mental hospital, triggering at least one speed camera along the way. Rover, her trusty old four-wheel drive, groans in protest as it veers off a dual carriageway and onto a country lane. I stare out into the forest as we follow the winding road that leads to the top of the hill. Not-so-distant memories come flashing back in a series of unwelcome images. This was the place where Ludvig – Blake's Pyromorph bodyguard – chased us, sending our car plummeting into the lake. Simply being here feels like an act of defiance against Blake and Ludvig and how they tried to destroy us that night. It's a miracle that we all survived, including Zara's old Land Rover.

'Did you check the car for bugs?' I ask, leaning into the space between the front seats. 'The last thing we need is a repeat of what happened last time.'

'I went over every inch, inside and out,' confirms Aaron. 'Twice.'

That's one thing less to worry about, but I'm still far from at ease. We're about to visit the man who tried to kill me. Our need for information is greater than my personal anxiety and I push the feelings down inside me, hoping they won't show on my face.

'Creepy looking forest,' says Dexter, staring out from the seat next to me.

'You should try being buried alive here,' I reply.

He laughs, thinking that it's some kind of joke, and I decide that it's a story for another time. Dexter has already endured enough tales of how cruel and twisted his father was. I decide to spare him that particular one.

Cane Hill Mental Asylum is exactly how I remember it. Even in daylight, the Victorian building looks dark and foreboding. From its hilltop location, the tall towers extend into the sky, piercing the heavy, grey clouds above. It's a place where tortured souls live out their remaining miserable days, scratching the walls and clawing their skin.

Zara pulls up in the gravel car park and turns to face us.

'Aaron and I will go in first. Give us ten minutes before you follow.'

'Hang on,' says Dexter. 'Shouldn't I be the first to go in? I'm the one who's visiting family, after all.'

Zara removes her designer glasses and polishes the lens, seemingly lost in her own thoughts.

'You and I have something in common. We both have a parent in residence here.'

It's a solemn reminder that this place also has great significance for Zara. Cane Hill is home to both her deranged mother and the man who was ultimately responsible for killing her partner. All that she loves and all that she's lost is contained within the asylum walls. I'm not the only one battling an inner turmoil. As strong as Zara is, I can't imagine how difficult this will be for her.

'This afternoon is open visiting,' she continues. 'All the patients will be in the day room. I'll go in first with Aaron. You two wait here for a few minutes and then follow us in.'

Aaron steps out and takes a sports bag out of the back of the car. A cold breeze rushes inside and Dexter pulls up the lapels of his suit jacket.

'Going to the gym?' he asks in an attempt to be light-hearted.

'Not quite,' replies Aaron. He pats the bag and gives us a wink. 'This contains the instrument I'll use to extract the Hangman Ghost from your father.'

Dexter flinches and I throw him a sympathetic glance. For an Empath, Aaron can be a little insensitive at times. He dashes off with Zara, battling through the swirling gusts as he strides towards the main entrance of the grim-looking building. I'm left alone with Dexter inside the car, doing my best to keep my nerves under control. It's hard to imagine what condition Blake will be in, let alone how he might react if we actually restore him to sanity. I try to reassure myself about why I'm doing this. Blake is the only person who knows the exact whereabouts of Kat. We need to extract that information from him. It's a transaction, nothing more. Business, not personal. Once we have what we need, we can leave this place – and Menzies Blake – forever.

I notice Dexter's leg bobbing up and down and it reminds me that I'm not the only one who is feeling apprehensive right now.

'Are you ready for this?' I ask him.

He takes in a deep breath, holding it in his chest before blowing out his cheeks.

'I think so. What about you?'

'If going through this can help us hunt down Kat, then I'm ready.'

I pull the Athame from my pocket, rotating it in my hand reflectively. The only time I've ever been able to use it was when I extracted the Hangman Ghost from my father. My actions saved both of our lives but by transferring it to Blake I'm directly responsible for him being here. Dexter and I have made our peace over what happened that night, but I'm not sure I'll ever be able to reconcile things with his father. Nor do I want to.

I stuff the Athame back into my pocket when I realise that Dexter is watching me.

'Whatever happens, I won't let my father hurt you,' he says.

It's a nice sentiment, but I don't need anyone to protect me anymore.

'I won't let him hurt you either,' I reply.

We make our way towards the old building and approach the reception desk. Dexter sifts through his various forms of ID like he's shuffling a deck of cards. To gain access, he must revert to his real identity and prove that he's the son of one of Cane Hill's most notorious patients. I cast my eyes around the walls, taking in a brass plaque which lists the names of former patients who were related to famous people, including Charlie Chaplin's mother. It feels like a distasteful way to demonstrate the merits of this hospital – even the rich and famous send their loved ones here. I arch my neck up and spot a CCTV camera where the wall meets the ceiling. Hopefully, by the time anyone has traced our whereabouts we'll be long gone from this awful place.

We're escorted into the day room and the first thing I notice is the stale smell of urine. The large, open area is sparsely furnished with rudimentary chairs and tables, all with safe, rounded edges. A TV plays quietly in one corner where several patients are transfixed on a cookery show. At the far end of the room, an old woman sits in front of a piano, her hands clasped together like she dare not touch the ivory keys. Further along, two younger men are playing chess, although some of the pieces are missing. Several nurses and orderlies wander around the room, gently touching the patients on the shoulder to check that they're awake, or alive.

Zara has taken a seat with her mother near a tall window, the sunlight breaking through its thick bars. She eyes us briefly before turning away to brush her mother's hair. Aaron stands awkwardly with his back pinned against the wall and a pained expression on his face. I wonder what could be bothering him, until I remember the last time we were here. His Empath senses spiked in the presence of so many tortured souls and the same must be happening to him right now. He nods to the far corner of the room, where two middle-aged men are huddled together in the shadows. When one of the men turns his head, I recognise the harrowed face immediately.

It's Menzies Blake.

Dexter grabs hold of my hand for support as we approach him slowly. I'm not sure which one of us needs the other most right now. As we edge forwards cautiously, I take in the details of the man who almost ended my life. His usual slick, jet-black hair is now grey, with greasy strands falling over his face. A swathe of heavy salt-and-pepper stubble covers his chin. In the few months since I've seen him, Blake looks like he's aged in an unusually accelerated fashion. He mutters away eagerly to the patient sitting next to him who appears to be half-comatose.

'I served King Charles the Second,' says Blake, jabbing a finger into his own chest. 'I took the head off the Duke of Monmouth!'

In between his slurred words, his jaw hangs half-open and slightly offset. I wonder whether it's Blake speaking, or the Hangman. Perhaps it's a disturbing combination of the two. When I glance at Dexter, his face has turned pale and his eyes are wide and anxious.

'Father?' he calls out, hesitantly.

Blake ignores him and continues to mutter into the ear of the other patient, who has started to dribble from the corner of his mouth.

'Father,' Dexter repeats, this time more forcefully. 'It's me, Dexter – your son.'

Blake turns to face him with bloodshot eyes.

'Don't you know who I am?' he asks. His expression suggests that he's taken offence at the interruption. 'I am a Necromancer!'

His last words are shouted and two of the nurses turn their heads in our direction. From the opposite side of the room, Zara knocks a jug of water onto the floor. The nurses rush to help her, falling for the diversion she's managed to create. At the same time, Aaron moves towards the patients playing chess, scooping up the remaining pieces as he walks by. The young men stare at the board in confusion, as though the chess pieces have just vanished into thin air. Without warning, one of them overturns the table and attacks the other. Chaos erupts, with almost every patient suddenly shouting and screaming. Several orderlies restrain the arguing men and struggle to remove them from the room with the help of the nurses.

Aaron appears at my side, dropping his sports bag onto the floor and quickly unzipping it.

'Pull that table over!'

I do as he says, wincing at the piercing shrieks which rebound off the bare walls. He whips out a wooden box, patched together crudely with duct tape and glue. I recognise it as the Ouija board he once used at The Agency.

'What's going on?' asks Dexter.

'No time to explain,' says Aaron. 'Get behind your father and brace him. Hold him tight!'

Zara dashes across the room to join us.

'We've got forty-five seconds before the staff return,' she confirms.

Her assured tone tells me that she's used her Precog senses to access a future vision of these events. Everything from knocking over the jug to stealing the chess pieces was carefully planned in advance. The ensuing chaos has provided a small window of opportunity for us to extract the Hangman Ghost but we have to act fast.

Aaron quickly sets up the Ouija board in front of Blake and places the small wooden pointer in the centre. He closes his eyes in concentration.

'Lord Russell . . . *are you there?*'

'Who's Lord Russell?' I ask, leaning in to speak to Zara.

'He's one of the Hangman's deceased victims, and he's very keen to bring him back to the underworld.' Her eyes are fixed on the wooden planchette as it drifts onto the word 'yes' as if moved by an invisible hand. 'We're using one evil spirit to dispose of another. Sometimes you have to fight fire with fire.'

'Will it work?' I ask, struggling to be heard over the noise of screaming mental patients.

'I don't know,' replies Zara. 'We've never tried it before.'

Aaron's eyes suddenly pop open.

'I can feel his presence. He's ready to do this.'

Zara takes hold of Blake's hand and forces it onto the wooden planchette. He immediately tenses up, the veins in his arm swelling.

'It's hurting him!' cries Dexter, his arms wrapped around his father to hold him in position.

'We have to do this,' says Zara in an uncompromising tone. 'It's the only way.'

I move alongside Dexter and help him to brace his father. The shrieks of terror within the day room seem to intensify and I notice that all the patients are now staring in our direction. I follow their gaze to see a swirling red orb forming above our heads. Blake's eyes bulge as he coughs up a black shadow; the malevolent spirit of the Hangman Ghost. At the same time, another dark, misty shape rises up from the Ouija board. The two shadows intertwine, like wisps of smoke. For a brief moment, the shadow forms into the hooded shape of the Hangman's head before being sucked up into the fiery red orb.

'Did it work?' I ask, peering cautiously at Blake.

Without warning, he projectile vomits across the Ouija board.

'I think it just might have,' says Aaron, pulling a sour face as he packs away the puke-covered board.

The nurses and orderlies burst into the room and attempt to restore order. Blake appears bemused but calm – he's the only patient who is. One of the nurses ushers us all outside and away from the chaos, allowing us to accompany Blake to his private room. Aaron and Dexter lower him into a chair as Zara examines his eyes, searching for signs of sanity.

'Do you know who you are?' she asks.

He looks down to his hands, flexing his fingers like it's the first time he's ever had control of them. For a drawn out moment he stares hard at the lines on his palms.

'My name is . . . Menzies Blake.'

Zara nods, satisfied with his clear response.

'Do you know who *we* are?'

He casts his eyes from Zara's face to Aaron's.

'You are both Agents,' Blake confirms. 'Gordon . . . and Hart.'

When his eyes meet mine he flinches and looks away. It's as though my presence is a harsh light shining into his eyes.

'*You*,' he says, the single word filled with venom. '*Sasha Hunter.* You did this to me, you and your father. Where is he?'

I open my mouth, determined to answer him, but words fail me. Blake attempts to stand but Dexter steps forwards, easing him back down into his seat.

'Father, don't. Please.'

Blake loses all fight the second he recognises his son. He reaches out to his face as though he needs to touch it to confirm it's not a hallucination.

'Is it really you, Dexter? It's been so long since I last saw you. Look at you, all grown up.'

Dexter palms his hand away, not yet ready for an emotional reunion. Somehow, he manages to stay strong and focussed, keeping his true feelings under control.

'Father, you need to listen carefully because we don't have long. I promise to visit you again, but right now you need to do something for us.'

Aaron produces a map from his sports bag, spreading it out across Blake's lap. I'm full of admiration for the way Dexter keeps his composure and softens his tone encouragingly.

'We need to know the exact location of Katalina's castle.'

Blake lowers his eyes onto the map. We gather around him as he traces a shaky finger across the paper.

'I'm afraid I can't tell you where it is.'

My heart sinks as our only lead turns into a dead-end. Blake leans back in his chair and steeples his fingers in a way that reminds me of the man he once was. He takes a moment to stare at Zara, recognising her as the leader of our group.

'But if you get me out of here I can *show* you where it is.'

Zara and Aaron exchange glances and I become worried that they might actually be considering his crazy proposal. It's one thing to restore Blake's sanity, but the prospect of freeing him is too much for me to bear.

'No way!' I snatch the map away from him. 'We'll find it on our own.'

Blake seems surprised at my rejection.

'That could take you weeks, or even months. I can provide a way for you to travel directly to Katalina, undetected, and in no time at all.'

He's manipulating the situation, just like when he was the leader of The Agency. I won't let it happen, not again.

'You're staying right here where you belong.' My words come out strong; I'm not the frail teenage girl he once knew. 'I know how dangerous you are, Blake. There's nothing you can say to change my mind.'

He raises his eyebrows in mock surprise.

'Do you think your mother can afford to wait much longer, Sasha?'

His assertion stuns me and I shake my head in denial. *Why is he referring to my mother in the present tense?* A feeling of panic overcomes me, a sudden awareness like being trapped in a bad dream, that same agitated helplessness.

'You mean you don't know?' continues Blake, staring from one frowning face to the next. 'None of you actually know?'

'Know what?' demands Aaron, grabbing Blake roughly by his collar.

'Ashleigh Hunter is alive and well . . .' He smiles and tilts his head, savouring his moment of complete control and allowing me a rush of hope before he finishes his sentence. '*For now.*'

Chapter 4

Zara

Somehow, I knew it.

Blake's words don't shock me like they do Sasha, who recoils and raises trembling fingers to her open mouth. I never wanted to fill her with false hope that her mother could still be alive after all these years. My Agency training has taught me to always work with the known facts and the evidence available. But we're also encouraged to use our sixth sense. For several weeks, I've been keeping something to myself: a fleeting vision of Ashleigh Hunter, alive and imprisoned in a dark place. That's how I know for certain that Blake's words are more than just the ramblings of a madman or a desperate lie to bribe his way to freedom.

I'm about to comfort Sasha when Aaron lifts Blake out of his seat and pins him to the wall.

'Is this some kind of sick joke?' he says, snarling into the side of his half-turned face.

I'm forced to switch roles from sympathiser to peacemaker, neither being my strong suit.

'Calm down Aaron.' I rest a hand on his forearm and encourage him to lower Blake back into the chair.

He reluctantly obliges and allows me to take over the interrogation in a less aggressive manner.

'Explain yourself, Blake.' I fold my arms and stare down at him. 'How can you possibly know that Sasha's mother is alive?'

'Because I was there when she was taken prisoner,' he replies, nonchalantly. 'Whether you choose to believe me or not, it is the truth. Ashleigh Hunter has been captive in Katalina's dungeon for several years.'

I search his eyes, desperately looking for the tell-tale signs of lies.

'Why would Katalina keep her imprisoned for all this time?'

Blake makes a pathetic attempt to smooth the creases from his shirt. It's clear that he's enjoying being the centre of attention, with everyone in the room hanging on his every word.

'When The Gathering of Witches failed on Dystopia Day, Katalina turned to an alternative method for creating her own supernatural force. For some time she has been incubating a colony of sentient creatures at her castle, those she refers to as *Porphyrians*.'

Blake's words dumbfound me. During all my research, I have never come across such a paranormal entity.

'And what exactly are *Porphyrians*?' I ask him.

Blake licks his lips, even though his mouth doesn't appear to be dry.

'They are the reanimated corpses of her ancient warrior ancestors.'

I glance towards Sasha whose eyes are trained on Blake. She balls her fists and slams them onto the table.

'What does all this have to do with my mother?' she demands.

'Porphyrians require the most powerful of lifeblood to overcome their afflictions and achieve rebirth . . . such as that of a White Witch.'

Aaron rushes at Blake once more. I struggle to restrain him by thrusting myself between him and Blake and using all of my strength to prise them apart. Aaron eventually relents and pummels the bottom of his fist against the wall in a release of aggression.

Dexter looks torn up, like he's not sure whether to defend his father or disown him. He came here to heal some wounds and I can't help but feel that this has only opened up new ones.

'This can't be true,' he mutters, aghast at the revelations.

'I'm sorry, Son,' says Blake, lowering his head.

I don't buy his contrition, not for one second.

'It all makes total sense,' says Sasha, her voice foreboding and her eyes bloodshot red. 'Katalina took an interest in me because she thought I was a White Witch like my mother.'

'I can help you,' says Blake, daring to offer an olive branch. 'I can provide you all with a way to travel directly to Katalina. You can free Ashleigh Hunter and put an end to all this madness.'

Aaron shakes his head stiffly and I notice a vein bulging in his neck.

'This madness is all your doing, Blake. You're more insane now than when we found you here.'

Sasha and Aaron are emotionally charged but something in Blake's words strikes a chord within me. During my battle with Katalina at the Tower of London, she tried to force me to drink a vial of blood and asked me to "join her". Those two words send a chill through my core. I had no idea of her plans to raise an army of warriors from the dead. It's a chilling prospect and I dread to think about what might have happened if I'd have drank from Katalina's vial.

I calmly move Aaron aside and stand squarely in front of Blake. My focus returns to the thing we came here for.

'What exactly did you mean when you said you can provide us with a way to get to Katalina?'

He sits upright in his chair and rakes a hand through the loose strands of grey hair that have fallen over his face.

'You always were the most intelligent, Agent Gordon.'

'Cut the bullshit, Blake. Explain yourself, or we'll leave you here to rot away. You might well have your sanity restored, but this isn't the kind of hospital where you simply discharge yourself.'

He lifts his hands in mock surrender until my stern expression convinces him to start talking.

'As you well know, since the events of Dystopia Day international movement is far from easy. What's more, I'm sure The Agency has not sanctioned your renegade mission.' He pauses for acknowledgement of his annoyingly accurate analysis but I refuse to give one. 'They will track and detain you regardless of how you travel, be it by land, sea or air.'

'This is useless,' says Aaron, throwing his arms out and casting me an exasperated look. 'That rules out every possible form of transport. Why are we even listening to him?'

'There is another way,' continues Blake, leaning forwards in his chair as though he's about to let us in on a delicate secret. 'A method which will allow you to travel from one point to another undetected, *and in a matter of seconds.*'

'He really is crazy,' mutters Aaron, turning away to comfort Sasha.

It is not in my nature to humour anyone, least of all Menzies Blake. However, I'm forced to concede that he is right about our limited options.

'Go on.'

His eyes grow ever so slightly when he senses that he has my attention.

'There are portals which provide access to the paranormal underworld. They are the doorways by which entities invade our society. These portals can also be used like a supernatural wormhole to travel from one place to another. All you need is someone who can open a portal and enable your transportation through it.'

I narrow my eyes at him, not because I don't believe him, but because I know exactly what he's capable of. I've witnessed Blake controlling spirits with his rare and uncanny ability.

'I suppose this is where *you* come into play.'

He nods slowly, the hint of a smile forming in the corners of his lips.

'As a Necromancer, I have such power. Katalina abandoned me and I would be only too happy to exact revenge. Time is of the essence and you need me. If you will only free me from here, I vow to help you.'

I suck in a deep breath, considering his bizarre proposal. His description of portals falls in line with what I have read during my studies, although I never knew they could be used in such a way.

'How do I know that you won't trap us in the paranormal underworld, or send us all to our deaths?'

Blake ponders my question briefly before surprising me with his answer.

'I will allow my son to accompany you. I would never place him in danger.'

I cast a glance at Dexter who has turned sickly pale. Sasha wipes her eyes and takes a moment to compose herself before stepping forwards.

'If there's a chance I can save my mother, I'm prepared to do whatever it takes.' She fixes Blake with a glare, her eyes a fiery red. 'I have one question: How can you be so sure it will work?'

He pauses before replying, allowing the dramatic tension to build. His confident expression tells me that he already knows the answer; he's just making us wait for it.

'Because it worked for your father.'

Sasha looks to me for an explanation but I'm as clueless as she is right now. I'm sure Lou would have told me if he had ever used a portal. Blake clasps his hands together and intertwines his fingers, enjoying our moment of confusion.

'Do you remember when Agent Hunter disappeared in the Tyburn tunnel? He was taken through a portal by the Hangman Ghost, a portal that I opened. If you can get me to Tyburn, I can open that same portal and send you to Romania. Then you will have your opportunity to destroy Katalina and her Porphyrians and save Ashleigh Hunter before it is too late.'

+ + +

We walk out of Cane Hill in stunned silence. The good news about Sasha's mother is severely tainted by the notion of the bloodthirsty creatures known as Porphyrians. Katalina now poses more than just the threat of a single Metamorph: she is building an army which grows stronger by the day. I wrack my mind, searching for options other than the one we're left with. The prospect of having to free Blake from his asylum prison leaves us with the worst possible dilemma. Katalina may have been the one who ultimately killed Lou, but it was Blake who sabotaged The Agency in a way that impacted all of our lives. He was the one who recruited Katalina and unleashed her on the Hunter family. He was the one who abandoned his son. He was the one who tried to initiate The Gathering, causing a world-wide blackout. And now we're left with his impossible ultimatum: to find Katalina, and save Ashleigh Hunter, we must free Menzies Blake.

Blake has Lou's blood on his hands, and I'll never let him forget it.

We trudge across the car park towards Rover. Sasha is supported by Aaron, his jacket wrapped around her shoulders. The news about her mother is almost too much for her to bear. For the last three years she has grown up to believe that her mother was lost forever. The missed birthdays. The years of high school. Aaron helps Sasha into the back seat and wraps his arms around her protectively. Two dark lines of makeup trace a path down her cheeks from the corner of each eye. I climb into the driver's seat, clenching the steering wheel like it's a stress ball. Dexter sits alongside me, the colour still drained from his face. I feel desperately sorry for him to have such a monster for a father, even if I don't quite know what to say to make him feel better. At the risk of sounding insensitive, I decide to break the heavy silence.

'We have a decision to make, and we need to make it now.'

Aaron stares at me in a way that makes me feel heartless.

'I think Sasha could do with a little time to take all this in.'

'It's okay,' she says, wiping her eyes. 'Zara is right. We don't have long. If my mum really is alive, I don't want to waste another second in finding her.'

Everyone nods in solemn agreement.

'Don't take this the wrong way,' says Dexter. 'But if my father can help then I think we should accept his offer. I want to give him a chance to redeem himself for all the terrible things he's done.'

'You would say that,' snaps Aaron. 'As far as I'm concerned, Blake will always be insane. He can rot in that place for all I care. We'll find Sasha's mother on our own.'

I meet his eyes in the rear view mirror. This isn't about taking sides and I hope my half-brother understands.

'It's not that simple, Aaron. The Agency has restricted our travel and we don't exactly have the luxury of time.'

Aaron turns his head away, shaking it in dismay.

'I can't believe you're actually considering freeing that monster . . . *then letting him send us through a portal!* Do you even remember how dangerous Blake is? He betrayed and almost killed every person in this car, not to mention those who can't be with us.'

His reference to Lou brings a lump to my throat. The windows of the car begin to steam up as the tension intensifies. I've already calculated the risk versus reward, having removed emotion from the equation.

'I understand the danger involved,' I reply, holding onto my composure by a thin thread. 'I'm not comfortable with the idea of having Blake help us but without him we're stranded. That's the only reason why I vote to free him.'

'And I vote no,' says Aaron angrily. 'Not in a million years.'

Sasha is the only one left to have a say, and it's clear to everyone that she should have the deciding vote. For her, the main motivation to hunt down Katalina has changed from revenge to rescue. Having lost her father, her mother's life is now on the line. She lifts her head and I notice the crimson glint sparkling in her eyes.

'Aaron is right. Blake is one of the most dangerous people on the planet. But so is Katalina, and sometimes we must fight fire with fire.' I nod at her observation. 'I trust you all more than anyone, and I know we can look after each other no matter what. For this reason, I vote yes.'

I'm awestruck by the strength of her words and the look of determination in her eyes. Aaron turns away to stare out of the window with a face of stone. I know that he hates the idea of placing Sasha at risk.

'Then it's decided,' I say. 'We'll free Blake tonight and then use the portal to travel to Romania. You all need to understand that once we do this, we can never go back to being Agents. We'll be international fugitives wanted by both the government and The Agency.'

The silence within the car is deafening, like the gravity of what we've just decided rests heavily on all of our shoulders.

Sasha and I return to the office while Aaron accompanies Dexter to collect Axel from quarantine. I can tell that he's reluctant to leave Sasha, but I reassure him that I'll look after her. It's important that Dexter makes it back from the airport safely, especially after being followed the last time. I encourage Sasha to stay busy, which will help to keep her mind from working overtime. We only have an hour to pack the things we'll need for our supernatural journey.

'I can't decide what to bring,' she says, stuffing items of clothing into a rucksack.

'Bring warm clothes,' I say as I dart from room to room. 'Romania is pretty cold at this time of year.'

I check through the contents of my bag, mentally ticking each item off my list: basic food rations, bottles of water, a GPS device and morning sickness medication. I quickly shove the box of tablets into the side of the bag before Sasha notices. Nobody needs to know about my personal circumstances right now, least of all Sasha. We've got much more pressing concerns: pregnancy can wait.

Finally, I pick up my expandable baton. The Police issue defence weapon is easy to conceal yet brutal when needed. I flick my wrist to engage the telescopic shaft, transforming it into a titanium bat. Sasha looks alarmed at my need for such a thing. She holds out her Athame and seems underwhelmed at its size.

'Maybe I should bring something else too.'

She rummages through a draw and produces a pair of nunchucks.

'Why not?' I say with a shrug. 'They worked pretty well for you last time.'

She shoves them into her rucksack then fiddles nervously with the drawstring. I watch as she picks up the picture of her parents and stares at their smiling faces. Her world has been turned upside-down. In the space of a few short months she's lost her father, her home and her life as she knows it. Now she's faced with the prospect of descending into the paranormal underworld through a portal. Despite all this, I don't want her to dwell on the overwhelming negatives, not when we've got such an important mission ahead of us.

'I can tell that you're nervous.' She nods, her jaw set. 'I am too. We need to remember that your father survived a journey through a portal. Our only focus should be the rescue of your mother. After that, we'll go to The Agency International HQ in Geneva. Hopefully, once we explain our actions they'll grant us a pardon.'

'Sounds simple enough,' she says, and her humorous sarcasm makes me smile.

She kisses the framed picture of her parents before carefully placing it between some folded clothes in her bag. In the time I've known Sasha, I've watched her grow from a vulnerable teenager to a confident young woman. She's faced such adversity and has taken it all in her stride. I'm proud of her.

In a way, I'm able to draw strength from Sasha's resilience. If we stand a chance of succeeding, we'll need to lean on each other. This mission has the potential to fail in so many ways, but I won't allow Menzies Blake to be the one who tries to destroy us. Not again.

We sit and wait restlessly for Aaron and Dexter to return. I check my watch every five minutes while trying not to show any sign of nervousness in front of Sasha. Mobile communication is too risky, so we have no way of knowing if and when they'll turn up. I pace the room, wandering over to the Agency computer where a new email is waiting in the inbox.

From: Edgar Levi
To: Zara Gordon; Aaron Hart
Subject: Daily reports

Agents Gordon/Hart,

I hope you are making good progress in rebuilding the UK Agency. The senior leadership team in Geneva have asked me to keep them updated. As such, I will need you to provide me with a daily progress report. I look forward to hearing from you.

Regards,
Edgar

I remove my glasses to rub the bridge of my nose. I hadn't anticipated this kind of micro-management from Edgar. If I'm not able to send him the daily updates, our cover will be blown. It's not the kind of task I can do remotely: Edgar will know if I'm not logged in to The Agency mainframe.

The office door opens and I quickly close the email. Axel bounds into the office, a bundle of energy and excitement. Dexter stumbles through the door after him, struggling to hold on to the other end of his lead. Then Aaron enters, with his mother alongside him.

'Janice?' I say, confused at her appearance.

'Hey Sugar,' she says. 'Be a sweetie and put the kettle on, will you?'

Janice looks like she might have got dressed in the dark, her bright blue coat clashing with a tartan skirt and orange tights. In her left hand she carries a plastic bag which looks like it contains bottles of wine. She plonks herself on the sofa next to Sasha and makes a fuss over Axel. I'm not displeased to see her. In fact, I grew quite fond of her during the time she put us up. But the timing of her visit couldn't be worse.

Aaron walks over and ushers me into the kitchen. I don't have the patience to wait to hear his explanation.

'What part of "quick and unnoticed" didn't you understand? Did you forget that we're about to break into a mental asylum and then leave the country? We don't have time for family reunions—'

'Did you see the email from Edgar?' he says, cutting me short.

'Yes,' I reply. 'I've just read it. Why?'

'It popped up on my mobile on the way to the airport. We need someone to send the daily reports from our office computer. That's when I had the idea to bring Mum over. She used to be an office secretary. I've briefed her on all she needs to know to send the daily updates to Edgar!'

I want to be angry with Aaron, but his enthusiasm is suffocating.

'It would have been nice to talk it through first.'

'We didn't have time. Besides, you said no mobile communication . . . so I made a decision on my own.'

He's right, on both counts, and that annoys me. As crazy as it seems, it just might work. I stare beyond Aaron as his mother chats casually to Sasha and Dexter while tickling Axel on the belly. Our team has just recruited another member, and the most unlikely of characters. It might have bought us the time we need to get to Romania, and I don't want to waste a second of it.

'Good work,' I say to Aaron, offering a grudging compliment for thinking on his feet. 'Now go and grab your things – we have a mental asylum to crash.'

Chapter 5

Sasha

Zara switches off Rover's headlights as we approach Cane Hill. I stare out of the car window and up at the full moon. A few months ago, my superstitious ways would have made me wary of such an ominous bad luck omen. Since losing my father, I've worked hard to try and master my fears, just as he encouraged me to do. *Fear only has power if you allow it,* he would always say. I read somewhere that a full moon pours down a tremendous amount of energy and it's important to remain in a calm state of mind to receive the positive effect. I'm sure that whoever wrote it didn't consider my circumstances, and what I'm about to do.

We allow our eyes time to adjust to the darkness, the engine's low hum the only sound in our ears. It's late, and most of the lights in the vast building are off. The moonlight illuminates the outline of the tall towers, which stand like giant stone sentinels on either side of the main entrance. This place looks imposing by day, but it takes on a chilling appearance under nightfall. Aaron, who is sitting next to me in the back seat, looks just as uneasy I am. I notice him biting his fingernails, so I pull his hand down into mine.

'You have no idea how many lost souls are walking these grounds,' he says.

His Empath senses must be picking up the presence of every former mental patient whose spirit hasn't yet passed on. His gift is remarkable but it can also be a curse. I squeeze his hand in a gesture of emotional support.

Dexter turns to face us from the front passenger seat.

'Can't you just switch your senses off, or something?'

'It doesn't work like that,' replies Aaron with an irritated tone. 'It's not as easy as controlling a dog, you know?'

Dexter raises his eyebrows, and Axel immediately pops up from the space in the back of the car to lick Aaron's ear.

'Cut out the nonsense,' says Zara, ever the serious one. 'It's time to get to work.'

'So what's the plan?' I ask her.

'All of the day nurses will have left by now. My mother told me that they're understaffed at night, which should make things easier for us. Blake's room is on the ground floor, around the side of the main building. We'll break in through the window and pull him straight out of his room.'

'But the windows have bars,' says Dexter. 'Thick, solid bars. The kind that would take hours to saw through.'

Zara reaches under her seat and produces a tow rope with a hook on the end.

'That's why I brought this. Rover to the rescue.'

It's the closest Zara has ever come to cracking a joke. She pats the dashboard and I smile at the human-like relationship she seems to have with her car. I try not to let the doubts creep into my mind about a vehicle that I've seen break down with alarming regularity.

We drive around the side of the building at a snail's pace, hoping that the crunch of gravel under the wheels won't disturb anyone inside. Dexter is able to point out Blake's room and I'm thankful for his excellent memory. When he helped to free Aaron from the hospital in Salem, he proved just how astute and meticulous he can be. The Agency shunned him as a potential Agent, but there's no doubting his value to our team. I only hope that his emotions don't cloud his judgement once we free his father.

Zara pulls up directly opposite Blake's room, positioning the car a few feet from the window. We creep out silently and help her attach the tow rope around the thick bars. She motions us towards her and we huddle together like a bunch of diamond thieves.

'As soon as I yank off the bars, Aaron will detach the tow rope. Sasha, Dexter: I need you to go inside and get Blake. I want to be out of here within thirty seconds, before anyone realises what's happened.'

Aaron places his hand out for a team high-five, retracting it when Zara fixes him with her grow-up stare. We watch from a safe distance as she moves Rover slowly forwards until the rope becomes taut. I fix my eyes on the window, hoping that we'll fit through the space created by the bar once it's been pulled from the frame.

Without warning, Zara stomps on the accelerator and Rover wheelspins, spraying gravel into the air. The car struggles to make any impact on the barred window, bellowing smoke from its exhaust. It looks futile, like the old 4x4 is trying to move the entire building. A light comes on in an upstairs room. This isn't going to plan and I'm certain that we'll be discovered. Suddenly, the car flies forwards followed by a tremendous crashing sound. A thick cloud of grey dust fills the air, settling to reveal a gaping hole in the side of the wall.

'Wow,' says Aaron. 'I guess that will do the job.'

'Untie the rope!' I shout, shoving him into action. 'We'll get Blake.'

Dexter is left wiping dust from his eyes, so I take him by the hand and pull him across the rubble. I expect to find Blake still tucked up in bed, but instead he's fully dressed, sitting in a chair on the far side of the room like he was waiting for a chauffeur to arrive.

'What took you so long?' he asks, looking down at his watch.

'Time to go,' I say, beckoning him forward. 'Let's move.'

I hear footsteps running along an upstairs corridor and the jangling of keys. I know it will only be a matter of seconds before an orderly arrives on the scene. Blake brings his hands together, arching the tips of his fingers as they touch.

'I've been reconsidering our deal. I'm not convinced that it's a fair bargain.' For some ridiculous reason he's talking like we have all the time in the world. 'On second thoughts, I think I'll decline your invitation to leave.'

I can barely believe his words. It makes me wonder if Blake might still be insane after all. Dexter moves towards him, placing a hand on his forearm.

'But Dad, we're here to free you!'

He shrugs off Dexter's hand coldly.

'Son, I have no intention to leave through a hole in the wall. Now that my sanity is restored, I can be out of here legally in a matter of weeks. It's simply a case of proving my stable condition. Why would I want to become a fugitive?'

An alarm rings out and I hear Zara shouting at us to hurry. I'm not prepared to let Blake destroy our mission before it's even got underway. I storm forwards and grab hold of him by his shirt collar, dragging him out of the chair.

'You're coming with us,' I say, snarling. 'I'm not asking you, *I'm telling you.*'

I pull the Athame from my pocket and wave it in front of his face. The last time he saw it was the moment I inflicted the Hangman Ghost upon him. Judging by his horrified look I know that my eyes are on fire. He doesn't need to know that I can't use the Athame; I just need to convince him I can. His arrogant demeanour is replaced by cowering submission, and with the help of Dexter and Aaron we bundle him into the car. Zara takes off before we've even had a chance to close the door. When several orderlies appear out of the hole in the wall, we're already screeching away from Cane Hill and away into the night.

+ + +

An air of tension fills the car during our short drive to Tyburn in the centre of London. We pass by the shops of Oxford Street where the only sign of life is a tramp rummaging through the boxes and bins left out for collection. It feels like no time at all since we were last here. I feel a sharp pang in the pit of my stomach when I recall the brief moments with my father spent searching for the Hangman Ghost. It was at this exact spot where we descended below street level only for my father to be whisked away through a portal. We managed to save him from Blake on that occasion, but I couldn't prevent Kat from taking his life in the most brutal way. *I can't bring Dad back, but I can still save Mum.* Drawing strength from hope, I remind myself why we're doing this. But when I glance across the car at Blake, I'm plagued by doubt. Will we ever be able to trust him?

Zara pulls up in a narrow side street nestled between two tall buildings and switches off Rover's engine. I step out into the damp midnight air with one eye on Blake. Dexter gives him his suit jacket to keep him warm, but I'd have let him freeze.

'I hope you all realise that the police will be looking for me,' complains Blake, self-centred as always. 'Your car was seen leaving Cane Hill. It's only a matter of time before—'

'Be quiet,' says Aaron, leaning towards him. 'When we need your input, we'll ask for it.'

'Hey, calm down,' says Dexter, placing a hand on Aaron's chest. 'If this is going to work we'll need to keep things civil.'

'Civil?' says Aaron, pointing a finger at Blake. 'He doesn't know the meaning of the word.'

Axel makes a low growl as he senses the tension rising.

'Can you guys keep it down?' says Zara, clearly irritated by the bickering. 'We don't need to draw any unwanted attention.'

I slip my hand into Aaron's in an effort to help him relax.

'Thanks,' he whispers. 'And don't worry, I won't let anything happen to you.'

I'm sure he has sensed my own uneasiness about Blake's presence.

Zara retrieves a crowbar from Rover's boot and marches towards a cobbled area. It's only when we arrive at a manhole cover that I realise the crowbar's true purpose.

'Your father disappeared in the tunnels below, right?'

I nod, shivering despite my warm jacket.

Aaron takes the crowbar, prises open the manhole cover and slides it to one side. A rancid odour wafts upwards and Blake immediately takes a step back.

'You don't need me down there with you,' he jabbers. 'I opened the portal from up here last time and I can do the same now.'

Zara narrows her eyes from behind her designer glasses.

'This isn't a democracy, Blake. You don't have a say. If you don't want to help us, I can drive you straight back to Cane Hill.'

Her harsh words are enough to convince Blake to drop his protests.

'I'll go first,' offers Dexter, flashlight at the ready.

Axel looks up at him and whines.

'Don't worry, boy,' says Aaron, ruffling the dog's fur. 'If I can carry Sasha up this shaft I can carry you down.'

Dexter nods appreciatively then descends into the damp darkness. One by one, we lower ourselves down the iron rungs.

Zara is closely behind Blake and watching his every move. I'm relieved when my feet touch down on the tunnel floor, making a shallow splash. As our flashlights illuminate the surroundings I'm reminded of how claustrophobic this underground passage is. This time, it feels safe to be part of a group. Except, that is, for the presence of one man.

'We need to follow the route of the old Tyburn River up to the crossing point,' says Blake, his voice distorted as he holds his nostrils.

I do my best to ignore the stale smell of sewage as we walk cautiously along the tunnel. A murky stream forms a channel and I do my best to avoid stepping in it. At one point, Axel lurches at something, making us all jump as his loud bark echoes off the walls.

'It was just a rat,' says Dexter with a chuckle.

The sound of running water grows louder as we descend further along the dank passage. Eventually the stream meets a much deeper river in a vaulted cross-section.

'This is as far as we need to go,' says Blake with an ominous tone.

'What now?' asks Zara.

I had hoped that she might have experienced a future vision, her Precog senses providing a reassurance that it will all work out fine. Obviously she hasn't, and what happens next is anyone's guess.

Blake rolls up his sleeves and shakes out the tension in his hands.

'To enable you to journey through a portal I must summon a guide. Last time, the Hangman Ghost protected Lou Hunter as they travelled through the paranormal underworld. This time, I will need to call upon a different entity.'

My heart starts to pound as the reality of what we're about to do sinks in. I squeeze Aaron's hand tightly.

'What if Sasha stays?' he suggests to Zara. 'I mean, maybe it's safer for her to stay if she doesn't have any powers?'

I shoot him a glare, unimpressed by him making decisions for me without even asking for my opinion. I know that he's only looking out for me, but I'm more than capable of looking after myself. Zara appears to ponder the idea so I decide to speak up before she can answer.

'No way, Aaron. My mother is being held prisoner in Romania, so that's where I'm going.'

I turn my attention to Blake as he approaches Dexter.

'Take this,' he says, offering him his wristwatch. 'I'm truly sorry for not being there for you all these years.'

Blake fastens the watch onto Dexter's wrist and it goes some way to reassure me. It's a gesture of genuine love and sorrow, not the actions of someone about to send his son to his death.

Zara steps forwards and hands her car keys to Blake.

'Look after Rover,' she says. 'He means a lot to me.'

Blake seems almost speechless, even more so when Aaron produces a small wad of cash and offers it to him.

'It's a couple of hundred, but it's all I've got,' he says. 'Try and stay out of trouble, for all of our sakes.'

If I didn't know him better, I'd have sworn that the Necromancer is touched. In a moment of reflective silence, I wonder if Blake really does have a heart. Maybe he regrets the path he chose in betraying my father and The Agency. If there was ever a time for him to make amends, it's now.

Blake clears his throat, pretending that the show of kindness hasn't affected him.

'Once you are in Romania, the portal will reopen at midnight each night at the exact same location. It will bring you home just as it will send you there.' He lowers his outstretched palms towards the dank water. 'Stand back. I am about to open the portal and summon the Ferryman.'

Blake performs a repeated Latin chant, gradually increasing in volume. His fingers touch the surface of the river and a wall of water rises up to form the shape of an arched doorway. The vision of the portal, and the thought of what we're about to do, brings my arms out in goosebumps. I watch in awe as a dark shape passes through the liquid arch and reveals itself as the helm of a boat. Standing on the vessel is a robed figure holding a bargepole, his face completely hidden by a long hood.

My experience of paranormal happenings has hardened me to such sights. I've fought against a Poltergeist and survived a battle against two Black Witches. Mentally, I should be able to handle just about anything. I'm not frightened, but I'm aware of my pulse rate rising as the strange apparition extends a skeletal hand with an upturned palm.

I cast my eyes around the rest of the group, checking to see if they're as apprehensive as I am. I have good reason to feel uneasy: I'm about to be sent through a paranormal portal by a man who we've just hijacked from a mental institute – the man who once tried to kill me. Blake seems to be the only person who is calm right now.

'Time for you to board,' he says. 'There's nothing to fear. I have instructed the Ferryman to protect you during your journey. I'd like you to go first, Son.'

Dexter's face turns an unhealthy milky white and I'm worried that he might faint. He takes a few cautious steps forwards, like he's walking the plank of a pirate ship. Axel releases a low whine as they climb onto the boat and sit on one of the benches before the Ferryman.

'Let's do this,' says Zara, encouraging us to board.

I have lots of questions that I want to ask. Too Many. But I'm aware that every minute that passes is another minute closer to my mother's fate. I remind myself why we're putting ourselves through this ordeal, and that pales in comparison to what she's been enduring.

I take hold of Aaron's hand as I step onto the boat. He puts his arm around me and squeezes my shoulder. It feels like we're the first unlucky people to test out a rollercoaster, only this ride has no safety bars. I glance back at Blake, trying to read into his solemn expression. He tosses an old penny to the Ferryman and I hear the sound of bone fingers clasping the copper coin.

The boat starts to move towards the archway of water.

Into the blackness.

I squeeze my eyes shut.

I'm coming for you Mum, I'm coming.

Chapter 6

Ashleigh

My shot at freedom is finally here.
    If only I had my Athame.
    I marvel at the tunnel's entrance, barely wide enough to squeeze my thin frame inside. My hands ache from the thirteen months spent digging. Inch by inch. Foot by foot. My only tool was the buckle from my belt and though it helped, it was a desperately slow process. I know exactly how long it has taken by the tally marks scratched into the walls of this pit that is my prison. After so many long years, I'm running out of wall space, but I'll never run out of hope.
    On scuffed hands and knees, I crawl inside the carved tunnel. The sound of my own heavy breathing echoes off the damp walls and fills my ears. This confined space does nothing for my claustrophobia but I'm not about to let it stop me now. Solitude has taught me how to deal with my anxieties. I've had lots of time to practice.
    The tunnel becomes smaller the further I go, forcing me to drag myself along on my stomach. My elbow catches the sharp edge of a rock creating a small open wound. It is a sight I am used to after

the years spent extracting my own blood. I always wondered why Katalina kept me alive when she could have so easily killed me. My presumption was that it was a form of torture. Every other day, a bucket was lowered containing food, water and a syringe. I was required to supply her with my own blood without ever understanding why. The thought chills me but the prospect of freedom propels me forwards.

I tear a strip of cloth from my shirt and bind the wound. It's nothing compared to what I've dealt with before. I recall how my resolve was tested a few months ago when help finally arrived. Or so it seemed. The voices of the Agents still resonate in my mind. I could hear them outside the castle, barely audible through the many metres of drainage pipes. It pains me to think that it was my mistake which might have cost them their lives. Weeks earlier, I managed to flush out my ID card and send it beyond the walls in the hope that it might be discovered. On that occasion, my plan backfired. Katalina took morbid glee in recounting how she brutally murdered each Agent before sealing the drain. She deprived me of food for almost a week, yet it only made me more determined to escape. And now here I am, clawing away the last of the loose rock as I crawl from the tunnel into a chimney shaft.

Despite my meticulous planning, it has not been an easy task. When I set about starting to dig, the walls of my oubliette cell gave me no indication of which way to go. In her arrogance, it was Katalina who revealed the direction of the chimney. During one of her daily visits, a momentary lapse revealed too much information. I counted her steps: Eleven paces from the door of the room above to the hatch high up in the bottle-necked ceiling of my cell. She peered down at me to sing her taunts. That was when I noticed the left hand side of her face illuminated by a nearby fireplace. In that instant, my escape plan formed. Every fire needs a chimney, and every chimney leads to an opening. The plan is everything. Designing one is like making a clock: all these little parts working together, turning, tugging, ticking. And at the end of the day, it either tells the time or it doesn't.

Either I escape, or I don't.

My hands press against the broken brickwork which forms the entrance to the chimney. *Keep going, I tell myself, you're almost there.* I've acted as my own motivational coach for so long. Sometimes the sound of my own voice is all that has kept me from going insane. During many cold nights, the futility of my task threatened to overpower me but one desire drove me on: to see my daughter again. The thought of Sasha warms my heart. I reach for the opal pendant hanging around my neck and kiss it for luck. It has kept me company for all of these dark years and acted as a bond to my daughter. I look forward to the day I can pass her birthstone onto her. With a renewed sense of purpose, and despite my shaking limbs, I climb inside the chimney.

I'm coming for you Sasha, I'm coming.

I dig my fingers into the gaps between the charred brickwork as I claw up the dark shaft. The walls feel cool under my palms and I'm relieved that a fire has not been lit. When I lift my head to peer into the blackness above, I notice a dim light. It must be the light from a room on a higher level and I decide to head towards it. The leathery flutter of a bat's wings startles me and I almost lose my grip. My heart pounds within my chest but I'm thankful for the adrenaline that pushes me on. As I reach an opening, the sound of a creaking door hinge makes me freeze.

'Come inside,' says Katalina, a voice that I have come to despise. 'Take a seat.'

At first, I fear that I might have been discovered and that her words are directed at me. It's only when I hear a second set of heavy footsteps treading across the floorboards that I realise she has company.

'I hope my journey here will not be in vain,' replies a male. 'As you know, my method of travel was . . . *unconventional*.'

It's been so long since I've heard another voice. The years spent in a dark underground recess have taken their toll on my memory. I wonder if it's my imagination playing tricks, but the eloquent accent sounds familiar. Sickeningly familiar.

'Don't worry,' says Katalina, interrupting my thoughts. 'Once you've seen what I'm about to show you, I'm sure you'll agree that it was worth the trip.'

My instincts tell me not to move a muscle for fear of revealing my position. The slightest sound could expose me and ruin the many months spent digging my way out. Despite this, curiosity triumphs over my better judgement. My daughter shares this trait and it has gotten us both into trouble over the years. I lift myself up, slowly and silently, just enough to peer through the grate of the fireplace.

The room is dimly lit by flickering candles, wax dripping from their iron prong holders. A leather studded chair is positioned near the fireplace with its back to me. The male visitor is obscured; I can only see his expensive looking shoes as he eases into the high-backed chair. Katalina stands at the far end of the chamber, her pale skin and red hair unmistakeable. The mere sight of her is enough to agitate me but there's something else even more unnerving in the centre of the room.

A coffin.

Katalina walks alongside the casket and strokes her sharp fingernails across the lid.

'Inside this sarcophagus is the culmination of many years of hard work and research. As you are aware, the last time we tried to form a Gathering it failed. The perpetrator of that treacherous act is now safely imprisoned.' I allow myself to smile at her delusion. 'Last time, we made the mistake of attempting to construct a paranormal army of Black Witches. It was an impossible task to try and control such disparate entities, each with their own twisted desires and divided loyalties. This creation of mine has great power, an unyielding nature and total allegiance.'

'How so?' asks the man, whose voice I try desperately to place.

I stifle a gasp as Katalina lifts open the coffin lid to reveal an armour clad corpse.

'Meet my ancestor, Baron Razvan. He was a great warrior of the Wallachia Principality who ruled this region some five hundred years ago. He fought for the Prince Draculesti, a man history remembers as Vlad the Impaler.'

The man sitting in the chair clears his throat.

'He is well preserved for being half a century old.'

I am surprised by his nonchalant reaction to such a revelation. His voice has an air of assuredness, almost arrogance. I turn my attention to Katalina who produces a glass vial of dark red liquid.

'This mixture of blood does more than simply preserve. Allow me to demonstrate.'

I watch with horrified fascination as she lifts the head of the corpse and tips the blood into its mouth. The room falls silent. When nothing happens, the man in the chair releases an impatient huff. Just as he is about to stand, the corpse begins to jerk. The sound of rustling chainmail fills the air as the armoured warrior rises from the coffin. Long, black hair flows over his steel-plated shoulders. A thin moustache adorns his top lip, with dark brows furrowed above two piercing eyes.

'Razvan is one of my *Porphyrians*,' announces Katalina proudly. 'They are undead warriors who feel no fear or pain and will obey my every command. This army will eclipse anything we could have ever achieved at The Agency.'

With the mention of these last two words, my memory immediately engages. I haven't been in action for a long time but the blade of my instincts hasn't gone completely dull. I suddenly feel hyperaware, and my mind cycles through images from the past. I recall a part my life before my captivity; it was my secret profession. As the memories form, my darkest thought is also the loudest. It confirms the identity of the man in the chair. Although I cannot see him clearly, I know for certain that it can only be one person.

Menzies Blake.

Chapter 7

Sasha

I'm only able to open my eyes when I hear Aaron's voice.
'It's okay, Sash. We made it.'
He pulls me in for a hug and seems as relieved as I am.
'Reconnaissance first, hugs later,' says Zara from behind us.
I uncouple from Aaron to take in our surroundings. We're no longer inside the boat. In fact there's no sign of the river, the Ferryman, the tunnel or Menzies Blake. Instead, we're all standing in the middle of a forest.
Zara circles slowly, scanning the area as she rummages in her bag. Next to her is Dexter, hunched over with his hands on his knees.
'Are you okay?' I ask.
'I'm fine,' he responds, summoning a liar's smile. Axel licks his ear by way of reassurance until he brushes away the dog's affection. 'Ok, not fine. I'm quite seriously considering throwing up.'
I rub his back but it only seems to irritate him so I decide to give him some space. My attention returns to the eerie forest which has somehow replaced the Tyburn tunnel. It's remote and

dense, with no discernible landmarks or footpaths in any direction. Dusk is settling in and the moon is out early. Trees tower over us with skeletal branches, reaching to the sky as if to drag the moon down to the ground and smother it in the dirt. My eyes are drawn to the largest tree which has a hollow trunk, like a gaping mouth.

When I check my watch, it confirms what I had already gathered.

'We've lost no time in getting here. Not even a second.'

Dexter wipes the dog slobber from his cheek.

'So it worked. My father did it – he got us here safely, just as he said he would.'

'Hang on a minute,' says Aaron. 'Let's not jump to conclusions. Blake said that the portal would take us straight to Katalina. I see lots of trees but I don't see a Metamorph or her castle. I mean, how do we know we're in Romania? We could be anywhere.'

'We're here,' says Zara, studying her GPS device. 'This forest is close to the border between Wallachia and . . .'

Her pause seems to frustrate Aaron, who throws out his arms.

'*And?*'

Zara casts her eyes around the group like she's making sure we can handle what she's about to reveal.

'Transylvania.'

You don't need to be a paranormal Agent to understand the associated meaning. It immediately conjures up thoughts of old Hammer horror movies with bloodthirsty vampires.

'You're kidding me, right?' says Aaron, laughing at the suggestion.

When Zara dead-eyes him, the laugh quickly dies in his mouth. The atmosphere changes again when Axel makes a low growl. His ears are pointed upright, his eyes fixed on something in the distance.

'What is it?' I ask Dexter.

He closes his eyes, allowing himself to access his dog's senses. We all watch in silent anticipation as he draws in a long inhalation through his nostrils.

'There's something out there. It's approaching us.'

Zara shoves the GPS into her rucksack and pulls out her small baton. With the flick of her wrist, it extends telescopically into a mean-looking weapon.

'From which direction?' she asks, like she's ready to wipe out the threat on her own.

Dexter's eyes pop open.

'From *every* direction.'

Aaron kicks at heap of dead leaves and curses.

'It's a trap. *I knew it*. Blake set us up and we all fell for it!'

Dexter shakes his head in stunned denial.

'No . . . it can't be . . . my father wouldn't do that.'

'Of course he would,' says Aaron. 'We're all fools for believing the rubbish about him caring for you just because you're his son. Menzies Blake doesn't care about anyone but himself. Don't you see it? This is his revenge.'

I place myself in between Aaron and Dexter, trying to calm the escalating situation. Zara is less subtle in her approach, grabbing Aaron by the lapel of his jacket.

'Switch on, Hart. Now's not the time. I need you focussed. And I need you all close to me. Form a circle and stay quiet.'

I swing my bag from my shoulder and rummage inside. My first instinct is to go for the Athame but instead I opt for the nunchucks. Aaron nods in approval as he picks up a large moss-covered log. Dexter backs up while holding on to Axel's collar, his attack dog at the ready. Whatever is coming for us, we're ready for it. Or at least as ready as we can be.

A sharp movement off to the left.

Then, a rustle in the undergrowth.

It's fast, and there's more than one.

'Look!' shouts Dexter, yanking Axel back as the dog starts to bark ferociously.

Three shapes dart across the forest floor. One of them stops to stare at us, its ears pointed upwards.

'Just rabbits,' confirms Zara as the harmless animals disappear beyond the trees.

Our group breathes a collective sigh of relief. I share a chuckle with Dexter but when I turn to Aaron, I notice a look of consternation on his face.

'What's wrong?' I ask, reaching out for his hand.

He's trembling and clutching the log like his life depends on it.

'I can feel something, Sash,' he whispers. 'It's a dark presence, and it's closing in on us.'

I follow his stare, straining to try and see whatever it is that's lurking in the darkness. Axel releases a low, guttural growl. With held breaths and unblinking eyes, we prepare ourselves once more. The sound of heavy, thudding footsteps becomes audible. I struggle to work out which way they're coming, until I realise that it's the sound of several pairs of feet, marching in unison.

'We're surrounded,' says Zara. 'Get ready to fight.'

'Fight what?' asks Dexter, his voice less certain than Zara's.

His question is immediately answered. From the gloom appears a tall figure. My pupils grow as I take in the strange colossus. It looks like a warrior from medieval times, covered in armour from head to foot. Strands of lank hair fall over its face, poking out from underneath a rusted helmet. Its body is covered in weathered chainmail and it holds a double-edged axe. My eyes are drawn to its bulging arms and the skin which appears to have a green mould-like tinge. A disgusting smell accompanies the strange beast, like rotting meat.

'Apparitions?' I ask, hopefully.

'No, they're physical entities,' says Zara, confirming what I feared.

The monster before me snorts, its foul breath pluming in the air. I dare to look away, quickly turning my head left then right. Only I wish I hadn't. Three more of the armoured freaks appear through the trees. Each of them brandishes an ancient and brutal weapon: a mace, a sword, a flail. They position themselves to block every possible escape route. Our gang seems hopelessly small and ill-equipped to deal with this kind of threat.

'Get back!' shouts Dexter in warning to our enemy. 'Get back or I'll release the dog.'

His threat does little to deter them. Instead, the four creatures begin to stomp towards us, their weapons raised. Our group shuffle backwards until our spines are pressed against each other. The ground between us and our enemy begins to rapidly shrink.

'Tell me you've got a plan, Zara,' says Aaron hopefully.

'No,' she replies. 'I'm improvising. Follow my lead.'

She breaks from the group and charges at one of the beasts. I gasp as a sword is swung at her, forcing her to duck to avoid the death-blow. She ducks and rolls past her assailant. With the flick of her wrist she whips the baton into the back of its legs. Her daring move seems to work; the creature collapses to its knees with a groan. Aaron quickly follows up, swinging at its head with the log. The wood explodes upon impact, showering me in splinters. Somehow, the kneeling beast barely falters. Worse still, its comrades begin to close in.

'Get him, Axel!' shouts Dexter as he releases his baying dog.

Axel leaps at the creature and bites into its exposed upper arm. Such an attack would cause any normal human to scream with pain, but the green-skinned warrior remains silent. I watch with horror as it takes hold of Axel by the scruff of his neck and tosses him aside like a rag-doll. Dexter looks on helplessly as his dog smashes into a tree trunk with a yelp.

'No!' he roars, balling his fists as though he's about to seek revenge with his bare hands.

I pull him back by the shoulder as I step forwards, the nunchucks swinging by my side. Everything is happening so fast that I don't have time to think. All I know is that our only chance of escape is to take out this kneeling creature before the others close in. I rotate my wrist to twirl the nunchucks, spinning them in a vicious circle. When I release the weapon, it cuts through the air in a blur, flying straight for the warrior's head. With surprising dexterity, the monster somehow brings up his sword. The blade cuts through the chain between the nunchucks, breaking my weapon in two.

The sound of a struggle makes me turn sharply.

'Dexter!'

He's been set upon by one of the armoured warriors, its muscled forearm wrapped around his neck. His face turns red as the life is slowly squeezed out of him. Axel is no longer able to help, while Aaron and Zara have been separated by the other beasts. It's down to me to save him. I thrust a hand into my open bag and pull out the Athame. It hasn't worked for me since the time I defeated Menzies Blake. Now I need it to help save the life of his son.

I extend my arm and hold out the Athame, pointing it at the head of the snarling creature. With every fibre inside me, I will the Athame to work, urging the blue light to shoot from the blade and destroy the monster. Dexter's feet kick in the air as he is lifted off the ground. The Athame trembles in my hand. *It's not working . . . I can't save him.* I shove the useless knife into my pocket and look around desperately for a better weapon. Something. *Anything.* As I search, a flash of red appears within the dark trees. *Red hair.* A female figure emerges, dark and stealth-like.

'Katalina.'

Her name slips through my curled lips and leaves a venomous aftertaste. Aaron was right: this must be a trap, set by Menzies

Blake and executed by Kat. She has sent her beasts to round us up then come to witness our demise first-hand.

Then something happens, something completely unexpected.

She draws a sword and drives it into the back of the monster who is strangling Dexter. It roars angrily and releases him immediately. I scramble towards Dexter and help to drag him free from the danger. When I look back, the red-haired female has leapt upon the back of the armoured beast. It reaches for her with clawed fingers but she reacts quicker, drawing her sword across its throat. As the corpse crashes to the ground, the female lands before me in a crouched position. We lock eyes briefly, long enough for me to see that it's not who I thought it was.

She wastes no time in dispatching a second warrior, slicing its legs to hamstring the enemy before unleashing a pirouetted decapitation. I shield my face as gore and blood flies off her sword. My eyes move across to Aaron and Zara who are both being throttled by another beast. The girl with the sword cuts through the two muscled arms, leaving the severed hands still clutching onto Aaron and Zara's throats. I'm relieved when Aaron is able to prise the dead fingers away and help Zara to do the same. When I turn back to the red-haired girl, she has already thrust her blade into the monster's armless torso.

'Watch out!' I cry, pointing to the final warrior as it closes on her.

She extracts her sword and turns, but it's too late. The armoured creature buries his axe into her stomach and sends her flying across the forest. Her sword is flung into the air and lands at my feet. Inspired by the sacrifice of the mysterious red-haired girl, I pick up her weapon and charge at the monster. Momentum helps me to ram the blade deep into its back, burying it up to the hilt. It howls and staggers forwards, taking a few slow steps before collapsing face down.

I take one second to breathe.

Then another to check my friends are okay.

Our enemies lie scattered across the forest clearing, cut down by the girl who came to our rescue and paid the ultimate price. I dash to her side, flinching at the gaping axe-wound across her stomach. Her eyes are open but vacant and lifeless. Aaron and Zara stagger over, equally bemused by our fallen saviour.

'Who is she?' I ask, not expecting an answer.

'*What* is she?' adds Aaron.

Zara lifts her arm to feel a pulse and notices a strange symbol on her wrist. As I stare at the girl's face, she blinks. I jump back with shock as she gasps and sits upright, gazing at me with wild eyes.

'She's an Amaranth,' says Zara, shaking her head in disbelief. 'She's an immortal.'

Chapter 8

Sasha

I stare at the red-haired girl like she's some kind of otherworldly being. For all I know, she is.

'Hello,' I mutter awkwardly. 'Are you . . . okay?'

It feels like a stupid question to ask. Moments earlier, I witnessed her take an axe to the stomach. It was a mortal wound. *I watched her die.* But now here she is, alive. And she's staring straight at me like nothing has happened.

'I was too slow with that last one,' she remarks as though chastising herself. 'There were only four of them.'

As she speaks, I pick up on a slight French accent.

'Only four?' says Aaron. 'We were struggling with just one until you showed up.'

'You took a pretty heavy blow,' says Zara. 'We need to get you to a hospital.'

The French girl pulls up her tank top to reveal a bare stomach.

'That will not be necessary.'

Somehow, there's no trace of the previous ugly wound. The only blemish on her pale skin is a dark bruising which is disappearing by the second. It seems impossible: I saw the axe blade thrust inside her; I saw the gaping wound as she flew back from the force of the blow. It's as though her body has healed itself in the space of a minute.

Zara offers the girl a hand to help her to her feet. When she accepts, I can tell that it's out of politeness more than necessity.

'I'm Zara, and this is Aaron and Sasha.' I nod in greeting during the pause in Zara's introductions. 'I couldn't help but notice that your wrist bears the ancient symbol of the Amaranth. I thought it was a legend, until now. Are you really blessed with eternal life?'

Dexter and Axel arrive just in time to hear Zara's last words. I'm relieved to see that they have no signs of permanent injury after our encounter. Other than a look of dishevelment, with twigs and leaves attached to both of their coats, they seem fine.

'You're an immortal?' he asks, grinning. 'Cooool.'

'My name is Julietta,' she replies, raking a hand through her long red hair. 'You are correct: I am immortal. But it has not always been a blessing. Not many people know of my kind, or the reason for our existence.'

As Julietta stands before me, I'm surprised to find that she has a slight frame and is no taller than I am. She's scruffy but in a particularly groomed way – it seems a controlled chaos. Her clothing looks old but functional: scuffed boots, cargo trousers and a worn leather jacket. The red hair which flows over her shoulders is much longer than Kat's and is a more natural shade of auburn.

'How did you find us?' asks Aaron.

I can tell he's a little suspicious of Julietta. Although I'm grateful for her help, I'm also mystified by her presence. I have many questions on my mind and Aaron has probably picked up on them while holding my hand.

'I was not looking for you,' says Julietta. 'I was following those Risers.'

She nods towards the remains of the four corpses.

'Risers?' It's a word I've not heard of before. 'What exactly is a Riser?'

Julietta looks straight at me before moving her eyes towards my hand, which is still holding her sword.

'It is an ancient name given to those who rise from the dead. They have been reanimated and instructed to do harm. It is my job to eliminate that threat. That is the way of the Amaranth.'

She opens her palm and I pass her the sword, its blade still dark red from the blood of the beasts. Her movements are slow and languid – the complete opposite to her fighting style. She wipes the sword on a moss-covered tree trunk before slotting it into a scabbard hidden underneath her leather jacket between her shoulders. Her eyes drift up towards the night sky, fixing on the bright moon.

'It is not safe for us to remain here. I have lodgings in a nearby village. If you want to live through the night, you should all come with me.'

I exchange glances with the others, unsure what to make of this mysterious French girl. She doesn't wait around for us to consider her offer. Without so much as a farewell, she begins to trudge off into the forest.

'She's incredible,' says Dexter, gawping.

Axel groans as though he has witnessed this kind of behaviour many times before.

'We don't know anything about her,' says Aaron. 'She could be dangerous. Scratch that – she's *definitely* dangerous.'

I look to Zara, whose face does nothing to reveal any inner turmoil.

'Julietta came to our aid when she had no reason to. If those monsters are our enemies, then she's our friend. Do you remember what Blake told us about Katalina incubating a colony of sentient creatures at her castle? I think we've just met some of them. We were taken by surprise and I don't want that to happen again. If

Julietta can tell us more about those creatures, then we should follow her.'

I glance back at the corpses of the four monsters. We may have been quick to assume that Blake had set us up, but I'm certain that Kat is the one behind this. The question is, what are these creatures, and if she sent them, how did she know we'd be here? I turn away from the mess of blood and severed body parts and catch up with the others as we follow the French girl. I hope that Julietta can give us the information we need, and soon.

+ + +

We are led through the forest at a steady pace; faster than walking but not quite running. The sense of urgency is worrying and makes me feel like this is too dangerous a place to linger. At the same time, I'm happy to hurry things along: somewhere out there, my mother is being held captive. I clutch her Athame in my hand, my fingers wrapped around its blunt blade. Yet again, it proved to be powerless in my possession. If it wasn't for Julietta's timely intervention, our mission would have been brutally ended before it even began. The sooner I can find my mother, and return this witch tool to her, the better.

Julietta leads us out of the forest and onto a thin winding road which descends into a valley. Up ahead, I can see the lights from a scattering of dwellings. A range of mountains provides a stunning yet eerie backdrop, making the houses appear small and insignificant. Julietta waits for us to catch up. Most of us are breathless and exhausted, yet she appears unaffected by our long and arduous trek.

'My lodge is in this village,' she announces. 'You can all rest once we are inside.'

Dexter shuffles along, dragging his feet and huffing like a kid on a school trip.

'Did we have to hike through a forest to get here?' he complains. 'There must be a highway nearby? Surely we could have hitched a ride.'

Julietta shakes her head dismissively.

'There are no major roads in this area. The nearest town is three hours away and many of the roads are inaccessible at this time of year.'

'Sounds great,' whispers Dexter under his breath. 'They have monsters here, but no roads.'

As we approach the village, the lack of modern technology becomes starkly apparent. There are no power lines and the street lighting is provided by old gas lamps. A horse whinnies as it stands tied up next to someone's house, much to Aaron's amusement. He pulls out his mobile phone to take a picture, and then frowns.

'Low battery,' he mutters. 'And no signal. I could really do with finding a telephone to check on my mother.'

'You will not find a telephone here,' says Julietta.

Dexter stumbles in a muddy ridge and lets out a sigh of exasperation.

'How do people live like this?'

'The villagers prefer this rudimentary lifestyle,' explains Julietta. 'Their days are spent working the land on the Carpathian Mountains. They strive to preserve a way of life that is hundreds of years old. It is a community based on farming, where horses and carts are more useful than cars.'

'No cars? No telephones? No internet? Sounds like a sad and lonely existence.'

'Not at all,' she replies. 'They believe that happiness is found within, not in the things that surround us. I like their way of life better than I do this modern age.'

I can imagine that this small village hidden by mountains and forests would be a perfect getaway for tourists. But right now, in the middle of winter and at night, it feels like we're stranded. In the wilderness of Romania, Kat has found the perfect location to retreat from civilisation. I can't imagine how we would have ever found this place on our own, let alone travelled here. I never thought I'd feel this way, but I'm grateful for what Menzies Blake did in opening the portal.

We pass by a small house with a weathered terracotta slate roof and a bearded man smoking in the porch. He says something to Julietta in a foreign language as he eyes us apprehensively. She responds to the man in in his native language and seems to put his concerns at ease.

'You can speak Romanian?' asks Zara.

'I can speak most languages.'

'She's awesome,' whispers Dexter, all doe-eyed.

Julietta guides us around the back of the house and towards a smaller residence, more of a wooden hut than a house. She opens the door and invites us inside. As she lights some candles, I cast my eyes around the sparse room. It has a long table with two benches, a single hob cooker and a sink.

'Nice,' says Dexter, rubbing his hands in an overly enthusiastic way.

Julietta motions for us to sit at the table as she lights the stove and stirs a large cooking pot. The air soon fills with the appetising smell of broth.

'My friend Marin owns this house. It is one of his more luxurious lodgings, with hot and cold water and an inside toilet.'

'Wow,' whispers Aaron, his cute sarcasm making me smile.

We sit in silence, grateful for the rest and the hot soup Julietta serves. It tastes kind of sour to me, although everyone else seems to enjoy it.

'This is good,' says Zara, adding way too much salt and pepper to her broth.

Julietta passes round a plate of crusty bread.

'It is ciorba – Romanian soup.'

I'm sure it's favourite dish for the people of Romania but the smell does nothing for me. Julietta is bent over with her back to us as she lights a log burner. Rather than appear rude, I lower my bowl beneath the table for Axel. Luckily, he gulps it down before she turns and sits with us. She waits patiently as the others finish their soup before speaking.

'I brought you here to keep you alive, but it seems to me that you were looking for trouble. Why else would a group of foreigners lurk in the middle of a forest at night? It is obvious that you did not travel here for the scenery. Few know that I am an Amaranth, yet you identified me immediately. Now that you know what I am, perhaps you could tell me who you are, and why you are here.'

We exchange glances with each other, wondering who should be the one to speak. Much like Julietta, our existence is secretive and not easily explained. After saving our lives, the least we owe her is an explanation.

Aaron wipes his bowl with a crust of bread, trying to capture every last bit of soup. Dexter is busy patting the edges of his mouth with a handkerchief. Eventually, Zara takes the lead.

'We are part of a secret agency that combats paranormal entities.'

Her description is honest, accurate and succinct. Julietta appears to mull over the answer, moving her eyes warily around the table. I can't help but notice how she also glances towards her sword leaning against the wall.

'You combat paranormal entities? You mean . . . people like me?'

It's a fair point. As an immortal, she is technically a paranormal being.

'No,' says Aaron, quick to reassure her. 'We only hunt down malevolent forces.'

Julietta's shoulders relax and her frown dissolves.

'Then we have something in common.'

Zara opens her rucksack, takes out a photograph of Kat and slides it across the table towards Julietta.

'Our target is a Metamorph. This is a picture of her in her human form. She resides in a castle not far from here. I am led to believe that those creatures from the forest are linked to Katalina. Our mission is to track her down, destroy her, and rescue Sasha's mother who is being held prisoner.'

She studies the photograph then lifts her head to meet my gaze.

'How long has your mother been imprisoned?'

'Three years and eighty three days,' I reply without the need for any calculation.

The mere act of saying the words causes a shock of pain deep in the pit of my stomach. It's a long time – maybe too long. Until now, I've held on to the belief that she is alive and well. That was before we encountered Kat's deadly creatures. When Julietta dips her head, I feel the need to voice the sense of hope I've been clinging on to.

'My mother's ID card was found at Katalina's castle a few weeks ago. It had the word HELP scratched on it. She's alive, I know she is, and we're going to find her.'

Aaron rests his hand on top of my balled fist. My emotions are plain for all to see, but he will always have a deeper connection with me.

'What can you tell us about those monsters?' he asks Julietta, steering the conversation away from the heart-breaking thought of my mother.

The room falls silent; the sound of crackling logs and Axel's panting breaths providing the only background noise.

'I have seen many varieties of their kind over the centuries,' she says eventually, lowering her voice. 'Unfortunately, I have also witnessed what they are capable of. I call them Risers but the locals know them as *Porphyrians*. The name is derived from their physical affliction which makes their skin prone to sunlight. Their condition is blood-borne, transmitted through a bite.'

I shiver at the thought of how close Dexter was to being bitten. For some reason, he seems almost amused.

'I've got this all worked out,' he says with a wide grin. 'They've risen from the dead. They don't like sunlight. They bite their victims. They must be vampires! I'm right, right? Tell me I'm right.'

Julietta shakes her head leaving Dexter a little deflated.

'Vampires are folklore but their existence is based on an element of truth. The legend of vampires was founded on the perceived similarities with Porphyrians. You were . . . half right.'

Dexter's smile quickly returns.

'My father warned us about them,' he says, leaning forward onto his elbows. 'He told us that Katalina is forming a colony at her castle.'

Julietta raises her eyebrows as she takes in this new information.

'I had tracked their source to a nearby graveyard. Are you sure your information is correct?'

'Who knows,' says Aaron with a scoff. 'This is Menzies Blake we're talking about.'

'The intelligence is good,' confirms Zara. 'I verified it personally.'

Julietta twirls a finger thoughtfully around one of her long, auburn locks.

'It seems that we all have the same goal: to eradicate the source of this evil. I will go to the graveyard at first light. After that, I would be happy to guide you to the castle. Right now, you should get some sleep until sunrise. There is a double bed in the back room and a bunk bed in the extension. Help yourselves.'

Julietta picks up her sword, places it on the table and starts to clean the blade with a rag.

'What about you?' I ask. 'Where will you sleep?'

'I do not need sleep. Any more questions?'

I have lots, especially about Julietta, but I'm not so rude as to ask.

'Actually, yes,' says Dexter, unsurprisingly. 'I've been wondering . . . exactly how old are you?'

Julietta doesn't seem to take offence. She smiles, like she might have been asked this before.

'I was born in 1527 in Gascony, France.'

'Wow,' says Dexter. 'That makes you . . .'

He pauses while doing the maths.

'Too old for you,' finishes Zara, much to Dexter's embarrassment. 'Now if you're quite done with quizzing our host we should all get some rest. Dexter and I will take the bunks.'

It's a nice gesture from her but it leaves me feeling slightly awkward. I've not yet shared a bed with Aaron, apart from the brief moments he came to me after a nightmare.

'Are you sure, because I'd be happy to—'

'It's fine,' says Zara.

Dexter can't seem to tear his gaze away from Julietta, so Zara helps him by taking hold of his shoulders and turning him in the opposite direction. His interest in this strange girl is bordering infatuation and it's amusing to observe. Axel makes a loud yawn then trots after them as they leave the room. I'm left standing next to Aaron, rocking from one foot to the other.

'We should go to bed too,' he says with heavy eyes. 'To sleep, obviously.'

'Yes, to sleep, of course,' I reply.

He opens the door and invites me through. I glance at Julietta to see if she took any notice of our stilted exchange.

'Goodnight,' I say to her.

She nods, the slightest of head movements, and continues to wipe the blade of her sword.

Chapter 9

Katalina

I stare at the portrait above the hearth. It is one of many which adorn the walls of this grand room within the tower keep. Each canvas depicts a forefather dating back to 1366; it was the year this castle was gifted to my family for their servitude to the Prince of Wallachia. The portrait which hangs above the fireplace is different because it contains not one but two figures: my parents. I gaze up at their faces, scrutinising the fine details of the lines and colours. I have my father's red hair and my mother's cheekbones. But when I focus on their stern expressions I feel nothing. Cold. Indifferent.

I was robbed of the chance to get to know them and that still rankles with me to this day. I was never able to show them what I am capable of. Both of my parents perished within days of each other after contracting a rare illness during the harsh winter of 1982. Maybe that is why I have such an obsession with biology. I was a medical marvel: a six-year-old who survived a deadly disease which killed two strong, healthy adults – and half the population of the village. I can still picture the face of the priest who visited me in the hospital. Three times he uttered the words of the Last Rites. In that moment, while I lay on my death bed, my human frailties succumbed. But they gave way to something much more powerful.

I pour another glass of wine from the crystal decanter. Petrus Pomerol, 1982 vintage. The year is particularly fitting. I raise the glass to my parents.

'In honour of those we have left behind. May your legacy endure.'

I rotate in a slow circle, holding the glass up to each of the portraits until I reach Baron Razvan. In his case, I am able to toast to the man in person. He is standing at the far end of the room, stock-still, like a seven foot mannequin dressed in armour. With a slow tilt of the head, he acknowledges my gesture. I take a sip of the wine before wandering towards him.

'Tell me, Razvan, what do you recall of your former life?'

He runs a finger down the long moustache which hangs from either side of his thin grey lips. When he first opens his mouth to speak, no words come out. Speech seems to be the hardest thing to master for those I reanimate.

'It was an age of brutality.' His words are forced out in a wheeze, like dust from an old book slammed closed. 'I fought in many wars. Not once did I lose a battle.'

It is easy to believe him. The mere sight of his hulking frame and gnarled features is enough to strike terror into any man. He is a walking abomination: ferocious, fearless and with a yearning appetite for blood.

I walk around him in a slow circle, admiring my creation and the pinnacle of my work. It feels good to have a companion, especially after my manservant passed away recently. Like Razvan, he wasn't much of a conversationalist either. He did his job diligently, looking after the castle while I was away in England, and ensuring my prisoner was fed and watered. Death comes to us all, but as my experiments have proven, it need not be the end. The five hundred year old warrior before me is testament to that.

Razvan is a sight to behold, even more so than my former Pyromorph partner. The thought of my time with Ludvig makes me smile, but life moves on. As much as I was fond of Ludvig, he was cursed with a fallibility which proved to be fatal. His sensitivity to water was his undoing at the hands of Sasha Hunter; it was too common a vulnerability to avoid. Razvan is a more robust prospect. His only weakness is the same as all other Porphyrians: photosensitivity. Exposure to daylight is easily avoided within the walls of my castle, where windows are few and the shutters remain closed. The density of the surrounding forest also provides cover from the harsh rays of the sun, which are limited during this cold season. My horde of warriors is an army of darkness and the Romanian wilderness is the perfect environment for them to thrive.

'Are you ready to fight again for your family?'

He slams a gauntlet against his own chest so hard that the chandelier above us shudders.

'I am at your command, my lady.'

'Good. Our army is growing by the day. A dozen of your brothers are sleeping in the crypt. I sent some others out to feed at dusk.'

He clears his throat. It sounds like an anvil being dragged across a stone floor.

'They have not yet returned.'

I check the grandfather clock. It is less than an hour to sunrise and it concerns me that my four Porphyrians are not back at the castle. I slam my wine glass onto a side table, so hard that it shatters. *Patience, Katalina. Your ancestors did not rise to power overnight.* It has taken me many years to perfect the reanimation process; it is by no means an exact science. After so many failed creations, I have no desire to lose more now.

'I will go out and look for them. First, you must feed, Razvan.'

I walk over to the wine cabinet and pull out one of the corked bottles. As I examine the contents in the candlelight, I am surprised to find it almost empty. A viscous, crimson residue clings to the glass but the liquid hardly covers the bottom of the bottle.

'We need to replenish the supply. Will you accompany me, Razvan? We must pay our guest a visit.'

He nods, his long hair swaying like chains over his steel-plated shoulders. Maybe I should braid his locks like the Norse warriors of the Dark Ages. Or perhaps I should dye it red, like mine.

Razvan follows close behind as I lead him out of the reception room and along the east wing corridor.

'We are not so different, you and I. Just as I am your leader, I too have a mentor.'

He grunts in reply. It is just as well that I did not bring him back from the dead for his conversation skills. While he might not be much of a talker, he is a willing listener.

'Menzies Blake found me when I was left orphaned in a facility for volatile children. This castle was taken away from me, and my inheritance was denied. Blake gave me my freedom and told me that one day I could become powerful enough to claim back my ancestral home. "I was once like you," he said. "Overlooked. Shunned. Denied what was mine by right. But, like you, I had abilities beyond that of the normal man. I can teach you to use your abilities to become powerful enough to take back what is yours."'

'And so you did, my lady.'

We ascend the spiral stone stairs, our footsteps in perfect synchronisation.

'It came at a cost. I was indebted to Blake. Over the years I slowly became his servant more than his pupil. It cost poor Ludvig his life and I have no intention of ending up the same way. You see, while Blake has been rotting away in a mental asylum, I have grown more powerful than he could possibly imagine. I do not need a Necromancer if I have my own army. I will never be left vulnerable again.'

'You words are spoken with wisdom.'

Razvan's arcane utterance pleases me. It feels good to have a companion to share my thoughts with once more.

I open the door to the oubliette room. The stone slabs are damp with moss gathered between the cracks. The click of my heels echoes around the circular chamber as I pace towards the well-shaped hole in the centre of the room.

'I am afraid it is time for your donation, my dear. This time, I brought a visitor for you.'

As always, my greeting is met with resounding silence. Ashleigh Hunter has proven to be an unbreakable prisoner, despite my best attempts to taunt her. I am truly surprised she has lasted for all of these years. Still, I will not need her once I have produced enough Porphyrians and built up their resistance. The blood of a White Witch was a vital ingredient for the reanimation serum but I cannot rely on it forever.

I place the usual three items inside the bucket: a bottle of water, some slices of bread and a syringe. Razvan looks on as an aloof spectator while I lower the rope attached to the handle of the bucket. I wait for the familiar tug of hands desperate for food. Instead, the bucket clangs as it hits the bottom of the oubliette.

'Do not play games with me, Ashleigh,' I warn her. 'Take the syringe and do your job.'

The last time she resisted I gave her the hose then starved her for a week. I shine a flashlight down into the dark shaft, its light reflecting back in a puddle on the rocky floor. If I am to feed Razvan before sunrise, I must hurry. For a dreadful moment I wonder if she might have finally perished.

'Go down there and find out what is wrong,' I order Razvan.

'As you wish,' he mumbles, removing his sword belt and the armour which covers his broad shoulders.

The rope attached to the bucket is old but thick and is able to support the Porphyrian's weight as he lowers himself. I angle the flashlight down; not for Razvan's benefit, whose eyes can see in the dark, but in the hope of glimpsing Ashleigh.

'If you are hiding from me, you will soon regret it,' I call to her in a sing-song voice.

The thud of boots-on-rock echoes up the oubliette shaft as Razvan drops the last ten feet. I stare into the darkness, waiting for Ashleigh's scream as she is confronted by my hideous creation.

Nothing.

Only the stomping of Razvan as he searches the underground chamber.

'Where is she?' I yell to him.

'Gone,' he replies.

'What do you mean, *gone*? There is no way out.'

He appears at the bottom of the shaft and looks up to address me.

'A tunnel has been dug. She has escaped, my lady.'

It seems impossible: the rock is several feet thick. Surely she was too weak to dig a tunnel on her own and without any tools. When Razvan holds up a metallic object – what appears to be a belt buckle – I am forced to accept the truth of what has happened. A sickening feeling churns within my stomach: a mixture of frustration and fury. It is released from my body in a wild scream

I will find you, Ashleigh Hunter, and when I do, I will drain every last drop of blood from your body.

Chapter 10

Sasha

I follow Aaron into the bedroom. It's small, claustrophobic almost, or at least that's how it feels to me. The cladded walls are bare and the window has its curtains drawn. Aaron lights an oil lamp as I stand and stare at the low bed covered with woollen blankets. Unless my eyes are deceiving me, the dimensions don't look right.

'The bed looks kind of small for two of us.'

'It's a single,' says Aaron, somehow not seeing an issue. 'It'll be cosy.'

He dumps his jacket and lifts off his tee shirt, leaving his hair a ruffled mess. I've seen him topless before, but being alone with him while he's half naked in this unfamiliar, solitary space makes my cheeks redden. Thankfully, he doesn't seem to notice. Instead, he kicks off his boots then pulls off his socks and jeans. I catch a momentary glimpse of his purple boxer shorts before he slides under the blankets.

'You're sleeping like that?' I ask him.

'Like what?'

He's not teasing; he genuinely doesn't see the problem.

'Without any clothes on.'

He laughs, like I'm the one being ridiculous.

'I can't sleep with clothes on – it's too uncomfortable. I normally sleep naked, you know.'

My blushed cheeks turn pure beetroot. I stand there fiddling with the zip of my jacket, trying to build up the courage to remove it. He clasps his hands behind his head and leans back against the headboard, trying to act casual. The shadows accentuate his muscular chest and shoulders and I have to blink hard to break my stare.

'Can you turn off the light please, Aaron?'

There's no way I am about to undress in front of him. Not here, like this, without any warning or time to prepare.

'Sure,' he replies, leaning away to blow out the flame. 'But hurry up, it's freezing in here.'

What's that supposed to mean? I think I can work it out. The best way to warm up is to share body heat, apparently. And the worst way to lose it is to remove all of your clothes. Which is what I'm about to do. Not all of them, but most of them. *Okay Sasha, you fought off monsters tonight, you can handle this.*

I take off each item of clothing like my hands have forgotten how zips and buttons work. At one point, I almost stumble and fall over and I hear Aaron chuckle. I manage to undress down to my oversize tee shirt and socks and then slowly climb into bed. Aaron shuffles over, making room for me to lie in a position which is as close to the edge as possible.

'That's better,' he says, his bare arm brushing against mine. 'Oh, you're nervous? Really, Sash?'

His Empath senses have finally picked up on my emotions as we make physical contact.

'I would have thought that was obvious without using your sixth sense. I'm . . . not used to sharing a bed.'

'And I'm not used to sleeping with underwear on.'

'Well you are! It's non-negotiable.'

He laughs, even though it wasn't a joke.

I pull the blanket over my shoulders and tuck it under my chin. The house is completely silent, except for the faint sound of someone snoring in another room. It could be Dexter, or his dog. It's hard to tell. Aaron breaks the quietness with an extended yawn.

'Are you tired?' I ask him.

'I guess so. It came on all of sudden. I can stay awake and talk to you for a while, though.'

He can barely get the words out without yawning again.

'It's fine,' I reply. 'I'm not sure I'll be able to sleep a wink in here anyway.'

'Is the bed not comfortable? Or is it me? Because I can take the floor.'

I shuffle a little closer to reassure him.

'No, really, you don't need to do that. It's this place. And the thought of Julietta, awake in the next room, sharpening her sword while we all sleep. Do you think we can trust her?'

Aaron replies with words that are slurred as they mix with the tail end of another yawn.

'She's an Amaranth, Sash. They are sworn to protect the innocent. It's in their DNA. Julietta is the best ally we could hope for.'

I wish I knew more about these strange immortal people. Zara recognised Julietta immediately as an Amaranth and I make a mental note to ask her about it. If knowledge is power, I've always felt kind of powerless as an Agent. I hope that I'll get to learn from my mother what my father never had the chance to teach me.

'Do you think Julietta will help us find my mum?'

I can hear his breaths slow down and become more drawn out.

'I'm sure of it,' he replies, so low it's almost a whisper.

I needn't have worried about any romantic notions Aaron might have had. Within a matter of seconds, he starts to twitch. It's unlike him to fall asleep so quickly. His dreams are often plagued by nightmarish visions which prevent him from drifting off. Back in London, he often sits up to the early hours watching TV or playing computer games. I decide not to disturb him; he could do with the rest. We've got the most challenging of missions ahead of us and everyone will need to be at their best if we're to succeed.

Despite all my best efforts, sleep evades me. I try every trick I know: breathing exercises, meditation, even counting sheep. I cuddle up to Aaron, hoping that his relaxed state and warmth will send me off. The truth is that my mind is too active. It feels like there's too much at stake to rest, even though I know that's what my body needs. It becomes even harder when my empty stomach starts to rumble and I regret not having any of the soup. 'You have to eat to keep your strength up,' Dad would always say to me as a child. He was right about so many things, I just never realised it at the time.

My thoughts linger on my father. They quickly darken and drift to what happened to him at the hands of Katalina. The vision of him lying outside the burning Agency headquarters is lodged in my head like an internal scar. It's an image I'll never be able to forget. I can't undo the events of that day, but I can save my mother and ensure that Kat will never harm anyone else ever again.

I check my watch to find it's 5am – still another hour or so until dawn. I decide to get up to go the bathroom. Aaron is normally a light sleeper but this time he's completely out. He doesn't move, even when I almost trip over the bed frame as I make my way to the door. I'm glad that he's able to get a decent night's sleep for once.

I move into the sitting room to find it empty, with Julietta nowhere to be seen. Her sword is on the table and a candle is burning, so she can't be far away. To get to the bathroom, I have to walk through Zara and Dexter's room. They are both fast asleep, with Axel snoring next to Dexter's bed. Zara must have been really tired as she has fallen sleep with her glasses on. I carefully remove them and place them on a side table. Her breathing is heavy and she doesn't move a muscle. Why am I the only one wide awake? Something just doesn't feel right.

I shake Zara gently, knowing that she won't mind if I wake her. I begin to worry when I can't rouse her. Dexter is in the same state of complete unconsciousness. I get no response even when I slap him on the cheeks. I nudge Axel but it's no use – the dog is curled up and in as deep a sleep as all the others. That's when something alarming strikes me: everyone had the soup except me, because I gave mine to Axel. And now everyone is in a total state of unconsciousness. There's only one logical explanation: *they've been drugged.*

I leap up and scramble out of the room, hoping that somehow I can revive Aaron. He is the only one who I haven't forcibly tried to wake up. Maybe his larger, more muscular body will be more resistant to whatever drug was in the soup.

As I rush into the sitting room, Julietta is standing next to the table, sword in hand. I come to a dead stop before her.

'You are still awake,' she remarks, curiously.

'I didn't have any of your soup. I gave mine to the dog.'

'Ah. That explains it.'

I can't believe she is admitting to it so calmly.

'You . . . *you drugged them?*'

Julietta shrugs in nonchalant acceptance.

'I gave them a non-harmful sedative hypnotic. They will all wake up in a matter of hours. In fact, it will be the best sleep they have ever had.'

'We trusted you. Why would you do that?'

'It is for their own good. I have seen many mortals die at the hands of those creatures. It is best that your friends stay here while I take care of things. You can wait for them to wake.'

I feel anger building within me. My eyes must be burning crimson.

'Don't you realise what you've done? We're not just here to destroy monsters – we're here to rescue my mother!' I take a step towards her, my voice rising. 'Every minute that passes is another moment she's in danger. How can we possibly save her if all of my friends are unconscious?'

Julietta places her sword on the table and folds her arms.

'Your shouting will not wake your friends, but it might wake our neighbours, or alert others to your whereabouts.'

I ignore her request to lower my voice.

'I didn't come here for my own safety; I came here for my mother. And I'm not wasting another second when I can be out there looking for her.'

I march towards the front door and then stop when I realise I'm still in a tee shirt and socks.

'Interesting,' says Julietta, as though she's talking to herself. 'I was once young and careless. You remind me of me when I was your age.'

It feels like a strange comment from someone who looks no older than me. Julietta might be an immortal but I'm not willing to defer to her authority. Not while my mother's life is on the line.

'We can stand here arguing all you like but I've made up my mind.'

Julietta shrugs and pulls on her leather jacket as though she's getting ready to leave.

'It does not have to be a choice between staying here or going on your own, Sasha. There is another option: you could come with me.'

Her offer catches me off guard. She drugged my friends to keep them safe but now she's willing to bring me with her. It doesn't make sense. I want to believe Julietta but after the past betrayals of Menzies Blake and Kat, I find it hard to trust anyone.

'I already told you – I'm not here to hunt monsters.'

'And I do not expect as much,' she replies. 'You are mortal, after all. But if the Porphyrians are linked to the Metamorph you speak of then we both have a vested interest in finding their source. I have been tracking the creature's movements for some time. They rise from a graveyard on the other side of the forest. If you come with me, I have one condition: that you observe only and do exactly as I say without question. Maybe we will both discover the answers we are searching for.'

I stare down at my stripy socks as I ponder her offer. It was rash of me to think I could go running out in the middle of the night, into a dense forest where bloodthirsty monsters lurk. If Julietta can eradicate Kat's army of protectors, I have no option but to trust her.

'I'll get dressed,' I say, hurrying past her.

'Good. I shall go and find you a weapon.'

Her comment makes me stop and turn.

'But I thought you said you didn't want me to fight?'

She slides her sword into the hidden sheath across her back and zips up her leather jacket.

'That is correct. I do not want you to fight. But that does not mean that you will not have to.'

Chapter 11

Sasha

I quickly dress in the bedroom without having to worry about making noise. A tornado wouldn't wake Aaron right now. I check his pulse rate and temperature, both of which seem normal. I'd feel better if I was able to talk to him and get his advice on what I'm about to undertake. I replay his last words in my mind: *Julietta is the best ally we could hope for.* I always feel safer with Aaron but at the same time I'm relieved that I'm going with Julietta on my own. Without the burden of a large group, we can move quickly and silently. Most importantly, I won't be placing my friends in a dangerous situation. It's *my* mother; it's *my* responsibility. I brush the hair away from Aaron's face and kiss him gently on the forehead. Before leaving, I pick up my Athame and shove it into my pocket. It's useless to me, I know that, but when I find my mother I'm sure she'll be glad to receive it.

When I walk back into the sitting room, Julietta is waiting for me. She nods to a large object on the table and my eyes grow as I take in the brutal-looking weapon.

'This is for you,' she says as I stand there gawping. 'It is a crossbow.'

My shocked expression no doubt led her to state the obvious. She picks up the crossbow and one of the blood-stained bolts.

'This goes here, in the flight groove,' she explains, slotting the shaft in place. 'The stock rests on your shoulder. Line up the sight with your target, relax, and then pull the trigger. Hopefully you will not have to use it. If you do, remember one thing: head shots only.'

It feels like a surreal moment: having a crash course in medieval weaponry delivered by an immortal in preparation to take on a host of vampire-like creatures. The moment doesn't last long; reality is handed to me in the form of the heavy crossbow which has clearly been used before, to murderous effect. I rotate the weapon clumsily, not totally convinced that I could use it to hit the door opposite, let alone a moving target.

'Why head shots only?' I ask hesitantly. 'Surely any vital organ is a good target?'

'You must kill the brain,' she replies calmly in her eloquent French accent. 'It is the only way to stop them. Porphyrians feel no pain and do not succumb like an average man, so anything else is a wasted shot. Remember: these creatures are already dead. We need to send them back to where they belong. You have six bolts. Use them, and reuse them, wisely.'

I nod, feigning confidence. Then drop the bolts and watch as they scatter across the floor. Julietta doesn't react as I kneel down to collect them but I feel the need to justify myself all the same.

'I've dealt with a Poltergeist before now, just so you know.' I snap the bolts into the holders near the grip. 'And some Black Witches too. I took the head right off one, actually.'

Julietta smiles, like she's humouring me.

'Ready?' I glance back at the bedroom door and she seems to read my mind. 'We will be back before dawn and before your friends wake.'

I wrap my fingers firmly around the crossbow and try to look like I know what I'm doing.

'I'm ready. Let's do this.'

We trek out of the village and back towards the forest which stretches out at the base of the vast mountain range. At one point, Julietta offers to carry the crossbow for me. I thank her but refuse, determined to carry my own weight. As I tread alongside her, I'm struck by her aura: serene, confident and wise beyond her years. Or rather, wise because of her years. She grew up in an age of savage warfare, where the act of killing was performed up close while looking directly into your enemy's eyes. It feels safe to be alongside her, although it's a misplaced safety; Julietta might be immortal but I am as vulnerable as anyone else. I build up the courage to ask the single most burning question I have about her strange existence.

'So . . . you can't be killed?'

She throws me a sideways glance and her pace quickens.

'If you must know, I will tell you. I can be hurt. I feel pain, just like you. My body can be wounded. The only difference is that I heal at an accelerated rate. And in answer to your question, I can be killed in the same way as the Porphyrians. If my head is removed, my eternal life will be over. Despite what you may think, Amaranths do not live forever.'

Her blunt statement hides centuries of conflicts, battles and near-misses. Julietta is like a cat that's on its last life.

'Then we'll both have to keep our heads.'

My unintentional pun makes me cringe. I blame it on spending so much time around Aaron and his bad jokes.

'I like that,' says Julietta, without showing any external emotion to suggest she actually does.

Rain starts to fall in a light drizzle as we carve a route through the trees. My jeans catch in a sharp thorn and I manage to tear them as I pull myself free. It feels as though the forest is trying to prevent my progress. If it's a warning, I choose to ignore it. My legs burn from the gradual incline; my arms ache from the weight of the crossbow; my mind is heavy with the thought of what lies ahead. It doesn't take long before I become breathless and I'm about to ask for a rest when Julietta comes to a halt.

'We are close to where I found you. The graveyard is not far from here.'

She drops to her knees and scoops up and handful of mud. I watch, mystified, as she starts to smear it over her face and hands. Before long, the only visible part of her is the whites of her eyes.

'Ah, camouflage,' I say, trying to find a nice patch of mud, if such a thing even exists.

Julietta waits patiently as I rub the earth over my cheekbones and forehead.

'Allow me,' she says, taking another scoop and roughly applying it to my face and neck in large clumps. 'Porphyrians have excellent senses. They will see, hear or smell you long before you realise they are near. The mud will help but we must be silent and fast. When the time comes, I will lead the attack and you will cover me from a distance. Do not shoot unless I tell you to. Understand?'

I nod and rake my wet hair back into a ponytail. Julietta doesn't seem to mind that her long, auburn hair dangles over her face. It gives her a menacing appearance, even before she draws her sword.

We press on as the rain begins to fall in heavy swathes, drenching the undergrowth. I hear a distant rumble in the gloomy sky. Julietta leads the way in a zig-zag route, eventually stopping behind the wide trunk of a tree.

'The graveyard is fifty yards ahead. It is within range of your crossbow. You will wait here while I investigate. If necessary, I will call out only two instructions: 'Shoot' or 'Run'. If you hear either word, act on it immediately.'

I unclip a bolt and place it into the groove of the crossbow, pleased with myself that I managed not to drop it this time. Julietta removes it, turns it around, and places it back in the groove the correct way around. I'm about to apologise when she places a finger to her lips. We peer around the tree trunk and towards the graveyard. It's so overgrown that it could easily be missed. Most of the crumbling headstones are leaning to one side and covered in moss. A rusted iron fence surrounds the square yard, at the centre of which is a small circular building.

I lean further out, trying to see through the darkness and rainfall. Julietta pulls me back sharply.

'Someone is coming,' she whispers.

I watch as a lone figure walks amongst the gravestones. It's too small to be a Porphyrian. Whoever it is, they appear to be looking for something, or someone. I take in the details: a slender figure, feline in her movements and with bright red hair. *It's Katalina.* My hands grip the crossbow tightly.

'It's her!' I say to Julietta in a hushed tone. 'She's the one who created the Porphyrians!'

My eyes narrow as I observe Kat creeping between the headstones, inspecting the graves of each.

'She must be searching for those we killed earlier,' replies Julietta.

I expect her to leap into action and charge at Kat but instead she remains still and silent. It's the first time I've set eyes upon Kat since she murdered my father. Adrenaline pumps through my system, combining with my emotions, fuelling me to do the thing I came here for. *With one shot, I can end her.* Nobody else has to die like my father did. My finger moves onto the trigger as I lift the crossbow to take aim.

'No,' says Julietta, lowering my weapon.

I shrug her hand away.

'If you won't do something, I will.'

Julietta positions herself in front of me and grips me by the shoulders.

'This is not how we work, Sasha. I cannot kill her until I have proof of her ill doings.'

I want to shove her aside and take the shot but another thought enters my mind. This isn't the only reason I came here. If I kill Kat, I may never discover the whereabouts of my mother.

As I stare past Julietta, a second shadowy figure appears. It's a large man, at least seven feet tall. He stomps through the trees decked in armour and as he turns I notice that he's carrying a broadsword. His ancient weapon is almost as long as an average person and impossible for any normal human to wield. Just as I'm sizing him up, he twists his head in our direction, like a predator that has caught a scent. A cold chill runs across my skin as he stares directly at us. Beneath his helmet, his face is flecked with green, rotting skin and two glowing eyes. A long, thin moustache dangles from his jowls. It's a Porphyrian but this one is much bigger and intimidating than the others.

'Is that enough proof for you?' I stammer, pointing towards the beast.

Julietta doesn't hesitate.

In the space of a breath, she darts forwards and closes on the monster. I watch, awestruck, as she propels herself into the air off a fallen tree trunk. With two hands on the hilt of her sword, she brings the blade down in a vicious arc, aiming for the neck of the armoured creature. He manages to bring his own sword up just in time, resulting in a mighty clash of steel. A brief flash of sparks lights up the dim graveyard. Julietta is thrown sideways by the strength of the parry, forcing her to roll and break her fall. She lands in between two headstones, with Kat behind her and the giant Porphyrian in front.

Instinctively, I lift the crossbow and lower my eye to the sight. The dark shape of the giant creature moves in between the crosshairs. I take the shot, surprised at the recoil effect of the string. The bolt flies wider than I intended, glancing off the Porphyrian's shoulder armour and deflecting it downwards. It hammers into a headstone, inches away from Julietta. I curse at my rash shot which almost did more harm than good.

'Don't shoot!' she shouts, rising from her crouched position. 'Run!'

I'm too transfixed to act on her instruction. My eyes won't shift from the battle between the undead creature and the immortal girl. The Porphyrian bears down on Julietta with his massive broadsword poised. The muscles in his exposed arms bunch like cannonballs. Further back, Kat is creeping up with her claws raised. *I'm not going run.* Despite Julietta's warning, I place another bolt into the groove of the crossbow.

My second shot is rushed; it flies wildly above the assailant and shatters a tile on the roof of the crypt. I fumble for another bolt, which falls from my fingers and disappears into the dark undergrowth. That's three arrows gone and only three left.

I'm startled by the repetitive sound of clashing steel. Julietta has launched a flurry of blows at the Porphyrian, forcing him backwards. A streak of blood splatters across a headstone as she slashes at his thigh. He doesn't seem the slightest bit affected by the wound but that's not the only problem.

'Watch out!' I shout to Julietta. 'Behind you!'

My warning comes too late. Kat rushes her and wraps her arms around her torso, pinning her arms to her sides. Julietta wrestles to free herself as the Porphyrian advances once more. At first I'm confused by Kat's actions, until she hisses an order to her creature.

'Razvan, take off her head.'

I can't let them destroy Julietta. I *won't* let them.

With a deep breath, I load another bolt and take aim. I train the crosshairs on the Porphyrian, aiming for the one place left exposed on his body. *You have to believe you can do this, Sasha.*

I relax
Then squeeze the trigger.
Slowly.
With meaningful precision.

The bolt cuts through the air and hammers into the Porphyrian's bare sword arm, the arrow tip burying itself deep into his muscle. He doesn't cry out in pain like any normal man would. Instead, he inspects the bolt which has lodged between his tendons. As he lifts his arm, an involuntary spasm causes him to drop his weapon. In the moment of stunned silence, Julietta reacts. She grabs onto Kat's arms and throws her over her shoulder. The Metamorph lands on all fours, her limbs like springs. She snaps her head in my direction. As I lower the crossbow, we make eye contact for the first time.

'Sasha Hunter,' she snarls, curling her lips into a smile. 'You should have run when you had the chance.'

I carefully load another bolt without breaking eye contact. I notice the long scar on one side of her face from her last clash with Zara. It's now up to me to finish what she started. My eyes are burning crimson, their fire fuelled by the months of compressed grief. In my peripheral vision, I can see the Porphyrian picking up his sword with his left hand and resuming his attack on Julietta. It just leaves me and Kat.

She marches forwards, ignoring the crossbow aimed directly at her.

This isn't a threat, Katalina. It's a promise.

She's less than twenty yards away and closing.

'I know why you're here,' she says. 'I know you, Sasha. You won't do it. You *can't* do it.'

Her mistake is to underestimate me.

'You killed my father,' I say to her, my words coming out strong.

I can see her twisted face as I line the crosshairs with the centre of her forehead. In my mind, I hear my father's voice. *Always face your fears head on.* Then an image flashes up of my mother. That's when I realise that I can't kill Kat. Not yet. Instead, I decide on a different course of action: to disable her and take her alive . . .

I lower the crossbow and unleash the bolt. It flies low through the air and hammers into Kat's thigh. She throws her head back and cries out. At the exact same moment, the Porphyrian delivers a thunderous kick to Julietta. A sickening crunch of snapping bones rings out as she crumples. I turn my attention back to Kat who is staggering and clutching her leg, the bloodied arrow shaft poking through the gaps in her fingers.

'Forget her, Razvan,' she calls to her beast. 'I want this one!'

The Porphyrian begins to pace towards me, his giant strides eating up the ground. I fire another shot, aiming for his head, but it glances harmlessly off his helmet. I've got one bolt left, and only a matter of seconds before the creature is upon me.

Julietta can no longer help. I prepare to make my final shot. *Make it count, Sasha.* Just as I'm about to fire, the Porphyrian suddenly leaps backwards like he just stood on a landmine. I'm confused, until I work out exactly what repelled him. It's the first rays of daylight breaking through the trees. I recall Julietta's explanation of their weakness: Porphyrians are photosensitive. He's unable to get any closer while I'm standing in the sunlight of a small clearing.

It's a satisfying sight to see the creature retreat into the shadows of the trees, growling with frustration. I keep my crossbow trained on him as he moves out of range and towards his injured leader. He picks Kat up and cradles her in his arms.

'The sun is rising,' he murmurs to her in a gravelly voice. 'We must go.'

As they disappear into the forest, I hear a shrill voice call out to me.

'Your efforts are futile, Sasha Hunter. I have a whole army . . . and they are coming for your blood!'

As soon as they've left, I lower the crossbow and dash to Julietta. In my panic to reach her, I snag my jeans on a thorn bush and manage to cut my leg. I ignore the pain and trickle of blood, which is nothing compared to Julietta's condition. She's groaning and clutching at her side. When I peel back her jacket, I'm sickened to see the shard of a broken rib protruding through her skin. She winces as she pushes it back into place.

'That beast was strong.'

'That's the understatement of the century,' I reply, trying not to vomit as she manipulates her broken bones.

After a few moments of heavy breathing to suck up the pain, Julietta manages to climb to her feet. I put a supporting arm around her waist and she uses her sword as a crutch. We hobble away from the graveyard, putting some distance between ourselves and our enemy until Julietta can recover. With each step her strength returns until she's finally able to walk unaided.

We stop near a small stream which Julietta uses to wash the dried blood from the blade of her sword. She seems to be lost in thought, perhaps reflecting on another clash without achieving the desired outcome.

'I have witnessed all I need to,' she announces, standing from her crouched position. 'That woman is controlling those creatures. As an Amaranth, I am sworn to protect the innocent. I will help you to eliminate her, Sasha.'

I'm grateful for her pledge of allegiance. We'll need all the help we can get.

'Kat might have escaped but she's injured and bleeding. Maybe we can head back to the graveyard and track her to the castle?'

I hear the crunching of footsteps behind me. Julietta shoves me aside and lifts her sword. I turn and point the crossbow at the figure that has crept up on us.

'Who are you?' demands Julietta of the man.

My eyes trace upwards from the expensive shoes, the finely pressed trousers and the long overcoat. As the shadows retreat from his face, I know exactly who he is.

It's Menzies Blake.

CHAPTER 12

AARON

A warm ray of sunlight softy wakes me as it shines through a slit in the curtains. I yawn and stretch, feeling like I've slept for days. And not a single nightmare. I reach across the bed for Sasha but she's not there. Maybe she got up to use the bathroom. But her side of the bed feels cold and I can't sense any of her residual energy, like she's not been there for a while. And all of her clothes are gone. She must have woken up much earlier. It looks like I might be the only one sleeping in.

'Get up, lazy bones,' I say out loud to myself in the same way my mother used to.

A dose of self-deprecation is enough to get me going. I throw on my jeans and shuffle into the sitting room, expecting to be greeted by judgemental stares. No Sasha. No Julietta. And no signs of anyone else. A glance at the clock tells me that it's 7am, so I've hardly overslept. The house is quiet. *Too* quiet.

I throw open the door to the far bedroom where I'm surprised to find Zara, Dexter and Axel still fast asleep. I call their names and shake the bunkbed until they almost fall out. It's only when I splash Zara's face with cold water that I finally manage to get a response.

'What the hell?' she says, squinting and wiping her face.

'What's wrong?'

'Sasha and Julietta are missing.'

'Ugh.' She reaches for her glasses. 'They're probably collecting firewood or something.'

'Zara, I slept really well. Not a single nightmare.'

She sits up in bed and angrily throws aside the wet end of her blanket.

'Did you really just drench me for that? Tell me there's more, because if not—'

'Something's not right. Look at Dexter and Axel – they're still dead to the world.'

Zara leans over from the top bunk to check, then swings her legs around and jumps down. She tries to wake Dexter, without success. I fetch another glass of water and do the honours.

'What are you doing, you idiot?'

Dexter springs up with water dripping from his scowling face.

'Easy buddy, I had to do the same to Zara. Something's wrong. I think there could be a carbon monoxide leak in here.'

Axel rouses at the same time as his master, which is good, because I had no desire to rile his bear of a dog. I've already felt the full force of its bite once before.

'It can't be carbon monoxide,' says Zara. 'We'd all be dead if it was. Besides, Sasha was obviously well enough to wake up and head out.'

I try to figure out why we all slept so soundly and deeply while Sasha apparently didn't.

'It's strange. Everyone went to bed at the same time after eating.'

'But Sasha didn't eat,' replies Dexter. 'I saw her feed her soup to Axel beneath the table.'

The dog dips his head, almost guiltily.

Zara throws me an alarmed glance before pushing past and hurrying into the kitchen.

'What are you looking for?' I ask her, my concern for Sasha growing by the second.

I watch, bemused, as she rummages through the cupboards.

'This,' she says eventually, holding up a jar of pills. 'Benzodiazepine.'

'Benzo... what?'

'They're strong sleeping pills,' clarifies Zara. 'Julietta must have spiked our soup.'

My stomach drops.

'She's kidnapped Sasha!' I yell, slamming my first onto the worktop.

After what happened in America, I swore to myself that I would never leave her in danger. I came so close to losing her. I can't let that happen again.

'We don't know that for sure,' says Zara.

I don't have time for her level-headedness, not when my girlfriend is missing in a place full of monsters.

'We shouldn't have trusted Katalina. I have to find Sasha.'

I hurry past Zara but she hooks me by the arm.

'Wait up, Aaron. I agree that we need to find Sasha but let me get dressed so that I can come with you.'

'We'll come too,' says Dexter, hopping around as he pulls on his jeans. 'Axel is awesome at tracking.'

He pats the dog on the head and Axel seems to grin back at him eagerly.

Zara lingers and I can tell her mental cogs are turning.

'Hang on, we can't all go. One of us needs to wait here in case Sasha returns.' I meet her stare with an uncompromising look. 'Fine. You three go, I'll stay.'

It's typical of Zara to know when to take a back seat and I'm grateful for that.

'But what if Julietta comes back?' I ask, my concern shifting from girlfriend to sister.

I don't need to spell it out. If Julietta was cunning enough to spike us, who knows what she's capable of.

'I can handle myself,' says Zara as she calmly fills the kettle.

I don't doubt that for a moment, but it doesn't make it any easier to leave her on her own.

'We'll find Sasha then meet you back here,' I assure her. 'We should never have trusted that Amaranth girl.'

Or anyone. Ever. Again.

I'm outside the house within sixty seconds. Dexter follows, still pulling on his jacket and bobble hat as he trails behind. As we trudge across the muddy path which leads to the road, I notice the bearded Romanian man, Marin, standing smoking on his porch. He eyes us silently as he blows a thick cloud of smoke into the crisp morning air.

'Hey there,' I call to him. 'Did you see Julietta?'

He stares back blankly, like I just spoke to him in a foreign language. Which is exactly what I just did.

'JU–Ll–ETTA,' I repeat, slowly and loudly, as if that will help.

Marin shrugs and takes another puff of his cigarette.

'Let me try,' says Dexter as he finally catches up with Axel.

I watch with a degree of embarrassment as he traces the outline of a woman with his hands before mimicking her walk.

'This is ridiculous,' I mutter. 'Let's go.'

'*Oui,*' replies Marin. '*Le Diable Rouge! Elle est allée au nord de la forêt.*'

'*Merci, Monsieur!*' says Dexter as the man disappears inside his cabin. He turns to me with a self-satisfied smile. 'Not bad for a high school French drop-out, huh?'

I throw my arms out in exasperation.

'So what did he say?'

'He told me that she went north to the forest. I think.'

I start to pace up the hillside road. Dexter pulls his dog's lead and then runs to catch up.

'Is that all he said?' I ask him.

'That was all that made sense,' he replies. 'He described Julietta as *Le Diable Rouge* . . . The Red Devil.'

I glance back at the cabin, narrowing my eyes at the bearded-man who is now peering at us from behind his front window. Can we trust him to point us in the direction of Julietta, or is he trying to throw us off the scent? My instinct tell me that Sasha is out there somewhere in the forest and I decide to trust it. When I find her, I won't let her out of my sight ever again. I clench my jaw tightly and quicken my step. We have to find Sasha, and fast.

I lead the way into the forest, following the same track that we used to get to the village. As soon as we're clear of the road, Dexter releases Axel from his leash.

'Find Sasha, boy!' he says in a high pitched, excitable voice.

The dog's tail wags furiously as he weaves from side to side with his nose close to the ground. It feels too much like a game to be of any help. I wait impatiently as the black dog searches the area in an ever growing radius. Just as I'm about to suggest we split up, Axel's head pops up.

'He's found something,' says Dexter, running towards the dog.

When I jog the short distance across the forest, the discovery sickens me. A small strip of torn denim is attached to a thorn bush. It's the exact same shade of blue as Sasha's jeans. Worse still, it has drops of blood on it. Dexter reluctantly hands me the shredded cloth. The moment I touch it, the terrible truth is immediately revealed.

'It's hers,' I confirm.

I want my Empath senses to be wrong, but they never are.

'It might have been an accident,' says Dexter hopefully. 'Axel has her scent now. He'll find her, I promise.'

He pats me on the shoulder and offers a forced smile. In the past, Dexter and I have had our issues, but I can tell this matters as much to him as it does to me. He might be the son of Menzies Blake, but he's a good friend to Sasha and he cares about her. If he wasn't here with me now, I'd probably lose my mind.

'Thank you, Dexter. This means a lot to me.'

'Don't sweat it,' he replies with a warm smile. 'Axel will track her down, just watch him.'

The dog takes off in a straight line through the trees. I focus on the action of placing one foot in front of the other, refusing to let any terrible thoughts creep into my head. Dexter seems to sense the burden of my worry and does his best to occupy my mind.

'You know, I came home to seek closure with my father. In my head, I saw two outcomes: either he would accept me as his son and see the error of his ways, or I would walk away safe in the knowledge that at least I tried. I want you to know that I feel responsible for what he did to Sasha and her family.'

'Dexter, please don't feel that way. Your father's actions are absolutely no reflection on you.'

'But I feel as though they are. I have to put right what he got so badly wrong. If my father won't fix things then I'll fix it on his behalf. I'll help you find Sasha and her mother. And if the opportunity presents itself, I'll destroy Katalina.'

After a short while, Axel comes to a stop. He points his nose to a clearing up ahead, where a circular building sits behind rusted railings. As we walk towards it, I notice a scattering of headstones. The feeling of nausea rises up once more as I realise where we are.

'This must be the graveyard Julietta talked about.'

Dexter nods solemnly and encourages his dog to proceed.

We walk through a gap in the fence and start to explore the grim surroundings. I try my best to shut out the residual energy which is always so prevalent in places like this. It's like white noise in my ears, a constant static screaming. I start to feel worse when we discover several open graves which look as though they were recently exhumed.

'I dread to think what happened here,' I muse.

When Dexter doesn't speak, I turn around. He's staring at one of the graves. The hairs on my arms rise as I see a splatter of fresh blood across the headstone. I don't want to consider what this means. It all feels wrong, like my nightmares have somehow filtered into reality.

Axel barks and breaks my fixated stare.

'What is it boy?' asks Dexter.

The dog takes off again, even faster than before. Dexter shoves me into action and we race after Axel. He swerves around the trees, barking persistently. When he eventually comes to a halt, I can see something up ahead in the distance. It's a female figure slumped against the tree. She has long, dark hair and a slight frame and she looks like she's in a bad way. Is my mind playing tricks on me?

'Sasha!'

She fails to respond as I sprint towards her. My heart is in my throat. I crouch before her and brush back her hair. Even before I see her face, I know it's not Sasha. The moment I touch her, I can sense it. It's an older woman, dirty and frail. Her face is drawn and she's barely conscious.

'Who are you?' I ask her.

'Help me,' she replies, reaching to me with a shaking hand. 'My name is Ashleigh Hunter.'

Chapter 13

Sasha

What the hell are you doing here? The shock of being confronted by Menzies Blake doesn't last long. It was naïve of me to think that I might have seen him for the last time. He doesn't answer my question straight away. Instead, he removes his hands from his pockets and shows his open palms to Julietta as if to prove he means no harm. The trouble is that he's a Necromancer and I've seen exactly what he can do with his bare hands.

'I had no intention of following you here, Sasha.' His voice is low and passive. 'You helped to restore my sanity, and my freedom. Most of all, you are a loyal friend to my son. He is the only thing which matters to me. I value Dexter's welfare above all else, which is why I am here.'

Another person might be fooled into thinking that he's being humble. Honest, even. But I know Blake better than most. It was only yesterday that he sent us through the portal; a broken man and a failed father. And now here he is, in the middle of a Romanian forest, uttering words more suited to a Dad of the Year Award speech.

'You knew this would be a dangerous mission,' I remind him. 'Dexter is his own man. He wants to be here. He wants to help.'

As I turn to walk away Blake takes a step forwards. Julietta grips the pommel of her sword in warning.

'That is close enough, stranger.'

'I'm no stranger,' he replies. 'I think you'll find that Sasha and I are old acquaintances.'

He chuckles nervously as though he's looking for some kind of acceptance. He won't get that from me. I feel my eyes burning red as I lean towards him.

'I'm here to save my mother, and my mother is here because of you. We freed you out of necessity. Don't mistake our actions as some kind of truce. I'll never forget what you did to me and my family, Blake.'

I feel a rage building inside me as I stare him down. My crossbow has no bolts but it would still work as a bludgeoning weapon.

'You need to hear me out, Sasha,' he says, almost pleading in his expression. 'I have received some new information which will greatly affect your mission. If not for your own sake, do it for Dexter.'

Blake knows me well enough to understand that my weakness is my family and friends. He's playing on the fact that Dexter is his son but also someone who I care about. I want to tell him where to go but – as always – he has dangled a carrot before me; one which is too important to ignore.

Julietta leans in and talks to me out of the side of her mouth.

'Do you want me to make him go away?'

I'm tempted to take her up on the offer. Instead, I bite down on my lip and decide to give Blake a chance.

'Say what you have to say, then leave.'

He thrusts his hands deep into the pockets of his overcoat. Julietta tenses, anticipating that he might pull out a weapon, but Blake simply smiles.

'Not here. What I have to say must be heard by everyone.'

And so the games begin. Only this time I'm not having it.

'It's right now, right here, or not at all. I can pass on your message to the others.'

Our conversations always seem to go this way: a series of moves and countermoves, jostling for power like a game of mental chess.

'I don't expect you to trust me, Sasha, so you'll forgive me for not trusting you either. I am aware that Zara Gordon is now the leader of the UK branch of The Agency. My message must be delivered directly to her. I also wish to see my son. If you take me to them, I will provide you all with the information I have – information that is vital to your survival.'

Blake lowers his head in a pious manner. His black hair, streaked with grey, is made slick by the morning drizzle. I look to Julietta to see if she's buying any of this crap.

'You don't have to do this,' she says, as though reading my thoughts.

Except I already know that I do. If Blake has information on Kat or my mother, I can't simply ignore it. We're short on leads and running out of time. He's the last person on this planet that I would choose to trust. However, I've come to learn that being able to choose who you trust is often a luxury.

'I'll bring you to the others,' I concede. 'Just remember what happened the last time you crossed me.'

Blake pulls up his collars and rubs his hands to warm them.

'How could I forget?'

We walk back through the forest in tense silence. I lead the way, with Blake following and Julietta close behind him. She insists on taking a position at the rear to keep an eye on things. Whenever I glance over my shoulder, I see her eyes boring into the back of Blake's head. I'm truly grateful for her company; it's reassuring to know that if Blake tries anything she will leap to my defence. It feels good to have an immortal covering my back.

My mind cycles through what crucial information Blake might hold. What could he have possibly discovered in the last twenty-four hours since we left him in London? And how did he know that Zara had been made leader of The Agency? I'm keen to find out, but at the same time I'm dreading returning to the cabin with our unwelcome guest. The atmosphere will already be tense, especially if the others have realised that Julietta drugged them. Aaron won't be happy about how I snuck off and left him. He was also dead-against ever trusting Blake in the first place. My decision to bring him before the group may well cause havoc at a time when we need to be most together. I just hope that whatever Blake has to say, it's worth it.

My heavy thoughts are broken when Blake appears alongside me and makes an interrupting cough.

'Who is your strange friend, Sasha?' he asks, nodding back towards Julietta. 'And why is she carrying a sword? And you a crossbow? It's like something out of the Middle Ages.'

His attempt to make friendly conversation only leaves me feeling cold.

'Her name is Julietta,' I reply, deciding against revealing her true identity. 'She has the same goals as we do.'

'I see. Then she will also be interested in what I have to say.'

There he goes again: tempting me with his guarded knowledge. I'm sure he wants me to beg him to divulge whatever information he has but I won't give him the satisfaction. Instead, I decide on a different approach.

'How did you find us?' I ask him. 'We stopped at the stream in the middle of the forest on our way back to the village. You had no way of knowing we'd be there.'

He shrugs off my perfectly valid point.

'It wasn't so far from the portal. Perhaps you forget that I have highly tuned senses.'

'You're a Necromancer. You talk to the dead.'

I hear Julietta quicken her step to close the distance between us. At least now she knows what we're dealing with.

'Indeed I am,' replies Blake in nonchalant admission. 'The dead see and hear everything. Luckily for me there are lots of lingering spirits in this area.'

'There are other things too. Terrible things which attacked us the moment we arrived here. You knew all about them.'

He drops his head, burying his chin inside the collar of his overcoat.

'All will be explained soon.'

I just hope that soon is soon enough.

It's an uneasy journey with Blake alongside me in such a remote place, despite Julietta watching his every move. I keep my head down, staring at my boots as they crunch over twigs and leave imprints in the soft earth. Then something catches my eye: the twinkle of a small metallic object half-buried in the foliage. It stands out for being out of place, as though the natural surroundings refuse to fully consume the man-made object. I reach down to pick it up and realise that it's connected to a chain. As I wipe the mud from the penny-sized object its identity is immediately revealed.

'What is it, Sasha?' asks Julietta, peering down at the pendant in my trembling hand.

I can't take my eyes off the small opal stone. I can barely speak.

'It's my birthstone. This belonged to my mother. *She was here.*'

It's the first real evidence of her existence since we've been out here. I'm filled with hope, followed by a rush of panic. Julietta places a supporting hand underneath my elbow.

'I thought your mother was imprisoned?'

'I thought so too. But how could her necklace have ended up here, in the middle of the forest?'

Blake glances at the pendant before wandering off.

'Where are you going?' Julietta says to him, her tone abrasive.

'Footprints,' he says, pointing to the ground. 'And there's more than one set. Look.'

Blake's right. If my mother was here, she wasn't alone. My mind betrays the hope which blooms in my chest by conjuring up the worst-case-scenario: What if she escaped only to be recaptured? Maybe she was being transported somewhere else? The chain of the necklace is snapped, which may have happened during a struggle. I try picture her and how she might look, but all I see is violence and terror.

'The footprints are human-sized,' says Julietta as she inspects the ground closely. 'They were not made by Porphyrians. I cannot see any sign of a fight here.'

It's good news and I cling to it like a child holding a doll.

'Can we follow the footprints and find out where she went?'

Julietta shakes her head and my optimism dies.

'The footprints can only be found in the soft earth where we are standing. They disappear as the undergrowth becomes thicker.'

'Shame,' says Blake.

I don't know if he meant to sound sarcastic but that's how I heard it. As much as I want to unleash on him, I refuse to be distracted by his mind games.

'There must be a way to track my mother from here?'

Julietta draws her sword and uses the tip of the blade to part the surrounding bushes.

'It is too dense here and any physical marks have been washed away by the rain. The only hope is to follow a scent trail.'

Axel. I've seen him do remarkable things before. Dexter's ability to remote view, combined with his dog's heightened sense of smell, would surely help to locate my mother.

I place the pendant inside my father's handkerchief and fold it carefully. It feels like a symbolic act – a way of bringing them back together. I close my hand around the folded cloth and clutch it tightly to my chest. For the first time since we arrived, I start to truly believe that my mother is alive and that we can find her.

'We have to get back to the village. Let's go!'

Chapter 14

Zara

Just because I'm a loner doesn't necessarily mean that I enjoy my own company.

I sit in the empty lodge, staring at the flames in the log burner, wishing that I was out there with the others. Doing something. Doing *anything*. Inactivity doesn't suit me, even though I know it's the best thing for me right now. I walk over to a grimy full-length mirror and gaze at myself in profile. My hand traces a path down my torso and over the small bump that I've been doing my best to hide from the others. Ever since I took the pregnancy test three months ago, I've kept my condition a well-guarded secret. My first reaction was denial, but two further positive tests confirmed what I refused to believe: I am having Lou Hunter's baby.

I rest my hand on the bump and try to imagine what I'll look like when it's grown three-times as big. Any other mother-to-be would be at home resting; I'm in the Romanian wilderness, hunting the creature that killed my baby's father and searching for his imprisoned wife. I couldn't talk to Aaron about it – there's no way he'd have let me travel here. As for Sasha, I'm dreading having to have that conversation with her. *Hey Sasha, you're going to have a half-sister. Want to go baby clothes shopping with me?* Then there's the added complication of Ashleigh Hunter. Who knows how she'll react to my child-bearing relationship with her husband? I turn away from the mirror and pull my jumper down, deciding to do the only productive thing I can right now: ignore my personal circumstances and focus on the mission.

The lodge is quiet without Aaron, Dexter and Axel and I'm already missing their presence. It was a difficult decision to stay behind and wait for Sasha and Julietta to return. The natural leader in me wanted to head out and organise the search party. Lou once told me that good leaders put themselves last. Now I know what that means. I just hope it was the right decision.

I boil a pan of water to make another cup of tea – my fourth within the last hour. It tastes awful without sugar. I wonder whether Julietta's neighbour, Marin, might have some. If nothing else, it will give me an excuse to talk to him and try and find out more about her. After the stunt she pulled in drugging us all, she has a lot of explaining to do. I'm not ready to condemn her but I do want some answers.

I head outside and trudge the short distance to the house near the road. The smoke rising from the chimney suggests that someone must be home. I hear a rumble in the sky and notice dark clouds gathering overhead, crawling over the mountains and towards the village. Does this place ever have sunlight?

I knock on the weathered front door and wait. Two threadbare curtains are drawn across the window and the gutter above the porch is broken and dripping. The middle-aged man with the greying beard opens the door ajar. A thick chain on the inside bridges the gap between door and frame, allowing him just enough space to peer through. His obvious paranoia is unnerving.

'Hi,' I say to the stern and shadowy face. 'I'm staying at the lodge at the back. Do you have any sugar?'

Marin stares at me with a blank expression.

'You know, sugar,' I repeat, miming the action of tipping a spoon into a cup.

I jump back as the door is slammed closed in my face. Seconds later, I hear the rustling of chains. It seems strange to have such precautions in a remote village where everyone must know each other. Unless, that is, he has happened to come across the creatures from the forest.

The door is thrown open and Marin invites me in with a reluctant grunt.

'*Oui, sucre,*' he grumbles, glancing up at the black clouds. '*Une tempête.*'

I haven't studied French for many years but I remember enough to recognise the words 'sugar' and 'storm'. If this guy only speaks French it might make it difficult to probe him for information about Julietta. Still, a bowl of sugar would be a result.

I fake a smile and step inside his dank house. The door slams behind me, making me jump and tense up. I'm already starting to regret not bringing my extendable baton, just in case things turn ugly. I watch with cautious eyes as Marin shuffles across the cluttered room, moving a pile of clothes so I can sit in a tattered armchair. As I ease into the chair, I feel a pang in my stomach, like a nervous twitch. My hand instinctively moves onto the bump and I realise what I've just experienced: I felt my baby's movement for the first time.

'*Bébé?*' asks Marin with one raised, bushy eyebrow.

The secret I kept from my closest friends for months is out of the bag instantly. I nod, seeing no point in lying to a stranger. He makes a grimace-like smile, revealing a broken front tooth. I smile back awkwardly, already regretting coming here.

'*Sucre,*' he mutters, parting the beads which hang from a doorframe separating the kitchen from the lounge.

Once he leaves the room, I take the opportunity to scan my surroundings. The house has the feel of a hunting lodge: animal furs cover the floorboards and the head of a stag is mounted on the wall above the charred-black fireplace. It feels like I'm being watched. That's because the eyes of stuffed dead animals stare out at me from their wooden plinths. My attention is drawn to some framed photographs on a side table. I recognise Marin; a younger version of him holding a rifle and resting his foot on a dead boar. Then I notice an old black-and-white photograph. It's a girl in Victorian attire, waving a flag with the Eiffel Tower in the background. It must be over a hundred years old, around the time the tower was constructed. Despite the grainy quality of the photograph, the girl is easily recognisable: it's Julietta.

The sound of rustling beads makes me drop the photograph.

'*Sucre*,' says Marin, holding a jar containing granules which have a colour somewhere between white and brown.

I pick up the frame to return it to its place on the side table. As I bend down, a wave of dizziness overcomes me. This time, I know it's nothing to do with my pregnancy. I grip the arm of the chair, preparing myself for what's about to happen. It's a premonition.

The front door of the house is kicked in by the foot of a towering man. Katalina limps inside; her leg is bound and she is using a stick as a crutch. Marin lifts up his shotgun. It's already loaded. Katalina drops to the floor as he fires at the intruders. The shot hits the giant armoured man in the centre of his chest, leaving a hole in his breast plate. He looks down, smiles, and then advances on Marin.

As the vision fades, the last thing I hear is the cracking of neck bones followed by a gargling sound.

'We have to go!' I shout at Marin as I leap from the chair. 'We have to get out of here, right now!'

He drops the jar in reaction to my wild yelling. Granules of sugar and fragments of glass scatter across the floor. I hope that he understands my body language and the urgency in my voice, if not the words. When I move towards him to urge him to leave, he reaches behind the door frame and grabs his shotgun. His eyes remain fixed on me as he cocks the barrel and loads two cartridges.

'They're coming,' I say to him. 'We don't have long!'

Marin slowly raises the shotgun and points it at me. In a moment of confusion, I had assumed that he was preparing to fight. Now I realise that he's protecting himself against the ranting foreigner standing before him. If he doesn't understand a word I'm saying, how can I possibly convince him of the imminent danger?

I don't have time to save you. I'm sorry.

It's a matter of seconds before Katalina and her monster arrive. If Marin won't move, I must find a way to get out of here myself. Somehow, I have to overcome our language barrier. An idea pops into my head. As ridiculous as it seems, it's one of the few words which sounds the same in both of our tongues.

'Toilet,' I say, crossing my legs and slightly bending at the waist.

He narrows his eyes suspiciously.

'*Toilette?*' he repeats.

I nod eagerly. My hope is to convince him that my bizarre actions were due to an urgent need for the lavatory, a hallmark of pregnancy. If he doesn't buy it, we'll both be dead.

He lowers the shotgun and pulls back the curtain of beads.

'*C'est dehors,*' he says, thumbing in the direction of a back door.

I rush past him, knocking over a bucket as I dash through the kitchen and out through the exit. To my despair, I find myself in a small yard with high walls lined by barbed wire. In the corner of the yard is the outhouse. Marin has protected this place like an apocalyptic prepper. I'm about to head back inside when I hear the sound of the front door being kicked down. *They're here.* I run into the outhouse and close the door behind me. The sound of a gunshot makes me flinch. There's a crack in the toilet door and although I can't see into the main house, I know exactly what's happening. I witnessed it play out moments earlier.

I gasp as Marin is thrown through the window. His limp body crashes onto the floor of the yard, his head contorted from a broken neck. I stare into his dead eyes, fixed in an expression of pure shock.

The back door of the house is thrown open. I hold my breath as Katalina limps into the yard followed by her colossal henchman.

'Was that really necessary, Razvan?' she says with a mocking tone. 'He was dead from the moment you crushed his windpipe. It might have been useful to question him before killing him.'

'He tried to hurt you, my lady,' replies the armoured giant in a hoarse voice. 'I will kill anyone who tries to hurt you. The red-eyed girl and the one with the sword will pay for what they did to you.'

He's talking about Sasha and Julietta. They must have tried to destroy Katalina. At least I know that they're working together. At least I know they're alive.

Katalina examines the blood-stained bandage around her thigh. Her dyed-red hair parts to reveal the horrible scar along the side of her face. Given the chance, she will do much worse than the wound I inflicted upon her in our last duel.

'The information I was given must be correct. Search the rest of the house, Razvan. Check every crevice. Sasha and the Agents were here. I am sure of it.'

I clench my fists together and tense as the pre-fight adrenaline rushes through my system. There's no way I can get out of here without a deadly confrontation. This time it's different because it's not only my life that's on the line. I barely survived our last battle, and although she's injured, Katalina is now accompanied by a murderous brute.

A clap of thunder breaks the silence. Razvan raises his head to the sky with a sudden look of wariness.

'The storm is passing overhead,' he groans. 'The sky will soon be clear and daylight will return. We must leave this village, my lady.'

Katalina turns in a slow circle around the small yard. As she faces the toilet door, I draw back from the crack, hoping that the darkness will swallow me. My hand rests protectively on my bump as my heart pounds against my rib cage.

'You're right, Razvan,' replies Katalina. 'But before we go, let's leave a message for our enemy. Burn this place to the ground.'

Chapter 15

Sasha

Don't be mad at me. As we jog through the last stretch of the forest, all I can think about is what Aaron and Zara's reaction might be when we arrive back. Julietta drugged them, and in going with her I was almost an accomplice to her plan. I just hope that they understand my motivation. We came close to destroying Katalina – she's now injured and on the run. And with my mother's pendant in my hand, I'm closer to finding her than ever before. If Dexter can use his Canisentient powers combined with Axel's natural tracking instincts, I have faith that we can achieve what we came here for. I hope that the others will forgive me for going alone with Julietta. My decision to return with Menzies Blake is a completely different matter.

'Hurry up old man,' shouts Julietta as Blake trails behind.

He stops at the bottom of a ridge and bends over with his hands on his knees.

'I'm not *that* old,' he wheezes, trying to catch his breath. 'I'm just not used to all of this physical exertion.'

I've been struggling to keep up with Julietta myself. She's like a machine, eating up the ground in large, consistent strides. Eventually I manage to close the distance and join her at the roadside beyond the edge of the forest.

'Don't worry about him,' I say to her. 'Blake will catch us up.'

'I am not worried about him,' she replies. 'I am worried about the others.'

Her usual neutral demeanour has changed to a stony expression. I follow her gaze towards the village in the valley below. A spiralling cloud of smoke rises up from the rooves of two dwellings. It's not the thin, grey wispy emissions of a chimney, but rather the thick, black smoke of a raging fire.

Aaron. Zara. Dexter. Axel. For all I know, they're still asleep inside the lodge. Helpless. Oblivious.

I drop the crossbow and take off running towards the village.

'Wait, Sasha,' shouts Julietta, picking up my discarded weapon. 'It might not be safe!'

Safety is the last thing on my mind. My friends came here to help me and I'm sickened to think that I left them so vulnerable.

As I race into the village, my worst fears are confirmed. There are two buildings on fire: one of them is Marin's house, the other is Julietta's lodge. I stare, dumbstruck, as the flames curl out of the shattered windows and lick up at the blackened roof tiles. Several villagers try to douse the fire with buckets of water but it's a futile task. If anyone was inside either building they wouldn't have stood a chance. My eyes begin to sting and my throat closes up but it's nothing to do with the smoke.

Julietta arrives as two villagers drag a charred body from around the back of the house. I want to run, or scream, or tear my hair out, but my body won't move. Shock has stiffened my limbs. I close my eyes, in denial over what I'm witnessing. The faces of my three friends revolve inside my head like a deadly carousel. I don't want it to stop. I don't want to know whose life has been taken.

'Marin.'

His name is exhaled by Julietta, more of a strained breath than a spoken word. She walks towards his corpse as it is laid out on a patch of grass. The villagers back away respectfully as Julietta crouches beside him. I will myself out of my trance and walk to her side, placing a hand on her shoulder.

'I'm sorry.'

'Marin was a good man,' she replies after a moment of silence. 'He did not die from the fire. His neck was broken. He was murdered.'

Until now, I hadn't considered that the fire might have been malicious. *We fought Katalina and hurt her, we sent her running away.* A saying crosses my mind, something about a wounded animal. Instead of destroying her, did we drive her towards our friends? I've witnessed the full extent of her wrath before. She killed my father then set fire to The Agency mansion. *This is her calling card.*

I'm distracted from my horrifying thoughts by the shouts of several villagers. They point towards the burning buildings. A lone figure staggers through the smoke and collapses on all fours.

'Zara!'

I dash forwards and help to drag her to a safe distance. She is wet through and the skin on her arms is shredded and covered in blood, but she's alive.

'Where are the others?' I ask her, supporting her into a sitting position.

She coughs and clutches her stomach.

'They're not here. It's just me.'

I slump to my knees as the massive build-up of tension is released from my body. Zara wipes away the black soot from around her glasses and flicks back her soaked hair. Julietta joins us and hands her a bottle of water. I know that I should give Zara some time to recover, but I need to know that the others are safe.

'What happened?' I ask. 'Where did Aaron and Dexter go?'

She tries to take a drink but coughs and spits it out.

'They went into the forest to look for you. While they were gone, Katalina turned up. She killed Marin and burned down his home and the lodge. I hid in the outhouse and doused myself in toilet water, then climbed over the wall to escape.'

She turns over her hands to reveal her badly lacerated palms and forearms.

'Zara, I need to explain why I left you all . . .'

'It's okay, Sasha. I know you went to hunt down Katalina. I might not agree with your decision, or Julietta's methods, but I understand. I'm just glad that you're safe.'

I'm grateful for Zara's understanding, especially considering her current condition. Although she has suffered from the smoke, her quick thinking to douse herself has minimised the effect of the fire, leaving only small, superficial burns. I'm more worried about the cuts on her hands and arms.

'I didn't have my weapon with me,' she groans. 'If I did, maybe I could have saved Marin.'

Julietta offers a sympathetic shake of the head.

'There was nothing you could have done.'

'It's true,' I add. 'You were alone and outnumbered. You were lucky to survive.'

Zara wipes her wet hair from her face, leaving a smear of fresh blood on her forehead. Her hands are badly cut up but I can see that it's her pride which is hurting the most.

We sit silently as the villagers continue to try and contain the fire using buckets of water. The two buildings are lost causes and their efforts have moved to stopping the spread of flames. As black emissions rise into the sky, I wonder whether Aaron and Dexter will see the smoke and return here. It's a slim hope; the forest is a dense canopy of trees and the village lies in a valley. I should never have left them in the first place.

I'm distracted from mentally kicking myself by Zara, who climbs to her feet.

'What is he doing here?' she snarls.

I turn to see Blake standing hesitantly, like he's as nervous of approaching us as he is the burning buildings.

'We found him in the forest,' I reply, somewhat sheepishly.

Zara walks towards him on weak and unsteady legs.

'Katalina said that she received information on our whereabouts.' She jabs a finger towards Blake. 'It was you!'

I have to stop her as she tries to lunge for him but almost falls over. Blake cocks his head back and holds up his palms innocently.

'I can assure you that this has nothing to do with me. I came here to help and to protect my son, that is all.'

Zara grips onto my arm, her bloodshot eyes bulging. Anger contorts her blackened and bloodied face to give her a fierce and wild appearance.

'Surely you don't believe him?' she asks me in a wheezy voice.

The truth is that I don't know what to believe. Bringing Blake here might have been my second bad decision of the day. One thing's for sure: I've had enough of his games.

I leave Julietta to support Zara as I turn to face Blake.

'You said that you had information crucial to our success. Zara almost died and the others are in danger, including Dexter. Whatever you know, you need to share it with us right now.'

He strolls forwards, far too casual for my liking.

'Our agreement was that I would tell everyone, including my son.'

I hear the sound of steel sliding from a scabbard.

'My friend was killed,' says Julietta, violence bubbling beneath the surface of her words. 'Do not think I would hesitate to slay you.'

Blake looks around. Most of the villagers have left, having reduced the fire to a smoulder. There's nowhere to run and nobody to help him. He walks closer, as though he doesn't want anyone else to hear what he has to say.

'After I sent you through the portal I got in touch with the only person I thought would help me. It was an old friend from The Agency: my former partner, Edgar Levi.'

The name rings a bell. An alarm bell. I share a brief glance with Zara. Unbeknown to Blake, Edgar visited us in London. If Blake is about to spew a load of lies, this might be his undoing.

'Go on,' I say, keeping my cards close to my chest.

'I confessed to my temporary madness and the terrible things I did and asked Edgar for forgiveness. He believed me and was good enough to invite me to be a part of his new vision for The Agency. He told me that he is in the process of rebuilding it under orders from Geneva.'

Edgar wouldn't help Blake. He's a good man.

'I accepted his kind offer,' continues Blake. 'That's when he told me about his plans to work with sentient beings.'

'We already know this,' says Zara. 'He told us himself.'

Blake leans in closer as if to emphasise his point.

'But do you know that one of the beings he is working with is Katalina? Edgar visited her and helped to prepare her Porphyrian army.'

I shake my head at his crazy assertion.

'That's impossible.'

'Is it? He knows that you are all here. This is a trap, and you are all walking blindly into it!'

My mouth hangs open in disbelief. Is Blake still insane, or is he lying to cover his own sinister motivations? Edgar helped me through The Academy. He made me an Agent even after he discovered I had no special abilities. He was also a friend to my father. But he was an older friend of Blake's. It's hard to separate the truth from fiction, especially when it comes from the mouth of Menzies Blake.

'It's all lies,' says Zara acidly. 'Edgar explicitly told us not to leave London. That doesn't sound like someone who is trying to ensnare us in a foreign country.'

'Don't you see?' says Blake, becoming more animated. 'He's been monitoring you the entire time. Edgar *knew* you would come here. The Agency is undergoing a revolution and he is leading it. You are all the last of the old kind, and he plans to wipe you out in a remote place where nobody can save you.'

I wish Aaron was here and not just so that he could read Blake's emotions.

'We have to find the others,' I say, stepping away from the madness presented by Blake. 'That doesn't change, regardless of whether you are telling the truth.'

Julietta nods in agreement and helps to support Zara with an arm around her waist.

'What about him?' she asks, still holding her sword in her spare hand.

'You have shared your secret with us,' I say to Blake. 'You can leave now.'

'I'm coming with you,' he replies in an uncompromising tone.

'Not a chance,' says Zara before descending into a fit of coughs.

I step between her and Blake, assuming her role while she's still in recovery.

'What if everything you've said is a lie and it's *you* who is leading us into a trap? I don't trust you, Blake. I'll never trust you.'

He clasps his hands together contritely.

'My son is in danger, Sasha. Once I find him, I will leave. Until then, you need me.'

'Why's that?' I challenge him.

He takes a moment to look each of us in the eye.

'Because I am the only one who can get you all out of here.'

Chapter 16

Ashleigh

Sixty seconds ago I accepted my fate. My escape from Katalina's castle had drained me of the energy to go any further. The first mile was a mad scramble through tangled bushes and thorny undergrowth, as though the forest was conspiring against me. My desperate attempt to flee also cost me my daughter's pendant, which I must have lost somewhere in the woods. After years of imprisonment and muscle atrophy, my body finally gave up and I slumped down against a tree trunk. In my moment of defeat, the sense of resignation brought an inner peace. At least my end would be here, leaning against a tree under a blue sky, rather than lying on the damp floor of a cell. When I heard footsteps approaching, I assumed the worst. *Katalina has found me.* But I was wrong. Instead, I'm staring into the kind face of a young man who seems to recognise me.

'*You're* Ashleigh Hunter?' he asks, even though I just confirmed as much. 'Sasha's mother?'

He's olive-skinned, with a mop of curly brown hair and the muscled physique of an athlete.

'Do you know my daughter?'

'Yes. I know her very well. I'm . . .' His sentence trails off, as though he changes his mind about sharing something with me. 'I'm an Agent. My name is Aaron and this is Dexter, and his dog, Axel. I can't believe we found you like this. We came here to rescue you!'

I smile briefly before my head rolls back and unconsciousness threatens to ruin the moment. Aaron quickly rummages in a rucksack and produces a plastic bottle. The water inside has never looked so fresh. He twists off the cap and holds the bottle to my mouth. My body responds as I gulp down the liquid, like it's a shot of life-fluid. I lick my cracked lips, savouring every last drop. The two boys stare at me, their faces a mixture of shock and concern.

'You're both brave,' I say to them. 'The last time some Agents tried to rescue me it didn't go too well.'

The boy named Dexter offers me a chocolate bar. I can barely remember what one tastes like.

'How did you end up here?' he asks.

'I dug my way out of an underground prison. It took a long time. Years, in fact.'

'That's badass,' replies Dexter, in what I assume to be a compliment.

'You're safe now,' says Aaron, taking off his jacket and wrapping it around my bony shoulders. 'Sasha will be over the moon to see you.'

'Is she with you?' My heart fills with joy, which is quickly overwhelmed by fear. 'It's not safe here. Katalina is preparing an army of creatures. She's working with someone from The Agency. I think it's Menzies Blake.'

The boy with the dog recoils in horror.

'No, it can't be. You must be mistaken. My father wouldn't do that. He helped to get us here.'

Although my body is weak, my mind is still as sharp as ever. As Dexter protests against my claim, I pick up on a single, significant word.

'Your *father*? Are you Menzies Blake's son?'

His cheeks redden and his dog seems to lean into him, like it's offering moral support.

'I know what my father did to you and I'm truly sorry. I was estranged from him for many years. He's a changed man now and he's trying to put things right.'

As I focus on his face, I notice that Dexter has the same eyes as his father. My instincts tell me that this boy has a good heart and that he's telling the truth. It's hard for me to accept that Blake could have turned a new leaf after his betrayal on Misery Island. I try to recall the details of what I witnessed before my escape from the castle. Katalina met with someone she knew: a well-spoken man whose voice I recognised. Although I didn't see him, I'm fairly sure it was Blake.

'You should try to eat,' says Aaron, opening the wrapper of the chocolate bar which is still in my hand. 'You need to get your strength up.'

He's right and it's nice of him to care so much. When I eventually take a bite I find it hard to swallow even the smallest bit. I stare into the faces of the two young men. They both look barely old enough to drive, never mind lead a rescue mission. The Agency must be recruiting people pretty young these days.

'We can't stay here,' I warn them. 'Katalina will be searching for me.'

'Don't worry,' replies Dexter. 'Axel will give us early warning of anyone approaching.'

'Finish your chocolate,' says Aaron with a warm smile. 'Then we'll get you out of here.'

I like these two kids. They are kind and determined and I can see why they would make good Agents. I try to draw strength from their optimism, even though it might not be enough right now.

'I'm not sure I can stand, let alone walk.'

'Then I'll carry you,' says Aaron. 'It's no problem. I've carried your daughter before.'

I let out a short laugh and the noise feels alien to me. Maybe it's because it's the first time I've laughed in as long as I can remember. Although my body is frail, my mind is racing. For so long, my sole motivation to stay alive was my daughter. Just a few minutes ago I had given up on that ever happening. And now, completely out of the blue, two young Agents have come to my rescue. They have provided food, water and the offer to take me to Sasha. The thought of seeing her energises me like a shot of adrenaline in the arm.

I gobble down the rest of the chocolate bar and climb to my feet.

'Let's go, boys.'

I insist on walking for as long as I can, which isn't very far. As we venture through the woods, Dexter sends his dog ahead to check for danger. The forest is dense and the sky overhead has darkened; anything could be lurking in the trees. When I realise that I'm slowing us down, I reluctantly accept Aaron's offer to carry me.

'Thank you, but this is kind of embarrassing. I'm old enough to be your mother.'

'You're never too old for a piggy-back,' he replies, cheerfully.

At least I'm not a heavy load for him. I've always had a slight frame, but the years of captivity have resulted in drastic weight loss. When I wrap my thin arms around him, I become conscious of the needle scars on the inside of my elbows. I pull down the sleeves of my shirt to cover them. Aaron doesn't need to know the horrors of what I went through and I don't want to have to explain it.

As we trek through the forest, a sudden flash of lightning illuminates the dark clouds and causes me to flinch. It reminds me of what happened on Misery Island six years ago. I can still recall the twisted face of the Elder Witch before she plummeted into the well. Her destruction caused a chain reaction which blacked out the daylight. A crack of thunder soon follows and before long the heavens open. We're quickly drenched by the downpour and our route uphill becomes dangerously slick. I scan the area, searching for somewhere to shelter, when I spot a hollowed out tree trunk.

'Let's stop and take cover,' I suggest to Aaron. 'Head over to that hollow tree. It's as good as any place we'll find around here.'

He calls over Dexter, whose dog is whimpering by his side.

'Axel is afraid of storms,' he explains as we make for the tree. 'Monsters? No problem. But a storm will turn him into a giant pussy cat.'

The black dog makes a whiny noise which almost suggests he's offended by his master's words. Dexter and Axel make for an interesting duo. While I could never trust Blake, I can sense that his son is genuine and not a chip off the old block. In a bizarre twist of fate, it's almost fitting that Blake's son is part of the rescue team, like he's here to put right what his father got so terribly wrong.

The hollowed tree is just big enough for us all to huddle inside. The cramped space soon smells of cologne and wet dog. My senses feel invigorated by being outdoors: I hear every raindrop and feel every crevice in the bark. I'm probably sugar-rushing, but right now I feel more alive than I have for years.

Dexter leans out and tilts his head towards the sky.

'No sign of the storm passing yet,' he says, reassuring his dog with a pat on the head.

Aaron is busy running the palms of his hands over the inside of the tree trunk. It's like he's searching for something, but his eyes are closed.

'Many have sheltered here over the years,' he mutters.

I recognise his behaviour; it reminds me of Lou.

'Are you a Clairist?' I ask him. 'No – you're an Empath.'

His eyes pop open and he breaks into a wide smile.

'You're only the second person who has ever recognised that.'

'Who was the first?'

His smile disappears the second I ask the question.

'It doesn't matter,' he replies.

I take the hint and decide not to press him on it. Instead, I turn the conversation on myself.

'Do you know what I am?'

'You're a Witch!' says Dexter, answering before Aaron is able to. 'A White one, I mean. Sorry.'

'Don't apologise. I'm a useless one without my Athame.'

'Sasha has it,' says Aaron, his face still sullen. 'She'll be glad to return it. You'll have a lot to talk about.'

The rain starts to ease from a downpour to a drizzle. Aaron steps outside, as though he seems to have become uncomfortable in my company. He paces up and down and looks as though he has the weight of the world on his shoulders.

'Everything okay?' I ask.

He arches his neck to peer up at the tree.

'I recognise this. It was near the spot where we arrived.'

It seems like a strange thing to say: how can you 'arrive' in the middle of a forest? A helicopter couldn't even get close with all the towering trees. I'm about to ask what he means when Dexter's dog starts to bark.

'What's wrong, Axel?' he asks.

The dog curls back its lips and releases a low, guttural growl. A movement in the forest catches my peripheral vision. Aaron sees it too and spins around to face it. I'm filled with a sense of dread. Everything was going so well. I was on my way to see my daughter.

Not now. Please, not now.

A dark shape forms in between two trees. It expands outwards, like a silent black gas. I watch with unblinking eyes as the shape forms into a rectangle the size of a door. A tall figure emerges through the mist as though he is stepping through a doorway . . . *or a portal.*

Aaron walks forwards slowly, approaching the emerging figure.

'What are you doing?' shouts Dexter.

His cries are in vain. It's as though Aaron can't hear him. He keeps walking towards the tall man. The portal disappears, retracting within itself until only the outline of the dark figure remains. I strain to see past Aaron as he squares up to the mysterious being. My first instinct is that it has to be a paranormal creature – it's extremely rare for a human to use a portal. When Aaron starts talking, I'm happy to be proven wrong. My nerves begin to ease as the two walk towards us side-by-side. I catch my first glimpse of the stranger. He's heavily built, with a bald head and a black beard.

'Good news,' says Aaron, his mood having lightened. 'This is Edgar Levi, a Director at The Agency. He's come here to help us.'

'Oh no,' says Dexter, his face suddenly ashen. 'I'm in trouble. *Big trouble.*'

The bald man steps forward and peers into the hollow trunk.

'Dexter Blake. I've been looking for you for some time. You can relax, this isn't about you.' His eyes move sideways and rest on me. 'It's nice to see you again, Agent Hunter. I'm glad we found you.'

A nauseous feeling descends on me as I listen to him speak.

His voice is instantly familiar.

It's an accent I've heard recently.

It's the voice of the man who met with Katalina.

Chapter 17

Sasha

Zara and Julietta stand either side of me as I square up to Menzies Blake. I can tell without looking that they both want to launch at him. It's hard not to feel the same. He duped me into bringing him here and I'm still not sure it was the right decision to do so. Now that he's finally shared his secret – information that I can't be certain is true – he has somehow found another way to remain in our company. Call me paranoid but this guy is either a genius or an evil schemer. Or maybe he's both.

With the fire finally under control, what's left of the buildings is little more than smouldering carcasses. Julietta pushes her way past Blake, eyeballing him as she passes.

'I am going to see what can be salvaged,' she mutters.

Zara remains at my side, a hand nursing her stomach. Her eyes are streaming and she's hoarse from the effect of the smoke. It's up to me to deal with Blake and I'm in no mood for his games.

'What do you mean, *you're* the only one who can get us out of here?'

He loosens his collar, as though his throat needs the room to process more lies.

'Everything I told you about the portal is true, except for one thing. I failed to mention that you need something to return through it. The Ferryman won't transport you without a coin, and not just any coin. It must be a penny which is at least one hundred years old.'

I can't believe he kept this crucial information from us until now.

'You're scum,' wheezes Zara, before turning away to vomit.

Blake recoils, like the sight of her being sick offends him. It's an expression I'd love to wipe off his face.

'Aaron was right about you. We were stupid to trust you.'

'I never lied to you, Sasha. I planned to be there when the portal opened and guide you back through it.' He produces an old coin from his pocket. 'This was my insurance, to make sure you didn't betray my son.'

'You'd know all about betrayal.'

He smiles, that same oily smile that he used on me the first time I met him at the hospital in London.

'Snide remarks really don't suit you, Sasha.' His fingers close over the coin and he slips his closed fist back inside his pocket. 'I'll hold on to this for safekeeping. Take me to Dexter and in return I'll show you the way to Katalina's fortress. Once we find my son, you can have the coin, and your revenge.'

I turn my back on him, which is all I'm able to do to show my resentment. Zara deserves my attention right now, not Blake. I hear him whistle as he wanders off. The sound of his cheery tune makes me want to draw the Athame and blast him back into insanity, if only I knew how. Instead, I focus on tending to Zara by helping to bind the wounds on her hands.

'We could just kill him,' she whispers, surprising me with her coldness. 'It might be the only way to get the coin from him.'

I peer over my shoulder, checking he's out of earshot.

'We can't, even if we know he's lying, which we don't for certain. It would crush Dexter.'

Julietta joins us and dumps a small sack on the ground.

'The fire did not leave much behind. I found a few bolts for the crossbow, some tinned food and a few other things.'

I delve into my pocket to find the Athame and the folded handkerchief with my mother's pendant inside. They are the only things that matter to me. When I eventually find my mother, I'll have the awful task of having to explain what happened to my father. I have no idea how I'll do it but it's not a priority right now.

'We need to find Aaron and Dexter before we can search for my mother.'

Zara nods.

'And then we need to destroy Katalina,' she adds, finding a home for her seething anger.

Julietta zips up her leather jacket in a way that looks like she means business.

'I will gladly help with that,' she says. 'And in the meantime I will keep an eye on that odious man.'

Blake is wandering near the roadside, kicking loose stones like he doesn't have a care in the world. Since the events of the blackout, every significant moment has revolved around him. Just when I think I've seen the last of him, his presence is thrust upon me once more. I'm beginning to feel as though I'll only escape him if one of us dies, and even then his influence extends beyond the realm of the living.

I gaze up towards the endless stretch of forest which covers the mountainside like an emerald cloak. Grey storm clouds hang low over the trees. My friends could be anywhere, searching for me as I'm searching for them, chasing each other's tails like mad cats.

'It's such a big area, and we have so little time.'

'We do not have to travel on foot,' replies Julietta. 'I have a better solution.'

It's not long before Julietta returns. To my surprise, she's accompanied by two horses; riding one while guiding the reins of the other. Her sword and the crossbow are strapped to the side of her saddle. She seems so natural in the way she handles two the powerful animals. Julietta is a girl of many talents although it makes total sense that she can ride so well: her upbringing was in the Middle Ages, when horses were the only form of transport.

'Where did you get the horses from?' I ask her.

'I bartered for them,' she replies, shrugging it off like it's nothing. 'During my existence, one thing has never changed – money can buy you most things. Luckily, I always keep an emergency fund.'

She pats her pocket.

'Very resourceful of you,' says Blake. 'You would make a good Agent.'

Like Julietta, I choose to completely ignore his false friendliness. Instead, I wander over to the spare horse which is saddled and ready to go.

'You can ride,' says Julietta, handing me the reins.

I grew up in a big city, my only riding experience being on a donkey at Clacton-on-Sea's beach. Animals and me don't get on, with Axel being the sole exception. I'm about to make my excuses when I realise that Julietta is not asking whether I can ride; she's telling me to. Zara is in no state to steer the horse and Julietta clearly doesn't trust Blake to ride alone.

'I want to take the reins, believe me,' I say to her. 'I'm just not sure I can.'

Julietta smiles reflectively, as though the art of learning to ride is a distant memory for her.

'Here,' she says, offering me a hand. 'Swing your leg over then place your feet in the stirrups, toes pointed upwards. Grip the reins just in front of the pommel and keep your hands low. Shoulders back and sit up straight. Good.'

I try my best to follow her instructions and feign confidence. The horse whinnies and circles restlessly, like it somehow knows that I don't know what I'm doing. Simply sitting in the right position seems to be a challenge.

'How do I steer this thing, or make it stop?'

'She is not a *thing*,' explains Julietta. 'Her name is Rua, a Huzul bred mare, perfect for the forest terrain. She is trained to ride and will follow my lead. Lean forward in your seat to accelerate, sit back in your saddle to slow. It is all in the legs. You will be fine, Sasha.'

That's easy for her to say. I only wish I had the self-assuredness that immortality must bring.

I stroke Rua's brown mane in an effort to bond as Julietta calls Blake forwards and offers him her hand. He folds his arms in petulant refusal.

'I sincerely hope that you don't expect me to—'

'Get up here,' she says irritably. 'This will be no more pleasant for me than it will be for you.'

I watch with a half-smile as Blake struggles to mount up behind Julietta. He makes for an awkward pillion rider, uncomfortable in his bulky overcoat and trousers. My humour is quickly lost when I realise that I'll have to do the same for Zara. It's one thing to put my own life in danger, but it's quite another to be responsible for someone else's safety.

'I trust you, Sasha,' says Zara as she climbs up behind me and wraps her arms around my waist.

'I trust you, Rua,' I whisper in turn to the horse.

It responds with a snort and throws its head back, almost unseating us. Julietta moves closer and uses her own horse to help steady Rua.

'Riding a horse is like doing anything for the first time. Believe that you can do it, Sasha, and you will. Remember, confidence is everything: whether animal or foe, make them believe you can be the master, and you shall be.'

It's good advice, although I don't have a great track record where self-belief is concerned.

'We should get going,' urges Zara. 'While we still have some daylight.'

I'm reminded that riding a horse isn't the most difficult thing I'll have to do today. My boyfriend, my mother and my friend are somewhere out there in the forest.

A forest which is crawling with undead creatures.

Creatures which come out at night.

We ride out of the village and into the woods, moving from a steady walk to a trot. It's not long before my thighs burn, my arms ache and my bum goes numb. I'm not convinced that using horses will save us time or energy at this rate. The one advantage they do provide is elevation. We can see further ahead on horseback, as well as being above the wild undergrowth and muddy ridges.

Julietta leads the way along a trail, the sodden ground churned up by her horse's hooves. As we progress, she twists her head from one side to the other, closely examining the ground.

'Can you keep still?' moans Blake who is jostled around behind her.

'Stop complaining,' she retorts. 'I am searching for signs that we can use to track.'

'This is ridiculous,' says Blake. 'It's a forest path which we've all used recently. There are lots of footprints – you'll never be able to find the right ones.'

Julietta twists in her saddle sharply, almost unbalancing Blake.

'That is true, but we are looking for the footprints of two males and a dog which have been freshly made since the storm. You are distracting me, old man.'

I can't help but smile at the way she leaves Blake speechless and fuming.

'I like Julietta,' I say to Zara.

'We need her,' she replies. 'I lost my baton in the fire and my hands are wrecked. I'm not sure how much use I'll be from here on in.'

'You're our leader. We don't need you fighting in the front lines, but we need you to hold us together.' She remains silent and I feel the need to emphasise my point. 'When Dad died, I fell to pieces but you stayed strong. Aaron and I were both numb with grief yet you found us a place to live and kept The Agency alive. You were the one who prevented us all from falling apart. You're our glue, Zara.'

I didn't mean for it to be such an emotional response. She shrugs it off in the most Zara-like of ways.

'Okay, that's good, I suppose.'

Zara has never been the best at receiving compliments and it's one of the many reasons I like her so much. It's rare to have these personal moments with her. I decide to take the opportunity to reassure her about something that I'm sure has been on her mind.

'I'll tell my mother what you did for me and Dad. She'll understand about your relationship with him, I know she will.'

I feel her arms tighten around my waist ever so slightly.

'Thank you, Sasha. When this is all over, we'll sit down and have a good chat.'

I miss our conversations, often about stupid girly things. Since my father died, it felt like Zara retreated within herself and started to keep things from me. I'm looking forward to having her back as my close friend once more.

Our route takes us deeper into the forest with no sign of any useable tracks. The longer I'm on the horse, the better I become at handling her, but it's time we can ill afford. I glance up at the sky where the sun has started its descent over the mountains. It won't be long before darkness falls. The thought of being stranded out here makes me anxious.

I'm about to voice my concerns when Julietta brings her horse to a halt. She leaps down from the saddle to examine the ground.

'What is it?' I ask her.

'Male footprints,' she says, pointing at the marks in the mud.

I recognise the zig-zag pattern and familiar logo of Adidas Superstars.

'They belong to Aaron!'

Julietta doesn't look quite as excited as she studies the surrounding area.

'We have paw prints too, but there are two more sets of male footprints. One is large, size eleven. And over here are some female footprints.'

I can feel Zara tense up in the saddle behind me.

'Kat and her creature,' she seethes.

That would be the obvious conclusion, and the worst possible outcome. It's only when I spot something else that hope rises within me. From my high position, I can see a glimmer of shiny metal poking out of the mud. I might have missed it if I was on foot. I jump off the horse to retrieve what turns out to be a small section of silver links.

'What is it, Sasha?' asks Julietta.

My heartbeat quickens as I compare the broken links to the chain attached to my mother's pendant.

'My mother was here,' I reply. 'I'm certain of it. These links belong to this chain of hers. It's too much of a coincidence that I found it on this path. I think she might have dropped it deliberately. She's leaving a trail for us to help find her.'

A rustling sound in the forest makes us all freeze. Rua's head shoots up, her ears upright. Zara is hunched over the saddle like she's unconscious. Her eyes are closed and her body is twitching.

'What's wrong with her?' asks Julietta.

'She's having a vision,' says Blake before I can answer.

Julietta slowly removes her sword from the saddle and passes me the crossbow. I load a bolt with a shaking hand, my eyes darting from left to right. Zara gasps as she rouses from her premonition. The look on her face extinguishes the hope within me, replacing it with a dark cloud of dread.

'They're coming.'

Chapter 18

Aaron

Edgar is talking, but I'm only half-listening.
'I want to reassure you that you're not in trouble, Agent Hart. I understand your decision to come here, I really do.' I trudge along the forest path at his side, my mind elsewhere. 'In fact, congratulations are in order for your rescue of Agent Hunter.'

At the mention of that name I think of Lou. Then Sasha. But I quickly realise that he's referring to neither.

'We didn't rescue Sasha's mother,' I mutter. 'We just happened to come across her while we were looking for Sasha.'

Edgar places a paw-like hand on my shoulder.

'As I told you, Sasha and Zara are safe at a nearby military bunker which The Agency has requisitioned. I will take you straight to them. They will be pleased to see Agent Hunter alive and well.'

I nod and smile but something doesn't feel right. As an Empath, I'm all about gut feeling. I should be relieved but instead I'm anxious, although I can't work out why. Edgar's voice fades into a background monotone as I go back over the events of the last thirty minutes . . .

When the portal opened I prepared myself for the worst. My fears were allayed when Edgar appeared and reassured me that he was here to help. It was when we walked back to Ashleigh and Dexter that the atmosphere changed. I could understand Dexter's concern after being on the run from Edgar for so long. But it was Ashleigh's reaction which I felt the strongest. She seemed... afraid.

'That's why The Agency's Senior Leaders in Geneva gave me clearance to travel here by such uncommon means,' continues Edgar. 'I have come to support you all, not to intervene. Your team requires an experienced hand. I'm sure you understand, Agent Hart.'

'Yes, Agent Levi. Of course.'

I look behind us towards Dexter, Axel and Ashleigh. They are following us but at the same time keeping their distance. Sasha's mother has my jacket around her shoulders yet she's still shivering. Her eyes meet mine and she appears to mouth something silently.

'Don't... trust... him.'

It doesn't make sense. Edgar is effectively our superior at The Agency. How could Ashleigh possibly have inside information on him when she's been imprisoned for the last few years? My mind drifts back to Edgar's first appearance as I try to piece together the clues.

Why did Ashleigh linger when Edgar was so keen to bring us to Sasha? Dexter had to retrieve her from near the hollow tree, where she seemed to drop something. Edgar had his back to her and didn't notice. It looked like a strange thing to do and I can't shake it from my mind.

'Agent Hunter will be fine,' says Edgar, demanding my attention once more. 'She is understandably scarred, both mentally and physically. Katalina will be neutralised for her crimes but first we must ensure everyone is safe. Sasha is worried about you all.'

Why does he keep mentioning Sasha? My mind is still racing and I decide to ask him one of the many burning questions.

'Where did you come from?' He gives me a quizzical look, forcing me to clarify my question. 'When you arrived through the portal, where did you come from?'

Edgar runs a hand over his bald scalp.

'That's a strange question, Agent Hart. We should hurry along; it's not safe out here after sundown.'

He's not giving me an answer and I refuse to let it drop.

'If you found Sasha and Zara before you found us, did you arrive through another portal?'

He chuckles and shakes his head.

'Portal travel is a complex procedure. I'm sure Menzies Blake failed to explain the finer details to you.'

Edgar might be right about that but his reply feels like deflection. There are too many unanswered questions for my mind to settle.

'How did you find out we'd travelled to Romania?'

He pauses before answering, just long enough to give himself some thinking time.

'I'm afraid Menzies Blake betrayed you all not long after he sent you here. I would have found out much sooner if your mother hadn't done such a good job of replying to my emails. She's an Empath too, correct? Perhaps I should make her position more permanent.'

First of all Edgar mentions my girlfriend and my half-sister and now my mother. If he's trying to stir my emotions, it's working.

'My mother's not right for The Agency. She has a very . . . independent lifestyle.'

'Shame,' he replies, without any obvious disappointment. 'I'm sure you're keen to complete your mission so you can return home and see her. The bunker isn't far now. We have rations and medical supplies. Once the team is replenished I will ensure everyone is sufficiently armed and protected to take on Katalina.'

This is all *way* too convenient. I find it hard to believe that Edgar located Sasha and Zara, took them to a refuge bunker and then found us straight away. The forest is enormous – we've been searching for Sasha for hours and despite the use of a tracker dog we've had no luck. Yet Edgar managed to do it immediately. If he's telling the truth, that is.

'Excuse me for a moment, Agent Levi.' I look back at Ashleigh and try to think of a reason to fall back and speak to her. 'I need some chewing gum and it's in my jacket pocket.'

Edgar frowns at my terrible excuse. I wish I had as good a poker face as Zara in these situations. Edgar reaches out and is about to say something but I quickly turn away. Dexter and Ashleigh come to a standstill as I approach them. It feels like they don't want to get any closer to Edgar than necessary.

I walk straight up to Ashleigh and pretend to search the pockets of my jacket. When my hand brushes against her, my earlier thought is confirmed: she's terrified.

'What's wrong?' I ask her in a low voice.

'He's lying to you,' she whispers back. 'He doesn't want to help us – he's working with Katalina.'

I'm shocked by her words. Her emotions tell me that she believes she's telling the truth. I don't doubt her conviction but I have to consider the fact that she's been locked away for years. Ashleigh is malnourished and exhausted and I must take that into account.

Dexter leans in, obscuring himself from Edgar's view.

'She told me everything,' he says, his voice as serious as I've ever known it to be. 'Edgar visited Katalina yesterday. This is a trap and we have to get away from him!'

'What's the hold up?' shouts Edgar as he takes the opportunity to light a cigar. 'We must hurry.'

I continue to pretend to search the pockets and buy us some time. My mind cycles through the options as I try to decide the best course of action. If we try to escape, we won't get far. Ashleigh is in no physical state to make a run for it. I'm also worried about Sasha and Zara. Did Edgar really take them to a bunker, and if so was it of their own free will? Even if Ashleigh is right, we have no way of knowing where Sasha and Zara really are and whether they're in trouble.

'I believe you,' I say to Ashleigh and Dexter. 'Stay back and keep your distance. I need to find out if the bunker exists and whether Sasha and Zara are there. If things turn ugly, I'll take care of Edgar while you two make a getaway.'

'Axel will have your back,' says Dexter, a steely look in his eyes.

'I can see what Sasha sees in you,' says Ashleigh as I pull the jacket closer around her shoulders. 'Be careful.'

I give her a small nod before I turn away. Edgar throws out his arms in exasperation as I make my way back towards him.

'Can we get going now, Agent Hart?' he asks, his patience clearly wearing thin.

'Sure,' I reply. When he looks at me suspiciously, I feel the need to offer an explanation. 'I couldn't find the gum. It must have fallen out of the jacket.'

Edgar huffs to show he's unimpressed before marching onwards.

'It's not far. Let's keep moving.'

With every minute that passes, the forest becomes darker and more foreboding. Edgar picks up the pace as we trek downhill, forcing us to bend our knees as a braking mechanism. The sound of rushing water becomes audible and grows louder with each step, eventually revealing a fast-flowing river at the bottom of a basin. Despite the growing darkness, I can see the white froth as the water carves a route through boulders and rocky outcrops.

Edgar comes to a halt and points towards a thin wooden bridge which spans the river.

'The bunker is just on the other side.' He raises his voice over the sound of the wild water. 'My eyesight is not what it used to be. Perhaps one of you could go first and lead the way?'

I don't like it. After what Ashleigh told me, I don't trust him. My instinct is to refuse his offer to cross, but I need to know whether Sasha and Zara are on the other side. I made a promise to myself to protect her, regardless of my own safety. I'm certainly not about to let Dexter or Ashleigh be forced into going first. It leaves me with no option other than to risk the crossing myself.

I'm about to step onto the bridge when a hand pulls me back.

'Axel will go,' says Dexter. 'He's got the best eyesight out of all of us. And he has an extra pair of legs.'

The dog gapes his mouth in a human-like grin, apparently happy to take on the challenge. Edgar doesn't seem too pleased as he steps aside to allow Axel across. We watch tensely as the dog takes slow, tentative steps across the wooden slats. Its black fur soon merges into the darkness and Dexter closes his eyes to access his dog's vision. All the while, Ashleigh keeps her distance, shivering at the bottom of the slope. I stare straight ahead at the bridge, ensuring Edgar is in my peripheral vision.

'He's almost there,' says Dexter, his eyes moving beneath his closed lids. 'I can see something on the other side.'

'Is it the bunker?' I ask, hopefully.

His face is tense, his jaw fixed.

'No, it's a person. More than one.'

'Is it Sasha and Zara?'

I notice Edgar toss away the stump of his cigar and slowly move a hand inside his overcoat. My attention snaps back to Dexter when I hear him gasp. At the same time, Axel starts to bark furiously.

'The Porphyrians . . . it's a trap!'

His eyes pop open and he races past me and onto the bridge.

'Dexter! Wait!'

I try to follow him but Edgar blocks my path. He steps onto the wooden slats, his large frame spanning the width of the bridge like a troll. In an instant I realise the terrible truth that has gnawed away at me ever since Ashleigh uttered her warning. He's not here to help us; he came to capture us.

Edgar pulls out a gun from inside his overcoat and points it directly at me.

'Don't do anything stupid, Agent Hart.'

I back away slowly, keeping myself between Ashleigh and the barrel of Edgar's gun.

'Why are you doing this?' I ask him.

I don't need an answer, but I do need to stall him while I work out my next move.

'The Agency is changing,' he replies with a shrug. 'It's too anarchic to have young people such as you and your friends with powers you don't fully understand. I'm sorry, Agent Hart. I liked you.'

His apology only makes me even angrier and I want to take it out on him. The last time I had a gun pointed at me it was in the hand of Ludvig at the Tower of London. I escaped that particular scenario with only a flesh wound, thanks to Sasha's intervention. I came here to save her but now I can't even save myself.

Beyond Edgar, on the other side of the bridge, I can still hear Axel barking and Dexter shouting over the sounds of the rushing river. He's stranded and in danger. I blame myself for following Edgar here. As much as I want to help Dexter, I'm left completely powerless.

Ashleigh suddenly grabs hold of my arm.

'There are more of them approaching behind us.'

I twist my head to see several dark figures making their way down the slope. The Porphyrians' shoulders are hunched so that their heads are lost within their muscled necks and body armour.

'It's over,' says Edgar. 'Don't let this turn messy.'

I hold my hands out submissively. His mistake is to assume I've given up. The moment he lowers the gun, I launch forwards. I kick at the bridge's tether rope with everything I've got. It's enough to unbalance Edgar and he falls back onto the wooden slats. It will buy us some time, but only a little.

I grab Ashleigh by the wrist and drag her forwards. My plan is to get past Edgar and make it across the bridge to Dexter. I'm forced to abandon that idea when he starts to climb to his feet, still holding the gun. The sound of the approaching Porphyrians drives me sideways, past the bridge and towards the edge of the river bank. We have two choices left and both are likely to result in sudden death. If this is the end, I want it to be an end of my own choosing.

'Take a deep breath,' I urge Ashleigh.

She casts off the jacket, allowing it to fall into the water and be swept away by the fast current. It's a sign that she understands what we're about to do.

'No!' shouts Edgar, readjusting his aim. 'Don't do it. I'll shoot!'

We hold hands and inhale.

Then leap into the rushing river.

As we plummet under the water, the last thing I hear is a gunshot.

Chapter 19

Sasha

'We're surrounded. They'll be on us in sixty seconds'.

Zara's rouses from her trance-like state, her words spoken with a chilling tone. My hands grip tightly onto Rua's reins. I feel the horse stiffen beneath me, like it can sense my own apprehension for what's about to happen. Zara's premonition has given us an advance warning of the predators closing in, but it might not help if there's no way to escape. In all the time I've known her, Zara's visions have often been the difference between success and failure; or life and death. Sometimes we can run, and sometimes we have to prepare to fight. This time, our group is stranded and depleted. Of those who remain, Zara is injured and Blake is, well, Blake. I wish Aaron was here at my side.

Julietta raises her sword as she circles her horse.

'How many?' she asks.

'I saw seven,' replies Zara as she stares into the darkness beyond the trees. 'Maybe eight. All of them armed and approaching at speed.'

My heart sinks into the pit of my stomach at the prospect of facing twice as many Porphyrians as last time. Zara slips her injured hands beneath mine to take hold of the reins, freeing me to load the crossbow. I don't have many bolts so I'll need to make each one count. *Head shots* I remind myself. *Only head shots will do.* My eyes flit from one direction to the other, hoping to catch an early glimpse of our enemy. This forest makes for a perfect place of ambush: dark, isolated, and lots of places for creatures to hide.

I'm distracted when Julietta's horse whinnies and rears up. I turn to see Blake on the ground and presume he has fallen. When he scrambles to his feet and runs away, it's obvious that it was no accident.

'Come back, you coward!' shouts Julietta.

But Blake has already disappeared beyond the trees, leaving the three of us to fight an overwhelming enemy.

'Let's hope he's their first victim,' says Zara.

I'm not worried about Blake's fate. What concerns me is how we'll get back through the portal without him.

'He's got the coin we need.'

'Don't worry about that,' replies Zara. 'Concentrate on the now. We won't be going anywhere if we don't make it through this.'

The sound of rustling leaves and jangling armour immediately sharpens my focus. A Porphyrian leaps over some nearby bushes, howling as it flies through the air with a dagger in its hand. I twist in the saddle and fire the crossbow. The bolt hammers into the monster's open mouth, cutting short its scream. Rua neighs with fright and retreats as the monster's lifeless body falls to the ground.

There's no time to bask in the glory of my shot. Another two Porphyrians appear from either side of Julietta, closing on her in a pincer movement. She brings down her sword to split the skull of one but the other latches onto her saddle in an effort to pull her down. Her horse makes an awful scream and I can see blood. Zara reacts by snapping the reins to send Rua into a charge. I kick my heels to urge our horse forwards. As we close in, I have no time to reload. Instead, I swing the crossbow at the Porphyrian, sending a spray of blood, chainmail and broken teeth flying upwards. It's not a fatal blow but it's enough to free Julietta.

'Two more!' she shouts, pointing her sword at the advancing enemy. 'I can take them.'

She lifts her sword to charge but her horse refuses to move. Ahead, a further three Porphyrians step through the darkness and line up alongside the others. Unlike the first two, these ones are armed with long spears and axes. The floored creature picks himself up and joins his comrades with a bloody, toothless grin.

As the six Porphyrians span out in a semi-circle before us, I use the momentary lull to reload my crossbow. It might well be a futile act. When the battle resumes, I'll only have time for one shot. There's no way Julietta can handle the other five on her own.

'Can we make a run for it?' I suggest.

'My horse is injured,' replies Julietta, pointing to a deep laceration on its flank. 'Yours carries two. If we turn our backs, we will be butchered.'

I hear a sound in the bushes behind me and spin around in the saddle.

'There's no escape route this way,' says Blake, positioning himself in the safe space between our horses. 'The forest descends to a river. It's too wild to cross.'

I'm surprised he's back, even though I know it's only because his pathetic attempt to flee has failed.

'I should use you as a human shield,' says Julietta to him. 'Only I doubt you would be much good.'

She dismounts and slaps her horse on the thigh, allowing it to canter away freely. The Porphyrians ignore the escaping animal and remain locked on us. They close in slowly and deliberately with weapons poised. Julietta plants her feet in a wide stance, twisting the heel of her rear boot into the ground.

'What are you doing?' I ask her, surprised at her actions.

'The horse was a hindrance. I will fight the old fashioned way.'

The Porphyrians move forwards, stalking us like a pack baying wolves. I hear Blake murmuring beside me. When I look down from the saddle, I notice that his eyes are closed and his hands are raised up high with curled fingers. He continues to chant in a strange language as he takes a step towards Julietta, his eyes still firmly shut.

'Are you mad?' she asks Blake, waving her sword at him.

He reaches out and grabs hold of the blade. With a swift movement, he jerks his hand to slice the skin on his palm. I've witnessed him act this way before. The bizarre ritual can only be one thing . . .

'He's using his ability,' confirms Zara. '*He's becoming a Necromancer.*'

I watch as Blake opens his wounded palm and throws a fistful of his own blood into the air. In an arcane language, he releases a roared command. The Porphyrians look perplexed as a swirl of mist appears before them. A tall shape forms from the coiling vapour. It becomes instantly recognisable by the sack-cloth mask with two eyeholes . . .

Blake has summoned The Hangman Ghost.

The Porphyrians snarl at the poltergeist before them and continue their advance. I watch in awe as The Hangman extends an arm and whisks an axe away from one of the beasts. A Porphyrian thrusts his spear at the ghost, but it harmlessly pokes through the transparent torso of The Hangman. With a single movement, the poltergeist sends the axe flying sideways in a vicious arc. Six heads fall to the ground and, soon after, six corpses join them. As fast as he appeared, The Hangman Ghost dissolves in a cloud of mist and the forest falls silent.

Blake slumps to his knees in exhaustion, his hand still oozing blood. It's hard to believe that he chose to save us and performed it in such a dramatic way. I dismount and approach him slowly, my finger resting on the crossbow's trigger.

'Are you okay?' I ask him.

He clutches his bloody hand to his chest and looks at me with an ashen face.

'That was . . . extremely difficult. Now, if you'll excuse me, I may need to pass out.'

Without further warning, he topples over unconscious. Julietta prods him with her sword but gets no response.

'I have witnessed many strange things in my time, but never anything like that.'

I move Blake onto his side and into the recovery position. He's breathing but completely out of it. It feels alien to be tending to him after all of the cruel things he's done in the past. But the past is the past. An inner sense of humanity compels me to help him, especially now that he's not currently a threat.

Julietta steps over Blake and wipes the blades of her sword on some long grass.

'He left us and now we can leave him. Search his pockets and take the coin.'

It seems like a harsh response to someone who just saved our lives.

'Trust me, I don't care much for Blake. But he came back and destroyed those Porphyrians when they were about to murder us. I made a pact to bring him to his son. I owe it to Dexter. We can't just leave Blake here.'

Julietta plants her sword in the ground, clearly unhappy with my response. I look to Zara; not for support, but for a rational opinion on what to do with Blake.

'I came here to find Sasha's mother,' she says. 'But I also came here to destroy Katalina. She's the one responsible for these creatures. Blake might be the only person who can lead us to her. We have no choice but to take him with us.'

Julietta picks up her sword and slams it angrily inside the sheath on her back.

'Your kindness may well be your undoing,' she grumbles. 'If that is your decision, then so be it, but we cannot wait until he wakes.'

Zara climbs down off the saddle and walks towards Blake.

'We won't. Help me to move him onto the horse and let's get going.'

It doesn't take Julietta long to locate the footprints and pick up the trail once more. With Blake laid across Rua's saddle, we move through the forest on foot. After a short while, the ground begins to slope downwards and I can hear the sound of rushing water. Julietta comes to a stop near a broad river spanned by a thin rope bridge.

'There are lots of fresh footprints here,' she says, studying the pattern. 'It looks like there was a commotion.'

I stare out across the bridge, unable to see through the darkness to the bank on the other side.

'Should we cross the river?' I ask.

'The footprints end here,' replies Julietta. 'I suppose we should.'

The bridge is far too narrow and lightweight to support the horse. Someone will need to go alone and act as the guinea pig.

'I'll check it out,' I say, stepping onto the first wooden slat.

'Wait,' shouts Zara. 'I can see something washed up on the riverbank downstream.'

I lean over the side of the bridge and squint. It's not a person, but I can see the sleeves of a jacket . . . *Aaron's jacket.*

I step off the bridge and run towards the sodden jacket which has snagged on a sharp rock. Aaron was here. My mother was here. But now the trail has gone cold.

I'm filled with dread at the thought of what might have happened. I clutch onto the jacket and stare into the swirling waters and sharp rocks. It's hard to imagine anyone could survive if they fell in.

I turn back towards Zara; hoping for reassurance, praying that she can make sense of this terrible scene. For some reason she's standing near a tree, inspecting a hole in the bark.

'What is it, Zara?' When she doesn't answer immediately I know that it's not good. 'Don't sugar-coat it. Just tell me.'

She removes a small metallic object which was lodged deep inside the tree trunk.

'It's a bullet.'

I try to swallow but my throat is too tight. Aaron and my mother were here, together, and shots were fired. Something has gone horribly wrong and I dread to think what might have happened. The sound of Julietta drawing her sword captures my attention.

'There are Porphyrians on the other side of the river,' she says, gravely.

I can see figures moving across the bridge. When I search for Blake and the horse, they're nowhere to be seen. It's as though the darkness has swallowed them up.

'There's too many of them,' says Zara. 'We have to move, right now.'

'What about Blake?' I ask, desperately scanning the area where we left him.

'He's gone,' replies Zara. 'And unless we get going, we'll be the next three victims.'

Chapter 20

Katalina

I grit my teeth and try to shut out the pain. Now that I'm back in my private room I can properly inspect the injury. Spots of blood have started to appear through the gauze padding which covers the crossbow bolt wound on my thigh. I stitched it up too quickly in the forest and one of the sutures must have broken. No matter, it's a mild inconvenience – more of an irritation than a hindrance. I replace the padding and wrap a bandage around it before pulling on my leather trousers. Although my leg feels stiff, I can still put weight on it and move around. I limp over to the drinks cabinet and pour myself a glass of chilled blood. As the thick liquid rolls down my throat, I can already start to feel its healing effect. Both Zara and Sasha made the mistake of not killing me when they had the chance. I'll make them pay for what they did to me in ways they wouldn't believe is possible.

A knock on the door makes me turn sharply with a wince. Edgar enters the room, a self-satisfied smile on his lips.

'You're back sooner than I expected,' I remark, shaking out the numbness in my leg.

'Your mouth is bleeding,' he says, pointing out the spot in the corner of his lips.

I wipe the drops of blood away then lick the remnants off the back of my hand. Edgar tries to hide the fact he's clearly repulsed. Humans are so easy to read.

'What can I do for you, Edgar?'

He doesn't reply straight away. Instead, he takes out a cigar and roles it beneath his nostrils, inhaling the scent of the tobacco.

'I've brought you a gift.'

'Unless it's Ashleigh Hunter's warm body, I'm not interested.'

He smiles at my blunt reply.

'Not quite, but I'm sure you'll be most interested in what I have to show you.'

Edgar steps out of the room, confident that I'll follow. I slam the chalice down and hobble after him. This better be worth the disturbance after a long and tiring day. Edgar's presence is becoming increasingly bothersome of late. I'm not sure that I approve of his frequent unannounced visits or the way he strolls the corridors of my castle like he owns the place. Our working relationship is meant to be a partnership but it's starting to feel as though I'm his subordinate. Edgar may well have influence within the upper echelons of The Agency but that is nothing compared to the army I'm harvesting.

I follow him down a spiral staircase and towards the row of unused chambers. Many centuries ago, these rooms were used as prison cells and I wonder how Edgar is so familiar with this part of the castle.

'Just in here,' he says, sliding a locking bar and swinging the door open.

I step into the room to find two prisoners chained to the wall.

'You brought me a boy,' I say, unimpressed. 'And a dog.'

The teenager gives me a simmering look of hatred. One of his eyes is surrounded by a fresh yellow bruise and he's sporting a swollen lip. The dog looks equally dishevelled as it growls at me with bared teeth.

'It's not just any boy,' says Edgar. 'This is the son of Menzies Blake.'

The mere mention of his name fills me with disgust. I've never gotten over the wasted years I spent working for him as a mole inside the Hunter household. When he was committed to a mental asylum, I was left to rebuild my life alone and in exile. I've never forgiven him for that and I never will.

'Blake was a victim of his own narcissism,' continues Edgar. 'He rose to a position of power too quickly and almost paid the ultimate price. However, he can still be of some use to us.'

I'm not sure that I share the same opinion of him.

'He's old and insane. He was useful to me once but not anymore.'

Edgar lights the cigar and sucks in a mouthful of smoke, swilling it around his cheeks before puffing it out.

'You might be interested to know that his sanity has been restored. What's more, he is here in Romania as we speak, helping the other Agents.'

This only serves to inflame my simmering hatred towards Blake. My reply is hissed through gritted teeth.

'Then he should be wiped out along with the others.'

Blake's boy snarls and strains at his chains like the feral animal next to him. Edgar paces the chamber in a wide arc, ensuring he keeps a safe distance from the growling dog.

'With all due respect, Katalina, I disagree. Blake's ability as a Necromancer is unparalleled. If he joined us, it would only strengthen our cause. We are powerful as two, but we could be unstoppable as three. In time, we would not even need the support of The Agency. I am Menzies' oldest friend and I know exactly how to motivate him.'

Edgar's gaze falls upon the boy who takes the opportunity to interject.

'My father has come to his senses,' he says, all blood and bravado. 'He'd never make the mistake of helping you.'

I walk over and crouch before the determined looking boy. As I bend down, I feel another stitch snap on my leg. It causes me to grimace and clutch my thigh. Blake's boy notices my momentary show of pain.

'Does your leg hurt?' he asks. 'I hope it's agonising.'

'Your father should have taught you not to provoke a dangerous creature.' I grab him by the jaw and pull his head closer to mine. 'He promised me the world. All I ended up with was this scar.'

I hear the rustle of chains to my side. Before I know it, the dog lunges at me. Its jaws clamp down onto my forearm, the incisors piercing my skin. A scorching pain shoots up my arm and I'm forced to release the boy as I roll backwards.

'Get her, Axel!' shouts Blake's son in encouragement.

The wild dog shakes its head from side to side as though it's trying to pull my whole arm out of its socket. Edgar draws his gun and aims at the wild animal. When the trigger clicks it becomes obvious that he's out of bullets. *The incompetent fool.* He kicks the dog hard in the ribs but it refuses to let go. Anger quickly replaces pain and I use it to morph the fingertips of my free hand. It's all that I need to defend myself. My fingernails extend into sharp, claw-like points. I draw my arm back and form my fingers into a dagger-like shape.

'NO!' screams the boy.

I ignore his pleads as I thrust my nails into the torso of the rabid dog. It yelps but remains locked onto my arm. It takes several more violent stabs, driven deep between its ribs, before the animal's jaw finally slackens. I withdraw my bloodied hand and kick the dog away from me.

'Axel!'

The boy strains at his chains as he reaches for the dog's limp's body. It rolls its eyes towards him and seems to make some kind of final connection. I'm fascinated to see such a bond between human and beast. The dog's eyelids close slowly and the boy releases a pained cry.

'You killed my dog,' he sobs with angry tears.

'Don't get so upset. You'll soon be joining your pet.'

I reach towards him with my clawed hand, the dog's blood still wet on my fingernails.

'Wait,' says Edgar. 'We need the boy alive. Blake will join us because we have the one thing he cares about more than anything. Better still, we have a hostage who will draw in the other Agents. Don't destroy this opportunity, Katalina.'

I wrap my hand around the boy's throat and place my claws against his jugular. I want to squeeze the life out of him, just to defy Edgar. *I'm in charge here. I can do as I wish.*

'I don't care about Blake, and I don't care about the other Agents. My Porphyrians will kill them all!'

'But you do care about Ashleigh Hunter,' says Edgar hurriedly. 'She escaped with one of the Agents. The easiest way to capture her is to draw her back in. Trust me, keep the boy alive, for now, and we'll reap the rewards.'

I glance down at the gash on my forearm, knowing full well that I'll need more of Ashleigh's life blood to recover from this new injury. Reluctantly, I remove my hand from around the boy's pulsating throat.

'Stop you're crying, you pathetic fool.'

He slumps back against the stone wall and draws his knees up to his chest. I stare down at him, unable to understand the ridiculous outpouring of grief over a dog. All humans seem to share the same weakness: an incapacity to control their emotions.

I turn towards Edgar who is staring at the puncture wounds on my forearm.

'Always keep your gun loaded,' I say to him. 'My Porphyrian guards would not have been so unprepared.'

He frowns and shoves his gun inside his belt.

'Your Porphyrians have proved to be little more than mindless savages so far, Katalina. You promised me sentient beings who would obey your commands. I am yet to see evidence of that.'

Almost on cue, Razvan appears at the open chamber door. Edgar takes a step backwards as my loyal footman ducks under the frame, his head almost touching the low arched ceiling.

'My lady, I bring news. We have captured a man in the forest. He would not talk until I persuaded him to reveal his identity. He goes by the name of Menzies Blake.'

'Dad,' whimpers the boy, lifting his head.

I turn to Edgar who seems to have suddenly lost his voice.

'You were saying?'

His eyes flick onto the cowering boy, then return to meet mine.

'I apologise for speaking too soon. Your Porphyrians have done well. This is perfect timing. We can use the boy to convince his father that the other Agents turned against him. Blake will join us and our combined powers will make for a perfect triumvirate. The world had a glimpse of what is possible on Dystopia Day when day turned to night. Unlike The Gathering of Witches, our partnership will not fail. Together, we can realise the full power of the supernatural.'

Edgar takes another drag of his cigar, revelling in his own words.

'I won't do it!' shouts the boy, tears streaming down his cheeks. 'I won't lie to my father. GET OUT OF HERE, DAD. IF YOU CAN HEAR ME, RUN!'

I press my boot against his neck to silence him. It would be so easy to crush the life out of him and drag his corpse to Menzies Blake. It would almost be worth it just to see the look on his traitorous face.

Edgar places a tentative hand on my shoulder.

'Remember, we need him alive.'

'Why? He has already told us that he won't cooperate.'

Edgar smiles, that same confident smile.

'Maybe you have forgotten about my own ability? Leave me alone with the boy. Once I have finished with him he will sing like a bird to any tune I choose.'

'Then do it,' I relent. 'But you should know that my patience is wearing thin. I played Menzies Blake's game for too long, humouring the Hunter family while he made promises to me that he couldn't keep. My ancestors were great warriors who fought valiantly for greedy, cutthroat leaders who betrayed them. In their name, I will seize power and rule over any province I choose to. Know this, Edgar: I answer to me and me alone. I will *allow* you to proceed with your experiment. But if your plan doesn't work, I will unleash my own form of justice.'

Chapter 21

Sasha

We follow the riverbank, heading downstream as fast as our legs will take us. I'm all too aware that we only survived the last encounter with the Porphyrians due to Blake's intervention. Now's he's gone and we're down to just me, Zara and Julietta. I'm still clutching Aaron's jacket in the vague hope that it will lead me to him and the others. They made it to the bridge near the river, which seems to be a focal point for Kat's creatures. I have a gut feeling that we'll need to cross that bridge to hunt her down. Our mission to destroy her feels like a long way off. Right now, we're scattered and running for our lives.

'Keep going,' urges Julietta, who has taken up a defensive position behind us.

As we flee, I can see Zara is struggling to catch her breath. She's cradling her stomach, like she might be sick at any moment. It's not been long since her escape from the burning building and she's not fully recovered. I drop back and take hold of her wrist, conscious of her injured and bound hands. Instead of helping her to move faster, I can feel her starting to slow down.

'I have to rest, Sasha,' she wheezes, slumping forwards with her hands on her knees. 'I feel ill.'

'Don't you dare give up,' I warn her.

Julietta stands protectively in front of us with her sword raised. Now that we're still, I can hear the rustle of noises in the forest. The pounding of heavy feet sounds like a beating war drum which is getting louder, and closer, by the second.

'I will do what I can,' says Julietta, rolling her shoulders and limbering up. 'But there are lots of them.'

I look around, desperate to find a solution in what is rapidly becoming a hopeless situation. There's nowhere to hide and we don't have the energy to run, or fight. I can only think of one way out, and it's far from ideal.

'The river – it's our only chance!'

Zara peers anxiously towards the fast-flowing water and sharp, rocky outcrops.

'Are suggesting a way to escape, or a way to commit suicide?'

Julietta runs to the edge of the bank to make a quick evaluation.

'Do it,' she says. 'I will wait and hold them off.'

'No,' I reply, firmly. 'We're stronger together. Stay with us, Julietta. Help us find the others.'

She nods and begins to remove her jacket.

'Lose any excess clothing that might weigh you down,' she instructs us. 'The river has a strong current. Our only chance is to stay above the surface and try to ride it out.'

The sound of the howling creatures shunts us into action. We dump our jackets and bags, keeping only our weapons. I sling the strap of the crossbow over my shoulder and check my pocket to make sure the Athame is safe. With held hands, we line up along the edge of the bank.

'Take a deep breath,' says Julietta. 'And try to hold on to each other.'

I glance back and see a gang of Porphyrians clamouring towards us. The green tinge of their rotting skin is visible beneath the rusted plates of armour and chain mail.

'I hope they can't swim,' I mutter as I grip Zara's wrist.

'I hope we can,' she replies.

We count to three, inhale deeply, and then jump.

The ice-cold water sends a shock through my system. I panic and lose grip of Zara and Julietta's hands. My head goes under and I accidentally gulp in some liquid. I kick for the surface and when my head breaks though I'm relieved to see the other two nearby. Julietta points behind me as the fast current propels us all downstream.

I spin in the water to see what's caught their attention. That's when I'm faced by a frightening sight: the Porphyrians are leaping from the bank and into the river.

'Swim for your life!' shouts Julietta.

I need no encouragement. I've never been a strong swimmer and my technique is made worse by my desperation to escape. My head moves from side to side as I pull through the water. A sharp bend in the river allows me to glance back at our pursuers. Of the half-dozen Porphyrians who jumped in after us, only three remain. I can see one of them thrashing his arms as he is sucked below the water. *Their armour is heavy and it's pulling them down.*

Zara and Julietta are a safe distance from the creatures but I'm losing ground and tiring fast. I feel something snag onto my jeans and fear that I might have struck an underwater tree root. When I try to jerk my leg back, I'm pulled in the opposite direction. It's only when I flip onto my back that I realise what's happened.

A Porphyrian has gripped hold of my ankle.

I scream for help but it's no use; Zara and Julietta are too far ahead and have no hope of swimming against the current to help me. I try to kick myself free, but my blows simply slide off the

Porphyrian's wet shoulders. He smiles at me as his head slowly submerges and I feel myself being dragged underwater.

Take a deep breath. You'll need it.

I'm pulled under the dark water, fighting for my life. My father's words drift inside my mind. *Stay calm, Sasha. Conserve your energy. Think of a solution.* I try to use my spare foot to stamp on the Porphyrian's fingers and loosen his grip. It doesn't work. Instead, he drags me deeper underneath the water, grinning as he sinks lower. I need to do something, and fast.

As I'm sucked further down, the crossbow strap becomes tangled around my neck. It's useless to me now and I'm about to cast it away when I notice something. A bolt is lodged on the flight groove – it's still loaded. The water slows my movements as I take aim at the head of the Porphyrian. My weapon is hardly designed for underwater combat but it's a case of having to improvise. I clench my jaw and pull the trigger. The bolt cuts through the water, leaving a stream of air bubbles in its wake. When the bubbles disperse, I catch a glimpse of the Porphyrian with the bolt lodged in the top of its skull. My leg is instantly freed and I kick my way to the surface.

My head breaks through the water and I fill my lungs with oxygen. Zara and Julietta are nowhere to be seen, but I still have one more Porphyrian giving chase. He is bare-chested, having discarded his chainmail to allow him to swim faster. I can't reload the crossbow and I won't be able to outswim him. My options are dwindling faster than my energy.

The river seems to flow wilder as it widens out. I hear shouts and can see Zara and Julietta standing on a nearby bank. Although I can't hear what they're saying, they seem to be gesturing at something up ahead. A wave rebounds off a boulder and throws me into the air. That's when I catch a glimpse of what's coming: the river is flowing directly towards a vertical drop.

I fight against the current as I desperately swim sideways towards Zara and Julietta. My energy is draining fast and I'm forced to dig deep with the Porphyrian in hot pursuit. Zara leans out from the bank with an outstretched arm, supported by Julietta. I'm just yards away when I feel another hand grip my boot. I'm too far away to grab Zara's bandaged hand. In a last ditch attempt, I extend my crossbow towards her to try and bridge the gap. Zara manages to grab hold of the crossbow string and pull me in. The string cuts into her already injured hands and she grits her teeth through the pain. I try to kick myself free but the Porphyrian hangs on to my leg, threatening to pull me loose. Just when I'm about to accept my fate, Julietta leans over me and brings down her sword, chopping the creature's arm in two. They pull me to safety as the Porphyrian drifts away.

I lie back and catch my breath as Julietta prises the fingers of the severed hand from my ankle. We watch from the bank as the green-skinned monster thrashes against the current, the surrounding water turned red. He tries to grip onto a boulder but the river carries him onwards and towards the waterfall. The last we hear is a fading howl as he disappears over the edge.

Zara crawls towards me, her wet blonde hair flattened and her glasses specked with droplets.

'Remind me whose crazy idea it was to jump in the river?'

I smile at her quip as I sit shivering under the moonlight.

'It worked. Kind of.'

Julietta shakes her head and chuckles to herself as she gathers up some firewood.

'For mortals, you two are pretty reckless. Just remember: you are not invincible.'

I'm impressed at how quickly she manages to start a fire from a tinder nest and some bark. Julietta is at one with nature, without the need for modern equipment and technology. And although her weapon is ancient, it's just as deadly in her hands as any firearm.

She encourages us to huddle closer to the flames. While my body desperately needs the warmth, my mind is anxious not to stop.

'Are we safe here?' I ask, still fearful of any lurking Porphyrians.

'The river carried us a fair distance,' replies Julietta as she blows into the fire to stoke the flames. 'The cold will kill you unless you dry off. I will fetch more wood while you rest. Later, we will resume our search for your friends.'

She walks off, leaving Zara and I to warm ourselves in front of the fire. I twist the water out of my hair while Zara rings out her clothes. Her wet top rides up as she bends over, revealing a bloated-looking stomach.

'Are you okay?' I ask her.

She pulls her top down defensively.

'I'm fine,' she says with a dismissive wave of the hand. 'You're pretty nifty with that crossbow.'

It feels like an awkward change of gears, like Zara is avoiding something. I decide not to press her and put it down to her usual guarded nature.

'I was improvising,' I reply. 'I got lucky, I suppose.'

'More good judgement than luck,' she says, the colour returning to her face. 'You seem to have a natural skill for weapons. Did you learn that at The Academy?'

Her comment makes me laugh. I've never been a natural at anything other than burning toast or putting my foot in my mouth. I think back to my time in Boston, which seems so long ago. When I used the nunchucks to destroy the Black Witch it was a case of having to make them work. Either that, or die.

'Beginner's luck.' I pull the Athame out of my pocket and rotate it in the firelight. 'It's just a shame that I never worked out how to use this thing.'

'It worked one time,' says Zara. 'When it mattered the most.'

Julietta returns carrying an armful of broken branches. She suddenly stops short of us, drops the wood and draws her sword. I grab the crossbow and climb to my feet, wafting away the smoke from the fire.

'What is it?' I ask her.

A figure appears, approaching us slowly through the trees.

'Sasha, is that you?' says Aaron.

I immediately drop the crossbow and race towards him. As I run into his arms, I almost knock him over.

'You're alive,' I say, my voice choked with emotion. I'm filled with a sense of pure joy as I hold onto him tightly. It's only when he doesn't speak that I know something is wrong.

'Aaron, what happened? Where are the others?'

Chapter 22

Sasha

'Where's Dexter?' I ask, searching the area of forest beyond Aaron.

Aaron's face darkens.

'Dexter and Axel were captured further upstream, near a bridge. They were taken by Kat's creatures. Dexter is the only reason I made it this far.'

'We'll find them,' I say, determined that nobody else will fall victim to Katalina or her monsters.

Aaron places his hands on my upper arms as though he's trying to steady me, or prepare me for something.

'Sasha, there's someone you should meet.'

He squeezes me lightly then moves aside. I'm left staring into the darkness of the forest. Another figure appears, walking towards me like an apparition. She's slim, with long dark hair like mine. *Exactly* like mine.

She speaks with a soft tone.

'Sasha?'

The sound of the woman's voice peels away the years. I'm transported back to my childhood, to a time when that voice was most familiar and reassuring to me. It still has that effect on me now.

'Mum?'

She moves closer, the moonlight revealing her features. Her frame is thinner than I remember and she's stooping slightly. Despite her sunken cheeks, it's a face I know and love. I blink hard to make sure that what I'm seeing is real.

Aaron places his hand gently on the small of my back.

'Go to her,' he whispers.

I draw in a wavering breath as I take several cautious steps forwards. She smiles, and that's when I know it *is* real, and that everything will be all right.

We embrace as mother and daughter for the first time in years. I leak a few tears of happiness as I rest my head on her shoulder.

'You've grown so much,' she says, stroking my hair.

It's true; I'm the same height as her now. But I'm no longer the innocent child I was when she disappeared from my life.

We separate but stay close, holding onto each other's forearms as though we're scared we might lose what has taken so long to find.

'I've got so much to tell you, Mum.'

She smiles, small wrinkles forming in the corners of her eyes.

'Aaron already told me about you two. I like him a lot. You have good taste, like me.'

My father. I can tell by the look in her eyes that she doesn't know. What were tears of happiness start to sting as the emotion changes: pain; grief; heartache. I turn away, wondering how I can possibly break the devastating news to her. Aaron has joined the others at the campfire, giving us both distance and time. I've only just got my mother back and now I'll have to deliver the most terrible news anyone ever has to.

I wipe my eyes and try to compose myself.

'Mum, there's something I have to tell you.'

'It's Lou,' she says. 'Your father has gone.'

I bite hard on my lip and fight to control my emotions.

'But . . . how did you know?'

'Katalina taunted me with many cruel things over the years. I learned to separate the truth from the lies. If he was alive, I know that he'd be here by your side. Your father and I had a special bond, Sasha. I felt it when he died. I've come to terms with it.'

She hugs me once more, her thin arms wrapping around me. I allow myself a moment of weakness, just one. As we stand locked together, I realise that there's not some finite amount of pain inside me. Maybe at times I tried to ride it out or wait for it to pass but that's not how it works. Grief is the worst kind of hurt because it hides in the deepest recesses within us. Our minds just keep producing more pain, and it never truly goes away. All you can do is lean on those closest to you and learn to deal with it.

Before I open my eyes, I picture my father looking over at both of us. He's smiling. He looks proud. He'll always be with us.

I reach inside my pocket and take out his handkerchief, using it to wipe my eyes as though it was his own hand. As I unfold it, my mother's pendant falls into my palm.

'You found your birthstone,' she says. 'You must have been drawn to it.'

'My birthstone?' I reply, confused. 'I thought this pendant belonged to you.'

She picks up the stone and hangs it around my neck, hooking the clasp onto one of the remaining good links.

'Your father gave this to me as a gift. It's opal, which represents the month of your birth. I always intended to give this to you one day. I'm so glad it found you.'

It found me? It feels like a strange way to describe how I came across it but I decide not to ruin the moment by questioning it. Instead, I produce the one thing I know for certain belongs with her: the Athame.

'Dad gave this to me. It saved my life once but I don't know how to use it.' I place it in her bony hand and close her fingers around the handle. 'This belongs to you, Mum.'

She stares at the small dagger like it's the most precious object in the world.

'Thank you for saving me, Sasha. I love you.'

I repeat the last three words back to her and have never meant something so much in my entire life.

We walk back towards the others hand in hand. Despite the years she has suffered inside a prison, and the fact I almost just drowned, we couldn't be happier right now.

I introduce my mother to Zara, and our new friend Julietta. Zara is understandably anxious – it's the most nervous I've ever seen her. It's not the right time to explain Zara's past relationship with my father but I know my mother will understand when we eventually discuss it.

Aaron stands up and clears his throat, a serious expression on his face.

'We've made a decision.' He turns towards me but avoids making eye contact. 'Sasha, you and your mother have been through enough. Julietta can direct you to the nearest village in the valley below while the three of us rescue Dexter.'

'And hunt down Katalina,' adds Zara.

'No way,' I reply. 'I'm not leaving you, *any of you*. We'll finish this together.'

My mother cocks her head back and looks a little shocked at my forceful response. She turns to the others and addresses them with a more conciliatory tone.

'Your offer is both kind and brave. I'm pleased to see that Sasha has such good friends and I thank you all for looking out for her. If we're going to rescue your friend, and defeat Katalina, we'll need every person here to do their bit. I might be a little frail and older than you all, but I'm a White Witch . . . and now I have this.'

She holds up the Athame. The blade glows in her hand, hinting at its latent power. Aaron's mouth drops open slightly.

'You're telling us that you can use it as some kind of supernatural weapon?'

My mother closes her fingers around the Athame's hilt and the blade responds by glowing brighter.

'It's been a while,' she says. 'Maybe if I had this with me all those years ago I could have stopped Katalina much sooner.'

Her words are filled with regret: the lost years, her lost husband.

'It doesn't matter,' I reassure her. 'You have it now.'

The blue light shines brightly in the darkness and reflects in every pair of staring eyes. I can tell that from this moment, every one of us believes we can achieve what we came here to do.

It's great to have Mum back.

+ + +

For the next thirty minutes, we sit around the campfire and update each other on the sequence of events since we arrived in Romania. Aaron describes how he found my mother and how Edgar appeared, only to deceive them. I'm shocked by my former Agency tutor's betrayal. I try to convince Aaron not to blame himself for what happened to Dexter but I can see that it weighs heavy on him. Zara recalls how Kat and her creature brutally killed Julietta's friend before setting fire to the lodge. My mother explains how she escaped from Katalina but remains quiet when the subject of Menzies Blake crops up.

Our conversation moves onto the task at hand and we gather closer to plan our assault.

'Preparation is the key,' says my mother. 'By failing to prepare, you are preparing to fail.'

She rises onto one knee and uses the tip of her Athame to trace lines in the ash. We all lean in to absorb the details of her hastily drawn map and try to commit it to memory.

'If we follow the river upstream it will lead us to the bridge,' she explains. 'From there, a track leads straight to the castle's main gate. However, if we veer off through the forest, there's a secret entrance around the back.'

Julietta taps her bottom lip.

'The forest near the castle will be crawling with Porphyrians.'

'That's why we'll need to split up,' replies Mum. 'It's too dangerous to try and take on Katalina and her army of creatures together. When I escaped from the castle, I passed an abandoned reservoir. It was a death trap – the water has turned thick and rancid and will swallow anyone who falls in. We know how recklessly the Porphyrians give chase, and also how much they struggle in water. If some of us can draw them to the reservoir, they can be wiped out in one go. It's our only chance.'

'I'll do it,' says Julietta without a moment's hesitation. 'It is why I came here in the first place.'

'And I'll help you,' adds Zara.

'But you're not well,' I point out.

'I'm okay,' she says, shrugging it off. 'My hands are injured but my legs work fine.'

As logical as my mother's plan seems, I'm uncomfortable with the idea of splitting up so soon after finally regrouping. Aaron places his arm around me and senses my wariness.

'Divide and conquer,' he says with a wink. 'It's a classic Sun Tsu military tactic.'

I have no idea what he's referring to but he seems fairly confident in the plan.

'What about Edgar?' I ask the group. 'If he's working with Katalina, he's dangerous.'

'We'll take him prisoner,' replies my mother. 'The International Agency leaders in Geneva will deal with him.'

'We need Blake too,' adds Zara. 'He has the coin we need to travel back through the portal.'

I sense a flicker in my mother's eye at the mention of his name. It suggests a history between them that I'm yet to fully understand.

'Don't worry,' she says, without malice in her voice. 'We'll find Blake and his son.'

Julietta kicks dirt to smother the campfire before we head off along the river bank. It feels safe to be part of a group once more, with Aaron on one side of me and my mother on the other. A part of me wishes that we were heading home to leave this place behind. I'm sure I'm not the only one who harbours this thought. At the same time, we all know the reasons why we're doing this: Dexter is imprisoned, just like my mother was, and Katalina is too dangerous to be ignored. She sought out my father to murder him and unless we deal with her, we can never sleep easy.

As we trek upstream, Aaron notices something washed up at the edge of the river. He climbs down to retrieve it.

'It's an axe,' he says, using his Empath senses to extract its origin. 'This is a few hundred years old but it's in near-perfect condition. It must have belonged to one of the Porphyrians who drowned.'

He brushes off the weeds and offers it to Zara.

'You should have it,' he says. 'For protection.'

'No thanks,' she replies. 'I'll need to move fast, not fight. You can keep it.'

He swings it in a circle above his head like a Viking warrior, a beaming smile on his face. Julietta shakes her head at his antics.

'Not like that. Hold it vertically and take a wide grip. It can be used to block as well as strike.'

Aaron doesn't seem to take offence to her instruction. If there's one thing I love most about him it's his ability to listen and take things on board. It could be because he's an Empath, or maybe it's just because he's a great guy.

My mother leans in close to me.

'Is he always this much fun?' she asks.

'Never a dull moment,' I reply.

She smiles and threads her arm through mine as we continue on along the riverside. I'm enjoying our time, although I know it's just a respite; the quiet before the storm of what's about to come. Soon, we'll arrive at the bridge where we'll cross into Katalina's territory. Life feels good, but death is coming.

I hope it's not looking for any of us.

Chapter 23

Katalina

Blake's son pulls at his chains and screams in protest as Razvan carries the corpse of his dead dog out of the chamber. The manacles cut into the boy's wrists as he reaches out with pleading hands. His pathetic display reminds me of Ashleigh Hunter's maniacal behaviour during her first few days in the oubliette. Humans are capable of making such awful noises when in distress. This boy is as distraught as I've seen anyone and I have to fight the temptation to put him out of his misery, if only to spare my ears.

Edgar follows as I step outside to the corridor so I can hear myself think.

'Give me five minutes alone with young Dexter,' he asks.

My mood is still unsettled from the dog attack. I bind the puncture wounds on my forearm with a spare length of bandage leftover from my thigh injury. From Ashleigh Hunter's escape to her daughter firing the crossbow bolt at me and now this; today has not been a good day.

'If you can't shut him up I'll rip his throat out.'

'I will do more than just quieten him.' Edgar blinks slowly, his demeanour as calm as ever. 'I will hypnotise him into a state of complete submission. Once he is under, I will reprogram his memory with a story about how he was betrayed and abandoned by the other Agents. Blake will believe every word of it. I will use his emotional state to bring him back on board to our cause. The end game is approaching, trust me.'

I roll my eyes, still not convinced that we need Blake at all. It would be easier to just kill him and his son. For some reason, Edgar believes that Blake is an asset we need. For now, I'll play along. The Agency is the only significant threat to me and I must do everything to pacify them. As their representative, Edgar holds the power, but the balance will soon shift in my favour.

I turn to Razvan, who is standing with the bleeding dog draped over his shoulder.

'Dispose of that dead animal then bring Blake down here.'

He makes a small bow before marching away, his armour clinking with each giant stride. While I might not be able to fully trust Edgar, I have faith in my reborn ancestor who will always have my back.

I swing open the chamber door, where the boy is kneeling with his head slumped onto his chest. Edgar's eyes grow. Where I see a victim, he sees an opportunity. I'm intrigued by his somewhat audacious claim to be able to manipulate the boy's memory. Perhaps this would be a good way to test both his skill and his commitment to our cause. If Edgar fails to make good on his promise, I can dispatch with him and proceed alone. If he is successful, I will continue with our working relationship . . . for now.

'Do your thing,' I say to him.

He removes his coat and hangs it on a wrought iron sconce attached to the nearby wall. I observe him as he unbuttons his cuffs and carefully folds back his sleeves. Finally, he rolls his head from side-to-side to loosen his neck. With a parting glance, he walks into the chamber and closes the door behind him.

I'm able to peer through a tiny barred opening in the thick wooden door. Dexter scrambles back against the wall as Edgar approaches him with an open hand. His fingers are splayed apart as he lowers his palm onto the boy's head. Dexter tries to fight him off, but Edgar's grip is far too strong. He tilts his bald head backwards and closes his eyes as he utters a chant:

'Spirits of the night, move among us. Be guided by the light of this world and visit upon us Relieve this boy of his recent memories and open the channel to his inner mind.'

As each word is spoken, Dexter becomes more passive. Eventually, his hands fall limply to his sides and he seems to sink into a stupor. The temperature drops within the chamber, sending a cold blast of air through the hatch. Edgar leans closer to the boy's ear and whispers in an ancient language which sounds like Latin. The strange ritual reminds me of something Menzies Blake would do when summoning spirits. I never trusted it then, and I don't trust it now.

Paranoia rises within me, gnawing at my insides like vermin in my stomach. I've always survived by eliminating threats before they become too powerful. Edgar Levi is a former Agency partner of Blake's. I'm suspicious of why he wants to work with his old colleague – who is damaged goods – and why he seems so insistent on keeping Dexter alive. Maybe his true allegiance is to Blake, and not me? Maybe he's planning on using Blake and his son to overthrow me? I refused to be used as a pawn again. I hold all the pieces; *I wield the power.*

I kick open the chamber door and storm into the room. Edgar continues to whisper into the boy's ear, feeding him with information that I'm not party to. I grab hold of his shoulder and haul him back.

'What are you doing?' he says, outraged. 'You must not interrupt the litany!'

I morph my fingers into deadly claws once more.

'If Blake is so important, he'll need a more compelling reason to join us.'

I turn to face the boy. With one swift move, I bury my claws deep into his stomach. In his trance-like state, he shows no reaction.

'Stop!' shouts Edgar. 'You'll kill him.'

I push harder, puncturing the vital organs with skilled precision. It's a calculated move and I know exactly what I'm doing.

'He'll die,' I reply in confirmation. 'But not for a little while.'

I extract my blood-drenched claws slowly. Edgar looks completely exasperated by my actions.

'You've ruined it. I can't possibly convince Blake that his son was betrayed now.'

I unlock the manacles around the Dexter's wrists and pull down his sleeves to cover the marks on his skin.

'Wrong. I've improved our negotiating power. Use your hypnotism to reprogram the boy – make him think that he was attacked by the other Agents.'

Edgar's eyebrows knit together in a fierce looking frown.

'How on Earth am I supposed to do that?'

I don't appreciate his negativity, or his lack of initiative.

'Sasha Hunter carries a knife. The boy's wound looks a lot like a knife wound to me. I have improved your narrative, now it's up to you to implant it in his memory. Once you're done, move him onto the bed in the next chamber.'

Edgar shakes his head.

'You're crazy, Katalina.'

'No, I'm ruthless,' I reply. 'There's a difference. Now hurry, Blake will be here soon.'

+ + +

It's amazing how well humans react under pressure. By removing thinking time, it forces them to focus on the task at hand. Edgar does remarkably well; he feeds the information to Dexter as he cradles him and carries him into the next room. Unlike the previous cell with its manacles and barred door, this chamber is more like a guest room. A bear-skin rug covers the stone floor and a wooden bed rests against the far wall. It's the perfect scene to create our illusion.

Edgar places the unconscious boy onto the bed. I remove the bandage from around my forearm and use it to bind his lacerated stomach.

'It's a little late for that,' says Edgar, still fuming.

'I'm not trying to save him,' I reply. 'It's all part of the illusion.'

In the years I spent masquerading as a housekeeper for the Hunter's, I became an expert in the art of deception. Humans are simple creatures and easy to manipulate.

'As long as Blake sees what he needs to see, and hears what he needs to hear, he will buy the lie.'

Edgar purses his lips and folds his arms across his barrel-like chest. I can tell that he wants to assert himself but to his credit he knows better than to try.

I finish preparing the boy just as footsteps can be heard on the corridor outside.

'It's time,' I say to Edgar. 'Make sure he is ready.'

I step outside the room to meet Razvan and our bedraggled guest. It's the first time I've laid eyes on Menzies Blake since the night he was defeated in London. His incarceration appears to have aged him by years, not months.

'Hello, Katalina,' he says, his voice lacking the inner confidence I remember so well. 'I often wondered when I'd see you again. Maybe you didn't hear but I spent the last six months rotting in a mental hospital. I hoped you would visit me. Did you lose your passport?'

I smile, briefly, before casting a more serious expression.

'We can talk later, Blake. Right now, time is of the essence.'

'Really?' he scoffs. 'What's more important that the incarceration of your old friend?'

He hasn't got a clue about what awaits him. I can't wait to see his reaction.

'We found your son in the forest. He had been attacked and left to die.'

Blake immediately loses the false facade. I can sense his pulse rising as the blood pumps around his system. Panic spreads across his face.

'What do you mean? Where's Dexter?'

I open the chamber door to reveal the carefully designed scene. Blake wanders inside like he's in a trance, completely ignoring Edgar. He approaches the boy, who is now awake and groaning in pain.

'Father, is that you?'

Blake falls to his knees at the bedside and grabs Dexter's hand.

'Yes, it's me, Son. I'm here. What happened?'

'I was attacked. They stabbed me. They did it because I was your son.'

Blake leans over the bed inspects the boy's mortal wound. Tears start to roll down his cheeks and fall onto the white sheet, mixing with the blood stains.

'Who did it, Dexter?' asks Blake, placing his hand on the boy's cheek. 'Who stabbed you?'

I shoot a glance at Edgar who gives me a nod of acknowledgement. My attention turns back to Dexter as he rises up from the bed, his face flushed red.

'SASHA HUNTER,' he shouts, his eyeballs bulging. 'SASHA HUNTER DID IT.'

He falls back onto the bed, his head rolling to one side. The room falls silent, perfectly punctuating Dexter's final words. It was a genius move to place the blame on the Hunter girl. To Edgar's credit, he managed to plant the lie perfectly. Perhaps he is worth keeping alive after all.

Blake gathers his son into his arms and rocks backwards and forwards as he sobs. I motion for Edgar to approach Blake.

'I'm sorry, Menzies,' he says, placing a comforting hand on his shoulder. 'We'll make sure Dexter's death is not in vain.'

Blake continues to weep uncontrollably as we retreat out of the room. Once we're outside in the corridor, I slap Edgar on the back.

'Good job,' I whisper. 'It couldn't have worked out much better.'

He turns to face me, his face darkened.

'You don't know what you've just created.'

I want to laugh at his response until a sound echoes from within the chamber. It's a piercing howl, forged from a mixture of pain and anger.

And something else otherworldly.

Chapter 24

Sasha

A heavy atmosphere descends over the group as we arrive back at the bridge. Without needing to verbalise it, we all know the danger of what lies ahead. My mother's plan is for us to separate and create a diversion. Zara and Julietta volunteered for the job of luring the Porphyrians away from the castle while the rest of us focus on a seek-and-destroy mission: to seek Dexter and destroy Katalina. I'm worried about Dexter. I'm worried about my mother, too. I hate that she has to return to the place she only recently escaped from. Most of all, I'm worried about Zara. She's as tough as anyone I know, but I can tell she's struggling physically. Occasionally, the mask of her brave face slips and reveals a pained expression. I have to stop myself from saying an emotional goodbye to her. Instead, I simply wish her luck.

'Did I just get a "good luck" from Sasha Hunter?' she says with a mocking smile.

Aaron bends down to tie the laces on Zara's boots into double knots.

'Stay close to Julietta,' he says, checking the bandages on her hands. 'Don't try to engage those creatures. Keep moving, no matter what.'

My mother gives detailed directions to Julietta on the whereabouts of the abandoned reservoir. Finally, she turns to address the group.

'According to Blake, the portal will reopen in an hour, at midnight. We all know what we need to do. We'll meet you back here with Blake, Dexter and Axel. Then we can all go home.'

It sounds so straight forward when it's compressed into a few short sentences. My mind fills with the unspoken horrors, such as Katalina and her army of Porphyrians. She's been the cause of so much death and misery for so long. All that will end tonight. *It has to.* With my mother at my side, I know we can do it.

We navigate the bridge in single file, walking slowly across the wooden slats which extend over the rushing waters. The opposite bank is clouded in a thick mist, like it's a warning from nature not to proceed. I clutch the crossbow with both hands, ready for an ambush. We're vulnerable on the rickety bridge and I'm relieved when we all safely make it to the other side. A solitary track dissects a route through the trees ahead. The mist parts, like an invisible hand drawing back a curtain. It reveals a turreted gatehouse in the distance.

With little more than a farewell glance, Julietta dashes off into the forest. Zara lingers for a moment.

'Don't worry, we'll find a way to lure the Porphyrians.'

'I know you will,' I reply to her.

'Go kick some ass, Sis',' says Aaron.

Her smile turns into a wince as she clutches her stomach. I want to say something, to ask once more whether she's well enough to do this. Zara doesn't give me the opportunity. With a deep breath, she turns and disappears into the dark woods.

Something tugs at my stomach, a nagging feeling that I shouldn't have let her go. I hope I don't regret it.

Our group suddenly feels much smaller without Zara and Julietta. Aaron rests the axe on his shoulder and reaches out for my hand.

'More than three of us would be too many,' he says, using his Empath senses to calm my anxiety. 'We've got a White Witch with us now and you're a crack shot with that crossbow.'

I look down at my weapon, which is already loaded and cocked.

'I only have one bolt left.'

My mother smiles and places a reassuring arm around my shoulder.

'Then make it count,' she says.

Our conversation is interrupted by a howling cry coming from beyond the castle wall. It sounds like a man has unleashed a wail at the top of his voice. I can hear pain and anguish mixed with an animalistic fury. I lock eyes with Aaron, who has lost his jovial expression.

'We should get going,' he says in a serious voice.

We climb down into a ditch which runs alongside the track, using it as cover as we scurry towards the gatehouse. I can't shake the anguished scream from my mind. It didn't sound like Dexter, which is some relief. Maybe it's the noise of a Porphyrian rising from the dead. Or perhaps it's some other tortured soul who is being held prisoner by Katalina. Either way, we need to get inside and find out exactly what's going on.

The ditch leads to a towering portcullis set within the gatehouse, with a crenelated wall extending in either direction.

Aaron pops his head up to scan the entrance.

'I can't see any Porphyrians,' he remarks. 'Maybe we could climb the wall like we did at The Tower of London?'

'That's not a good idea,' replies my mother. 'Do you see those thin slits in the turrets? They're called arrow loops. We can't see in, but whoever is behind them can see out. If we follow the perimeter wall east, I can guide us to the hidden entrance. Stay close and follow me.'

We take a sheltered route through the trees, maintaining a safe distance from the castle's outer wall. I'm tempted to ask my mother about the layout of the fortress but it's more important that we remain silent. After the years spent planning her escape, I feel confident that she'll be able to lead us inside safely. What happens after that is another matter.

Eventually my mother comes to a halt and calls us to gather in. We crouch behind a thorn bush as she points out a small arched doorway built into the wall.

'That's the hidden entrance,' she whispers. 'I used it to escape from the castle's grounds.'

It's not nearly as impenetrable-looking as the gatehouse but it's still a heavy-duty door built of solid oak.

'How do we open it?' I ask.

Aaron lifts up his axe.

'Allow me.'

My mother places a hand on the blade and lowers his weapon.

'I don't doubt that you can do it but we don't want to attract attention. I've got a better idea.'

She produces the Athame. I immediately notice a glint of excitement in her eye. I've carried the blunt dagger around for so long yet I've been frustrated at my inability to use it. The knife belongs in the hands of a White Witch and I can't wait to see my mother finally unlock its power.

I watch with an unblinking stare as she points the Athame in the direction of the door. The blade begins to glow, a cool blue colour. In my mind's eye, I envision her blowing the door apart, or even destroying an entire section of wall and anyone behind it. I flinch as a shaft of blue light shoots from the tip of the blade and impacts the door near the handle. I brace myself, but there's no explosion. Instead, I hear the turning of a lock followed by the creak of the door opening ajar. The blue light retracts and the glowing blade returns to its usual dull colour. It was effective, in the most understated of ways.

'Discretion is the better part of valour,' says my mother with a satisfied smile.

We approach the now open door silently, moving through the undergrowth with careful steps. Aaron is clutching his axe with both hands and I've got my finger poised on the crossbow's trigger. My mother keeps the Athame drawn and at the ready. Just as we're about to enter, she turns to face us.

'This is enemy territory,' she whispers. 'Every step you take will be fraught with danger. Once we're inside, we need to make our way to the main tower. The oubliette I was kept in is inside there, at the bottom of a vertical shaft. It's accessed from a higher level within the main tower, which is Katalina's private chamber. Whatever happens inside this place, I need you to control your emotions. If I don't make it, you two head straight for the portal. Do you understand?'

Her words come as a reality shock. Having only just been reunited with my mother, I'd never considered the possibility of losing her so soon. I don't want to give her the confirmation she seeks, because I know what that means. This was always a rescue mission more than an assassination; it's more important for me that my mother lives than Katalina dies. As I stare into her eyes, I know it's something she will not easily concede.

'Sasha, *do you understand?*' she asks again, this time more forcefully.

'Yes, Mum,' I reply, with fingers crossed behind my back.

We move through the doorway in the perimeter wall, surprised to find the castle's grounds completely empty. A nearby cart provides cover and allows us to take in the surroundings. The inner walls are lined with flaming torches which illuminate the vast courtyard in a flickering light. From our hidden position, I'm able to see the full extent of Katalina's castle for the first time. The main keep rises up as though it has grown out of the bedrock beneath. It's an imposing sight with its blackened stonework, like it's been charred by fire. The only sign of life is an orange glow in the uppermost window of the tower. A wooden staircase leads to an arched entrance at first floor level. I glance across to the left and can see the main gatehouse. The portcullis is now raised as though someone has recently left, or recently entered.

Aaron swings the axe by his side restlessly.

'It's quiet,' he muses.

'Too quiet,' I reply.

My mother's eyes are fixed on the entrance to a tunnel at the base of the keep. A pair of barred gates have been pushed open and left resting against the wall.

'If Katalina is holding your friend prisoner, he'll be in one of two places: the dungeon chambers, or the oubliette. The only route to both of them is through that tunnel.'

'Sounds like a plan,' says Aaron. 'Let's go and find Dexter. I never thought I'd say it, but I'm actually starting to miss him.'

Aaron is eager to get going but I can tell that something is making my mother uneasy. It seems to be more than just the fact she's back here, at the place of her incarceration.

'What's wrong, Mum?'

She narrows her eyes and moves them up to the glowing window at the top of the tower.

'The portcullis is up and the tunnel gates are wide open for us to walk straight inside. There's not a soul here. It doesn't feel right, Sasha. I've always found that if it seems too good to be true, it usually is.'

The very moment the words leave her mouth, the sound of grinding chains breaks the silence. I snap my head towards the gatehouse to see the portcullis lowering. A slamming noise nearby makes me turn, and I notice that the entrance door in the wall has closed. I can't see anyone but I can hear rasping breaths and the shuffling of feet. Lots of feet.

'What's happening?' asks Aaron, his head jerking in different directions.

My mother pushes us away from the wall and draws her Athame, her jaw set.

'It's a trap,' she scowls. 'And we just walked straight into it.'

Porphyrians. Not just a few of them. It's all of them. Dozens of creatures pour through the gatehouse and circle the courtyard, bristling with brutal tipped weapons. They remind me of a bunch of crazed chimpanzees at feeding time. We become stranded as they form a ring around us, leering at us with slack jaws and hungry eyes. I'm distracted by the sound of someone clapping. I spin on my heels to see Katalina walking out of the tower and down the wooden stairs. She's flanked on either side by two imposing figures: one of them is a giant Porphyrian warrior, the other is Edgar Levi.

'Bravo,' she says with a mocking tone. 'I was so worried that you might have drowned, Ashleigh. Your blood is so precious to me. I'm grateful that you've saved me the trouble of hunting you down.'

I move from behind my mother and raise the crossbow, aiming at Kat. She's fifty yards away but in a clear line of sight.

'I've got a shot,' I whisper.

The giant Porphyrian tries to shield Katalina with his own body but she shoves him aside.

'Look everyone, it's Sasha Hunter and she's trying to shoot me again.' She tilts her head back and laughs. 'I thought we were best friends, Sash?'

I feel my eyes burning crimson, reflecting the simmering hatred within me which is urging me to shoot. My mother moves alongside me, her hip brushing against mine.

'Control your emotions,' she whispers, concealing the Athame at her side. 'Don't shoot – not yet.'

Edgar walks further down the stairway, a gun in his hand.

'Where's Agent Gordon,' he calls.

'She's far from here,' shouts Aaron. 'You're a traitor, Edgar. You'll pay for this.'

'How pathetically brave,' says Kat, enjoying the moment. 'You're completely surrounded and vastly outnumbered. Despite your hopeless situation, I'll offer you a deal. If you lower your weapons and surrender, I'll allow you all to share the same cell for the remainder of your pathetic lives. I'm sure Ashleigh will testify to how lonely imprisonment can be.'

I can feel the glow of the Athame nestled between mine and my mother's leg. There will be no deal made. It's freedom, or death. I only hope we can destroy Katalina before her horde of Porphyrians descends upon us.

The silence is broken by a high pitch sound. It's the blast of a horn, like a hunting call. The Porphyrians react by snapping their heads in an easterly direction. I keep my crossbow trained on Katalina as her giant guard leans in to speak to her.

'The scouts have found someone, my lady.'

Zara and Julietta. I want to believe that this is part of their plan but the giant's reaction suggests otherwise.

Katalina giggles and makes a fluttering clap.

'Very good, Razvan. It will surely be Agent Gordon and the red-headed Amaranth girl. I underestimated both of them before. We should take no chances this time. Send all but twelve of your men.

Instruct them to kill them, and bring me back the blonde girl's head.' Katalina runs a hand across the scar over her eye. 'I want to see the last expression on her face.'

Zara.

I have no time to dwell on Kat's threat. The towering creature gestures to several ranks of Porphyrians who immediately charge through the gatehouse. The remaining dozen close in around us. When I turn my attention back to Katalina, she looks different. Her hands have become claws; her skin is all gnarled and leathery; her face is contorted into an animalistic scowl.

I hear Aaron make an audible swallow.

'She's morphed into her altered state,' he says. 'We're in trouble.'

Chapter 25

Twenty minutes earlier

Zara

I turn my back on Sasha, Aaron and Ashleigh and race into the forest. There's no time to think about the danger we're about to face. I can't allow myself to consider the unborn baby I'm carrying inside me. If I did, even for a moment, I'd stop dead in my tracks. Sasha and Aaron are relying on me and I won't let them down. My sole motivation is to preserve the lives that mean the most to me. To do that, sometimes you have to run away from danger. This time, I have to run towards it. I won't leave this place until I've eliminated the threat that took the life of my baby's father.

It's simple.

All we need to do is draw the Porphyrians away from the castle.

Then kill every single one of them.

Julietta darts through the forest, nimbly jumping over fallen tree trunks and chopping her way through tangled bushes. I can picture her doing the exact same thing hundreds of years ago, clad in armour and chainmail instead of a leather jacket and slim-fit jeans. Her ancient sword is the only reference to her past medieval life. She wields it with such ease, like it's an extension of her own arm.

I dig into my energy reserves and do my best to keep up with her. I've always had a good level of physical fitness but pregnancy has severely reduced my cardio. The wounds on my palms have also reopened, with traces of blood seeping through the bandages. To add insult to injury, my vision is obscured by a crack across the lens of my glasses. All in all, I'm in pretty bad shape. It's not an option to feel sorry for myself and I'm determined not to be a hindrance.

Julietta comes to a stop and thrusts the blade of her sword into the ground. I catch up with her, grateful for the chance to catch my breath. When I stare into the valley, I'm relieved to see that we've located what we're looking for. Down below, a few hundred metres away, the tree line circles a large, sludge encrusted reservoir. A thin walkway dissects the filthy lake, stretching out from an abandoned water tower.

'We found it,' I sigh.

'Yes but we already have company.'

Julietta points out a group of three figures lurking near the iron framework which supports the rusted water container.

'Porphyrians,' I remark. 'But I only count three of them.'

One of the hideous creatures puts a horn to his mouth and blows out a short blast. Two more Porphyrians appear from within the forest and join their group.

'They use the horn to call each other,' observes Julietta. 'If they see us, they will alert the others.'

'Isn't that what we want?' I ask.

'Yes,' replies Julietta. 'But it must be on our terms and when we are ready to ensnare them.'

I check my watch, anxious for us not to get into a waiting game. If there are only a few Porphyrians out here in the woods, it could mean that the rest are at Kat's castle . . . which is where Sasha, Ashleigh and Aaron are headed.

'We have to do something,' I urge Julietta. 'We can't just hang around watching them.'

'Agreed,' she says, picking up her sword. 'I will kill them all and retrieve their horn. I will use it to call the rest once we have inspected the reservoir and prepared a trap. You should stay here.'

Five against one; I don't like those odds. And I don't like being a passive observer.

She's about to dash off when I grab hold of her arm.

'Wait,' I say to her. 'I have a better plan.'

She gives me the exact same look that Aaron does whenever I say it to him. She needn't worry, my plans usually work. *Most* of the time.

My ploy is as simple as it is effective. Julietta will approach the Porphyrians from behind, signalling me when she's at the water tower. I will appear on the far side of the valley and goad them onto the walkway. Once they're in a vulnerable position, Julietta will strike and cut them down before they know what's happened. It's a classic decoy manoeuvre, and I'll be playing the part of the decoy. It's just about all I'm capable of right now.

With the plan of action agreed, we separate and I make my way around the edge of the valley. I move fast, racing through the forest to get myself into position. I'm not far from the reservoir when I feel a sharp, agonising pain shoot up my leg. I fall to the ground under the weight of something heavy gripped onto my ankle. The pain makes me dizzy and I clench my teeth to stop myself from screaming out. It feels like I've been bitten, and whatever it was is still clamped onto my leg.

The pain is blinding, radiating up from my leg in waves of agony. When my vision finally clears, I dare to look down. The silent perpetrator is revealed.

I've stepped onto a bear trap.

I dig my hands into the earth and try to claw myself free but the iron jaws have locked onto me. I try to prise open the mechanism but it won't budge an inch. The jagged teeth are embedded in my calf, just above my ankle. These things are designed to trap huge animals; a small human with wrecked hands has no chance of escape. My whole leg feels like it's on fire. I lie back and swivel my head to look for something to use as leverage: a stick, a rock, anything. That's when I notice something that sends an ice cold chill up my spine.

I'm lying in a shallow pit which is scattered with human bones.

I push the terror aside and start to join the pieces together: scavenging Porphyrians; a bear trap; human bones. The horrendous realisation slowly sinks in. This is some kind of feeding nest.

I'm left with two choices.

Lie here, accept it, do nothing.

Or *fight*.

Julietta needs me. Sasha needs me. My baby needs me.

I roll onto my stomach, ignoring the excruciating pain. If I can't remove the bear trap, it will have to come with me. I use my knees and elbows to claw myself forwards, inch by inch. The iron contraption drags along the ground like a plough. At this rate, it will take me an hour just to get to the reservoir.

I hammer my first into the ground and curse my bad luck. In the silence that follows my expletives, I hear a noise. It sounds like breathing.

I twist my body and roll onto my back. I'm faced with a sight which almost makes me vomit. A Porphyrian is standing there with a headless human body slung over its shoulder. A bear trap is clamped onto the corpse's leg. The victim must be some poor villager who wandered into the forest and stepped onto an iron trap, just as I did. The Porphyrian's eyes grow at the sight of fresh prey.

It feels like there's no way out. My hand relaxes from a defiant fist and rests on my bump. *I would have called you Louis after your father, or Louise if you are a girl.*

The Porphyrian drops the body and grins, revealing a mouth of blood-stained teeth. My instincts force me to scramble backwards but it's a hopeless effort. The bloodthirsty creature approaches me, drooling in anticipation. It knows I'm trapped and going nowhere. Julietta is on the other side of the reservoir. Nobody can save me.

I won't give up on us, bump.

I rotate onto my side and try to reach for a nearby rock to use as a weapon. My fingers scrape the edge of the stone but I'm too far away to grasp it. The Porphyrian kneels next to me, ready to lunge. My fingers claw at the earth and I catch onto a long, sharp object. It's a splintered human femur.

I grab the bone and twist my body. As the monster jerks his foul head towards me, I thrust the sharp edge of the bone under its open jaw. It penetrates the rotting flesh. I push harder, sliding it up inside its skull. The eyes pop wide open in a moment of disbelief before rolling upwards.

I'm almost crushed as the heavily armoured corpse flops down on top of me. Adrenaline courses through my system, giving me the strength to shove the Porphyrian aside. I use the weight of its body to press down on one of the trap's springs. By shuffling into a sitting position, I'm able to use both hands to prise the iron jaws apart, just enough to move my leg. The pain is excruciating as the metal teeth slowly retract from my calf.

We're still alive, my little bump.

There's no time to dwell on my latest injury. Using my one good leg, I hop from tree to tree until I make it to the low concrete barrier which forms the edge of the reservoir. I can see Julietta standing on top of the water tower, waving her sword above her head frantically. The group of Porphyrians have started to move away from the tower and Julietta risks being spotted at any moment.

'We have to do this,' I say to myself, and to my bump.

I stand upright, using the wall for support, and cup my hands to my mouth.

'HEY, I'M OVER HERE! COME AND GET IT!'

The five helmeted heads turn in my direction. I continue to hurl insults and wave my arms. They take the bait and start to move towards me. To my frustration, they decide to circle the reservoir rather than take the direct route across the walkway. Maybe these creatures are not as stupid as they seem. It takes every ounce of my strength to climb over the wall and drag my lame leg onto the walkway.

'COME ON, YOU UGLY BASTARDS!'

It works, and the Porphyrians turn back and run onto the bridge in an effort to cut me off. Julietta waits until the last one of them has stepped onto the crossing before making her move. I watch in awe as she launches herself off the water tower and rolls out of her landing. The five beasts are too focussed on me to see her sprint up behind them like an assassin.

With her first strike, Julietta thrusts her sword through two heads, skewering them like cherries on a cocktail stick. She uses her foot to prise the sword free then kicks the lifeless bodies aside. One of the Porphyrians turns, but only in time to see her blade bite into his neck. A fourth hurls himself at Julietta and grabs hold of her sword hand. They become locked in a struggle as the remaining Porphyrian continues across the walkway. It's the leader – the one with the horn . . . and a huge axe.

I'm stranded; too injured to run and with no way to defend myself.

'Come on Julietta,' I whisper, willing her to overcome her foe.

But she's too far away with too little time to make up the distance. I can do nothing except snarl at the Porphyrian who is charging towards me. My hands move protectively over my stomach. If this is going to be the end, the creature won't see fear on my face . . .

I brace myself for impact. The colossal beast raises his axe to strike. The weapon pauses in mid-air, and then slips from his grasp. His face contorts with an expression of confusion as he falls onto his knees. When he slumps forwards I can see the bronze sword buried deep into his back. Julietta is twenty yards further down the walkway, standing over a headless corpse. *She threw the sword like a javelin.*

I shuffle forwards and pull the sword free. With a single, merciless blow, I remove the Porphyrian's head.

Julietta jogs the distance, surprised to see me in such a bloodied state.

'You would have made a good medieval warrior,' she says.

I hand her the sword.

'And you would make a good Agent.'

I lean down and take the horn from the dead Porphyrian. The headless torso slips over the side of the walkway and submerges slowly into the swamp-like water.

Julietta rolls her shoulders, like she's just getting warmed up.

'Blow the horn and bring on the rest,' she says. 'I'll take them one at a time on this walkway.'

I'm about to do it when another idea pops into my mind.

'I might have thought of a way to even the odds.'

Chapter 26

Sasha

The shrill sound of the horn fills the air as we stare down our enemy. All around us, twelve Porphyrians sway and drool, waiting for the order to attack. Beyond them, on the wooden stairs which lead into the tower, stands Katalina. It's a hideous version of her I've never seen before. Her fingers have become long, pointed claws and her teeth resemble the canines of a wild beast. If it wasn't for the dyed red hair she'd be completely unrecognisable. On one side of her is her ancestral guard, Razvan – a seven foot monster wielding an impossibly large broadsword. On the other side is Edgar, a man I once trusted, who is holding a revolver. I've faced perilous situations before now, but nothing quite like this.

My mother takes a step forwards, keeping the Athame hidden behind her back.

'When it happens, get on top of that cart,' she says in a low voice.

'When *what* happens?' I ask, panic rising within me.

'This.'

She whips her arm out and points the Athame directly at Katalina. A bolt of blue light shoots from the tip of the blade, blasting aside two Porphyrians as it streaks towards their leader. Katalina's guard reacts by dragging her sharply to the side. The blue light grazes the leathery skin on her shoulder and she howls in pain. My mother curses at her aim which was intended to do so much more than a glancing wound. The neon light hammers into the tower behind Kat, shattering the masonry and sending chunks of rock flying into the air.

Aaron pulls me back towards the cart as the remaining ten Porphyrians close in. I don't want to leave my mother's side, but I know I have to follow her plan.

'Climb up!' he urges me. 'We need to take the higher ground.'

I throw my crossbow up first before hauling myself onto the top of the cart. The baying mob of monsters surrounds us in seconds. Aaron is set upon before he has time to hoist himself up. A Porphyrian lunges at him with a spear, thrusting the barbed tip at his throat. He manages to react in time, blocking the jab with his axe. I pick up the crossbow and take aim at Aaron's attacker.

'No,' he yells, locked in a struggle. 'I've got this!'

He kicks the Porphyrian back and then follows up with his axe, burying the blade into the creature's neck. I flinch at the sight of the gruesome beast as it collapses in a heap of limbs and gore. The other Porphyrians step over the body of their fallen comrade as they advance. I reach out and help Aaron to climb up, preparing to make our stand.

From my elevated position, I can see over the creature's helmeted heads to where my mother is locked in battle. Katalina dives for cover as Razvan moves forward to attack. As he marches closer, my mother unleashes a blue blot from her Athame. The giant Porphyrian takes the full impact on his chest armour. The powerful blow makes him swivel but it's only a momentary setback. He recovers quickly, his breast plate singed black but unbroken. Like a mechanical warrior with impenetrable armour, he continues to advance.

I become distracted as a Porphyrian grabs hold of my ankle and tries to pull me off the cart. If I fall, I'll be devoured before I can so much as scream. I lower my crossbow to within inches of the creature's face.

'Eat this,' I hiss, pulling the trigger and surprising myself with my brutal causticity.

The bolt goes straight through his mouth, spraying me with blood. He slumps forward onto the side of the cart. I place my foot onto his head and extract my one remaining bolt from his skull.

'My mum's in danger,' I shout to Aaron. 'She needs help!'

Aaron is busy warding off more Porphyrians as they try to climb onto the cart.

'Razvan is too heavily armoured for the Athame,' he says. 'We're fighting the wrong enemy. I've got an idea!'

Without warning, he launches off the cart. In a display of impressive athleticism, he jumps over the heads of the bemused Porphyrians. The reach up and try to grab a limb as he flies through the air. He lands behind them and whirls his axe over his head is a show of bravado.

'Hungry?' he asks, taunting the creatures. 'Then come and get me!'

They take the bait and turn their attention away from the cart and towards Aaron. He's impossibly outnumbered. With only one shot, I've got no way of helping him. Instead of engaging them, he turns on his heels and runs towards the centre of the courtyard. The Porphyrians give chase like a pack of hunting dogs. Aaron sprints in the direction of my mother. At the same time, Razvan closes on her with his broadsword raised.

'Ashleigh!' shouts Aaron. 'Switch!'

My mother glances back over her shoulder. She seems to read his intentions immediately. I watch in awe as she rotates and flicks her wrist at the charging Porphyrians. The Athame releases another powerful bolt of light. It flashes past Aaron, narrowly missing him before engulfing the eight remaining creatures. Without the same protective plate armour as Razvan, they are devoured in a neon blast. Green-skinned limbs are torn from bodies and heads roll across the courtyard. As the blue light fades into bright particles of dust, I see Razvan about to bring down his sword.

'MUM!'

My warning shout is too late. She locks eyes with me as the blade descends on her. At the moment of impact, Aaron slides in front of her and raises his weapon. The clash of steel-on-steel rings out as he blocks the mighty strike with his axe. Although he manages to deflect the blow aimed at my mother, the mighty blow sends him reeling sideways. Razvan lowers the visor of his helmet to cover the only exposed part of his body. My mother clutches the Athame, searching for a weakness she can exploit.

Each second passes slowly, dream-like. I'm transfixed on the battle until a movement in my peripheral vision catches my eye. A flash of red. While my mother and Aaron are busy fighting Razvan, Katalina has leapt onto the courtyard. She charges towards them without them having seen her, preparing to spring an ambush from the side. It's typical of Katalina to wait for the moment of distraction before she strikes like a serpent. I raise my crossbow and track her as she dashes towards my mother.

You've got one shot, Sasha. Make it count.

I'm about to pull the trigger when my mother rolls away from Razvan's sword, blocking my target. As she rises to her feet, Katalina pounces onto her back. My mother cries out as the vicious claws dig into her shoulders.

I don't have a clear shot and I can't risk hurting my mother.

Katalina wraps her arms around my mother's neck, the sinews of her muscles tightening. I'm helpless to intervene as my mother falls to her knees, the life being strangled out of her. I jump off the cart and run towards them, hoping to find an angle to shoot. Katalina sees me coming, and smiles.

'Don't worry, Sasha. I won't kill her – I'll just put her to sleep. Her blood is too precious to spill.'

I look to Aaron, who is exchanging blows with Razvan, doing his all just to survive. Nobody else can save my mother. It's all on me.

I take aim, trying to find an exposed limb or shoulder. Katalina shifts her body to align herself behind my mother, forming an impossible target. My mother looks as though she's about to lose consciousness when she does something truly shocking. With barely any room to move her arm, she rotates the Athame and plunges it into her own thigh.

'No!' screams Katalina, horrified at the sight of my mother's blood.

Her reaction is enough to loosen her grip and allow my mother to breathe. She makes the most of the opportunity and hauls Katalina over her shoulder. The Metamorph lands heavily on her back.

She's down, and vulnerable.

I fire the crossbow and watch as the bolt sails towards her. Somehow, Kat reacts in time and flips out of the way. The bolt hammers into the ground in the spot where she was lying half a second ago. My mother groans as she removes the Athame from her leg and points the dripping blade at Katalina.

'There's nowhere left for you to run, Metamorph.'

It's a moment of poetic justice: my mother is about to destroy my father's murderer.

It feels as though the battle has turned.

Until a single gunshot rings out.

My mother drops the Athame as Katalina scampers towards the tower. I move my eyes towards the source of the fire. Edgar is standing on the stone steps, the smoke rising from the nozzle of his gun.

I turn back towards my mother, who collapses to her knees. In one fatal moment, everything has changed.

Chapter 27

Zara

I lower the horn and toss it into the reservoir, watching as it slowly sinks beneath the murky water.

'Are you sure it will call them?' asks Julietta.

I shrug, not exactly giving her the confident affirmation she was looking for. The response, however, is almost immediate. From the direction of Kat's castle we can hear the distant rumble of armoured feet and howling beasts.

'They're coming.'

'Good,' Julietta replies. 'I do not like to be kept waiting.'

She turns and dashes along the walkway, heading towards the water tower beyond the reservoir. I'm left standing on the thin bridge, suddenly feeling very alone and exposed. All around me is a swamp-like expanse of water. I couldn't escape even if I wanted to. I begin to wonder whether my plan will translate from theory to practice. A plan is only as good as its outcome. I would have preferred to have had a vision to reassure me of the end result. Our preparations were made quickly, without the luxury of time to carefully plot our ambush. From experience, the best plans are not usually the ones made in haste.

Julietta moves into place near the water tower and waves to me from her hidden position. I'm sure she's worried that I might pass out at any moment. I give her the thumbs up to let her know that I'm fine. I'm not – my body is trembling and I feel like throwing up. If our plan doesn't work, projectile vomit might be my only defence. My leg is badly cut up from the bear trap and practically useless to me. I'm injured, unarmed and completely vulnerable. I'm also carrying an unborn baby and putting it directly in the line of danger, not for the first time today.

On cue, the baby kicks inside me, almost as though it's reminding me what's at stake. I can't allow myself to dwell on the sheer craziness of it all. We're out of options, and out of time.

When I notice Julietta duck down for cover, I know the Porphyrians are close. But it will all be for nothing if the horn has only summoned a few of them.

I needn't have worried . . .

An army of around fifty Porphyrians comes charging through the trees. I didn't expect so many and I hope our plan still works. At first, they look confused, as though they were expecting to find their comrades. I wave my arms in the air to catch their attention. They approach the edge of the reservoir cautiously.

'Keep coming,' I say under my breath. 'A little closer.'

The Porphyrians gather near the walkway as they decide how many to send against me. I see Julietta slip through the bushes behind them and silently move into position.

This is it.

I hold the handrail on either side and brace myself. Julietta grips her sword in both hands and approaches the water tower. With one mighty swing, she cuts into one of the structure's four rusted legs. The steel doesn't break, but it folds. Some of the Porphyrians turn at the sound of the sword strike. Before they realise what's happened, it's already too late. Under the weight of the container above, the steel pillar collapses. The tower topples over and crushes some of the closest creatures. It's a bonus, but it wasn't the ultimate goal.

Thousands of gallons of water are released in a tidal-like wave. It spills over the Porphyrians who are thrust backwards by the sheer force. I watch with glee as the thrashing creatures are washed into the murky reservoir. The tidal-like wave of water shakes the walkway, almost throwing me over the side. A couple of the Porphyrians manage to cling on but Julietta is quick to follow up and decapitate them.

Within the space of twenty seconds it's all over. The surface of the reservoir settles to its former crusty stillness and everything falls silent. In one swift blow, the enemy has been eradicated. It all seems too good to be true and the pessimist in me always worries when I feel this way.

'We did it,' says Julietta, standing on the walkway with a beaming smile. 'It worked out just like we planned.'

I throw my head back with relief. It's not over, but we've done our part. I start to feel dizzy and black spots cluster in the corner of my vision. It's a premonition: a strong one; an imminent one.

Julietta is walking towards me on the walkway when a hand reaches up and grabs her leg. I try to hobble towards her to help, but it's no use. She loses balance and falls into the reservoir. I can only watch as she is sucked under the surface. A few bubbles rise up. And then nothing.

I open my eyes and snap my head forwards.

'Julietta – stop!'

She gives me a quizzical look.

'Is something wrong?' she asks.

'Please listen to me. Turn around and go back. Don't ask why, just do it. NOW!'

'But you are injured,' she says, pointing to my leg. 'Let me help you to cross.'

It's too late. A slime-covered hand reaches up from the water. The fingers wraps around her ankle in vice-like grip. Julietta stabs her sword over the side of the walkway in an attempt to free herself. I try to limp towards her, hauling my useless body forwards. The bridge sways and Julietta loses balance. At the same time, the submerged Porphyrian yanks sharply. For a brief moment, I lock eyes with Julietta and I see something in hers which I haven't before: resignation. I watch in horror as she tumbles into the reservoir and is pulled under the surface.

I saw it all play out in my vision.

Now I've witnessed it happen for real.

With gritted teeth, I shuffle along the walkway, dragging my injured leg behind me. Every passing second is crucial and I can't waste a moment. In a series of slow, painful movements, I reach the point on the walkway where Julietta disappeared. There's no sign of her except a few air bubbles which rise to the surface. And then nothing.

Seconds pass. And then minutes. I know Julietta is an immortal, but that will count for nothing if she's trapped at the bottom of a swamp. She'll have no way to defend herself against a Porphyrian who has nothing to lose. Even if she somehow survives, I don't have the time – or the ability – to find her.

I slump onto my knees, cursing myself that the premonition didn't give me enough warning. Julietta saved us all so many times. With her last courageous action she wiped out Kat's entire Porphyrian army.

Except that's not going to be her last action.

I grab a broken section of the walkway's handrail and twist it until it breaks free. If I fall into the reservoir, it's game over. But it's a risk I'm willing to take. I lean over the edge and thrust the handrail into the froth at the exact spot where Julietta disappeared. Foot-by-foot, I lower the metal pole, hoping that I'll somehow prod Julietta and provide the lifeline she so desperately needs. If it was anyone else, it would be too late. But Julietta is an Amaranth, and a fighter. She'll never give up and neither will I.

My hands work their way to the end of the pole. I stir it around, moving it slowly like a spoon in soup. *Come on Julietta, just reach out and take hold.*

I feel a tug. Then another one, a stronger one which almost pulls me in. Is it Julietta, or have I found a drowning Porphyrian? It's a chance I'll have to take.

I lean back and haul the handrail out of the murky water, using every last bit of strength within me. My eyes remain locked on the surface. I dare not blink as each inch of the pole is retracted.

A green hand appears and I almost drop the pole. But the skin isn't green; it's just covered in slime.

'Julietta!'

I shout her name as I haul her out of the filthy lake. Somehow, I find the strength to pull her onto the walkway. She rolls onto her back and coughs, expelling a lungful of sludge.

'Are you all right?' I ask her.

'That was unpleasant.' She mutters a few expletives in French before switching back to English. 'Thank you, Zara. You just saved the life of an immortal.'

It's a huge relief to have found her but I can't relax just yet.

Not until the lives of my friends are safe.

Not until we all make it out of here alive.

Chapter 28

Sasha

In a fight against a Metamorph and her army of monsters, it's a single bullet which has turned the battle.

Everyone stops, like time has frozen. Edgar and Katalina look on from the top of the wooden staircase in front of the tower. Aaron and Razvan separate and turn to look at the fallen victim.

I race towards my mother. She's curled up in a foetal position, clutching her stomach.

'Mum, I'm here. Try not to move.'

I press my hand down on top of hers. Blood oozes through the gaps in our merged fingers. She gasps and winces, like she's been winded. But it's worse than that. Much worse.

'Pass me the Athame,' she says with an outstretched bloody hand.

I reach for the small knife and place it in her palm. She wraps her fingers around the handle loosely, barely able to hold on to it. Behind me, the clash of weapons resumes as Aaron and Razvan continue their duel. From across the courtyard I hear the sound of mocking laughter.

My mother presses the Athame's blade to her forehead and then puts it in my hand.

'No,' I protest. 'It's no good to me. I can't use it. I can't do this without you, Mum.'

'Trust me,' she says. 'We'll do it together, but I need you to help. Are you ready?'

I feel anything but ready. The Athame has been a burden to me, a constant reminder of my lack of inherent ability.

'What should I do?' I ask.

She closes her eyes gently, as though she's meditating.

'Clear your mind of all emotion. Take aim and stand strong. Now!'

I whip around and point the Athame towards Katalina. Edgar reacts to my movement and steps forwards with the gun raised. It's quicker for him to squeeze a trigger than it is for me to extend my arm and take aim. He fires and I close my eyes at the sound of the gunshot. When nothing happens, I dare to open them.

My mother is lying next to me, still in a meditative state. I can see a fading trail of blue light tracing a line from the tip of the Athame to Edgar. It has somehow absorbed his bullet before it could reach me. Better still, the bolt of light has struck Edgar's gun-hand, disarming him. He briefly examines his right hand which is reduced to a bloody stump. The sight overwhelms him and he collapses, toppling down the wooden staircase. Katalina howls, abandoning Edgar as she flees inside the tower.

'It worked,' I stammer, hardly able to believe it.

'Six o'clock,' says my mother. I don't understand what she means, until she says, 'Behind you!'

I spin around to face Aaron and Razvan. The giant Porphyrian is distracted by what just happened on the staircase, searching for Katalina through his visor. Aaron takes advantage and swings the axe at him, sending his helmet flying into the air.

'Now!' shouts my mother.

I point the Athame at Razvan's exposed head. Another blast of blue light shoots from the tip of the blade and obliterates the Porphyrian's skull. For a moment, the headless giant remains standing, swaying gently, before finally keeling over.

Aaron punches the air.

'You did it, Sash!'

'I don't know how,' I reply, staring at the Athame in my hand.

My mother rolls onto her back and brings her knees up. Aaron and I gather at either side to support her.

'I can use the Athame remotely,' she says with dry lips. 'But only through someone who I am connected to.'

She rests a shaking hand on to the pendant which is hanging around my neck.

'For many years I poured my heart and soul into this opal stone. You might not have inherited my ability, Sasha, but we have an emotional bond. There were times when I felt it during my captivity and I willed my powers to you.'

My memory recalls those moments like they were yesterday: the battle against Blake at the Tower of London and the time I was buried underground. It was in those moments of extreme emotion – times when I yearned for my mother – that she must have felt it, and reached out to help.

She coughs and her tongue is red.

'We have to get you out of here,' I plead to her. 'You need help.'

'No, my love. It's not finished yet. Your friends are imprisoned in the tower. Katalina is in there too. Save them, and destroy her.'

'But Mum, you've been shot. You're bleeding badly.'

'Don't try to move me,' she replies firmly. 'Take the Athame and go quickly. It's only powerful while I'm conscious. I need to feel it when you want me to transmit my energy.'

It feels like information overload at a time when I'm least able to cope.

'How do I do that?' I ask her.

'Channel your emotions in the most positive way you can. Just remember, when fighting monsters be careful not to become one yourself. You can do this, Sasha. I believe in you.'

I turn to Aaron; not for support, but to ask him to go against all of his instincts.

'I can do this. Please stay with her.'

He looks at me and I know exactly how he feels.

'Sash, don't ask me to let you go in there alone. I have to protect you – it's the only thing I'm any good at. It's the only thing that matters to me.'

He doesn't want to let me go, just like I don't want to leave him.

'Please, Aaron. Do this one thing for me. I promise I'll make it back to you.'

I can see the torment in his eyes. He opens his mouth but can't seem to find the words, or can't bring himself to say them. Instead, he gives me a small nod, which is all I need.

'Look after my mother,' I ask him. 'Keep her alive. I'll be back as soon as I can.'

He places his hand over my hand as it clutches on to the Athame.

'*Come back to me,*' he says, tears forming in his eyes.

'I promise I will.'

I stand up and walk away from him, knowing it's a promise I can't keep.

+ + +

Each step feels heavy, as though I'm weighed down with worry. Zara and Julietta are out there, left to face a horde of Porphyrians. My mother is badly injured and bleeding out. The portal will reopen in fifteen minutes and the only hope of saving my mother is to get her home through it. I push my emotions to the side and force myself to focus on the task at hand.

Save Dexter and Axel.

Find Menzies Blake and the coin he possesses which will get us home.

Kill Katalina.

Any one of those acts is challenging in isolation. Combine them and they become much harder to achieve. Throw in the fact I only have a matter of minutes and they amount to being almost impossible. That's never stopped me before.

I approach the tower but avoid the stairs, where the body of Edgar is laid at the bottom. Instead, I enter through the tunnel at the side. This is where the prison cells are said to be and it's where I'll most likely find Dexter.

The tunnel walls are lined with candles which give off a shadowy light. I move quickly but cautiously, ready for anything that might jump out on me. The Athame is in my left hand and the crossbow is in my right. My last shot missed, but I was able to retrieve the bolt. It feels good to have a weapon in each hand, but they're no replacement for my friends. After living for so long as a loner, I never thought I'd miss anyone so much as I do right now.

The tunnel takes a left turn, following the square outer wall of the tower. I walk past several closed doors on either side, each with barred windows. I'm forced to rise up on my tiptoes just to see inside. A sound from behind makes me jump and I almost fire the crossbow. When I turn, I realise that it's just a rat. I notice that the Athame's blade has a faint glow. *My emotion is the trigger to my mother. I have to control my feelings and harness them only when I need them most.*

'Dexter, are you here?'

I whisper shout his name as I move from chamber to chamber, each one as silent and empty as the last. As I near the end of the corridor, one room in particular draws my attention. The door is wide open and I can see inside. There's a bed and the sheets are stained with blood. Something terrible has happened in here and I dread to think what. If Aaron was with me, he could use his Empath senses to read the room and its dark history. It might have been used as a jail cell over the centuries, but those blood stains are fresh.

If Dexter isn't down here in the cells, there's one other place he could be. My mother described the oubliette where she was kept for all those years. She described it as being accessed from a higher level within the main tower.

I reach the end of a corridor and ascend up a spiral staircase. My steps echo upwards and there's little I can do to dampen the sound. If Katalina is on a higher floor she will surely hear me coming. I stop to catch my breath on a landing, taking a moment to inhale the fresh air coming in through a small arched opening. The window looks out over some stables on the opposite side of the courtyard. As I lean my head outside, I notice something lying on the ground: it's the body of a dog.

Axel.

I feel a sudden pang of sorrow for the poor dog, immediately followed by concern for Dexter. Axel was his soulmate; they would never leave each other's side. The Athame's blade glows bright blue as my emotions peak and I force myself to stay calm. There will be a time to grieve for Axel later. Right now, I have to concentrate on my mission. With a deep breath, and a clear mind, I continue up the stairs.

I pass through several dark floors with sparse furnishings. One of the eerie rooms has an open sarcophagus and I steel myself to check inside only to find it empty. When I return to the spiral staircase, an orange glow from above confirms my hunch: the things I'm looking for are on the top floor and I must face them all together.

I creep up the final few stairs. From a crouched position, I peer around the corner. My blood turns cold when I see Katalina at the far end of the room. She's searching through a cabinet of glass vials, frantically checking each one before tossing it to the ground.

'There's no Witch blood left,' she mutters to herself, panic in her voice. 'I've ran out. That idiot Edgar has destroyed my supply.'

She's referring to my mother and I have to fight to contain my rising anger. Instead, I scan the rest of the room. I can't see any sign of Dexter, but there seems to be a small opening in the centre of the floor. *The oubliette.*

I withdraw and lean back against the wall, preparing myself for what I have to do. Katalina is like a wounded animal: she's injured, desperate and at her most dangerous. The moment I reveal myself, she will charge at me. I'll only get one chance to destroy her.

I carefully place the crossbow on the floor. My survival now depends on the Athame, this small knife which contains an otherworldly power. I press it to my forehead, just as my mother did. *Please work for me.*

In one fluid movement, I spin from the wall and into the doorway. My stance is side on, with the Athame extended and pointed at the target. Katalina turns, her eyes growing as she fixes on the tip of the blue blade. I throw open the mental gate which has been holding back all my recent emotions: concern for my mother and Dexter, sorrow for Axel, hatred for the Metamorph that has caused so much pain. *Don't become the monster.* I hold back the hatred, allowing the rest to flow through my body. The Athame glows a bright blue and Katalina is frozen in my crosshairs. Then something appears in my peripheral vision which distracts me. When I realise what it is, the controlled flow of my emotions is immediately broken.

Menzies Blake walks into the centre of the room carrying Dexter in his arms. He looks at me with pure fire in his eyes.

'Sasha Hunter – you killed my son.'

Chapter 29

Sasha

Blake stands in the space between me and Katalina, unwittingly providing her with a human shield. He cradles his son, whose head is flopped back. I can tell from the grey pallor of Dexter's skin that the life has been drained from him. My friend is gone. I feel completely crushed and no longer able to control the swell of emotions building inside me. A tear forms in the corner of my eye and I try to blink it away. It's only when I meet Blake's stare that I notice the burning hatred in his face. His eyes move down and fix on the blade of the Athame. That's when his last words finally sink in. *He thinks I killed Dexter.*

Katalina moves to the side and peers over Blake's shoulder, a wicked smile on her lips. I can't destroy her until I can regain control over my emotions. I can't destroy her while Blake is standing in the way.

'Dexter was my friend,' I say to him, lowering the Athame. 'Whatever she told you, it's a lie.'

Blake shakes his head furiously, his nostrils flaring.

'You're the liar!' he shouts, spraying spittle. 'With his dying words, Dexter explained to me exactly what happened. How you never accepted him because he was my son.'

He tilts Dexter's body to reveal the bloody wound on his stomach. My throat tightens and I have to force myself to stay strong and not break down at the sight of my friend. I dip my head and squeeze my eyes closed in an effort to force the vision away. It won't change what's happened. Dexter is dead.

Blake moves closer, threatening me with his proximity.

'My son was everything to me and you've taken that away.'

I force myself to respond but when I speak the words come out choked.

'I was nothing but a friend to Dexter.'

'LIAR,' he roars. 'Dexter told me himself. He told me that YOU stabbed him.'

I struggle to process the accusation; the thought that Dexter himself blamed me. It seems impossible. He must surely have been drugged or influenced somehow. I shake my head in denial and dismay. Blake has already made his mind up about what happened and there's no changing it. He'll never accept how close my friendship with Dexter was. None of it matters right now. All I know is that he's gone and his father blames me. I can't alter that, but I can finish what I came here to do.

I try to angle my head to see past Blake. In my prolonged moment of shock, Katalina has disappeared. I scan the room, desperately searching for her.

'LOOK AT ME,' screams Blake, his face turning purple with rage.

I take several small backwards steps, all the time maintaining eye contact. The Athame is by my side but it feels cold and useless. *I've lost control of my emotions and I've lost control of the Athame.* I need to retrieve the crossbow and at least give myself some form of protection.

With another backwards step I hit something solid. I turn around, hoping that I've made it to the door frame. Katalina is standing inches away from me, holding the crossbow. Her finger is resting on the trigger and the steel tip of the bolt is pointed directly at my heart.

She tilts her head and smiles with a sickening serenity.

'I want you to know that after I kill you, I will morph into your form. Your mother and boyfriend won't realise that I'm not you until it's too late. I will cut Aaron's throat and watch him bleed out. In your mother's case, I'll be sure not to waste any of her blood. Unlike yours, it won't be a quick death. You Agents are all the same: your obsession with the paranormal world is your undoing. I will destroy every last one of you.'

I can't beat her to the draw. If I try to raise the Athame, she'll pull the trigger.

If this is my last moment, I refuse to let it be one of fear or submission. I stare her down, the crimson burning in my eyes. *I won't become the monster.*

My hand suddenly feels hot.

The Athame is primed.

An unexpected bolt of blue light shoots from the tip of the blade and blasts onto the floor. Several flagstones crack and sharp bits of rock fly into the air. Katalina flinches and is thrown off balance. She tries to fire the crossbow but the bolt flies wildly upwards and ricochets off the ceiling. A wide crevasse opens up in the floor between us. Katalina tries to swipe at my face but she can't reach me. I lift the Athame to strike but she leaps onto the wall and then springs off, somersaulting over my head.

I twist on the spot, the blade of the Athame extended as I search for her.

Stay calm. Stay in control.

She appears behind Blake, once more using him as cover. My line of sight is blocked and I can't get a clear shot. I can only watch as Katalina walks up behind him with her claws raised. Blake has his head nestled into his son as he holds him, too lost in grief to realise what's happening. She's used him all along and now she's about to dispose of him. Her actions reflect her words: '*I will destroy every last one of you.*'

I point the Athame at Katalina, doing my best to aim at her rather than Blake. A bolt of blue neon light shoots from the tip. It sears past Blake, scorching his shoulder as it passes, causing him to drop Dexter. Katalina doesn't see the strike coming. The blue light hits her on the chest. Unlike the Porphyrians, she isn't obliterated upon impact. Her body seems stronger, her skin thicker, like leather armour. She tries to fight it, swiping at the light with her claws. *I'm not the monster, Katalina, you are.* I keep the light trained on her until it knocks her down. She slides across the floor, scrabbling against the stone slabs with her claws. The opening of the oubliette gapes like a hungry mouth, ready to swallow. She senses where she's headed and unleashes a guttural scream. With a final push, I power her into the dark hole. Her screams fade as she tumbles down the long shaft. It's cut short when she hits the bottom to the sound of bones shattering.

The blue light retracts into the blade and the Athame returns to its dull form.

Kat's gone.

I did it.

I destroyed the Metamorph.

A voice calls up from the courtyard: It's Aaron.

'Sasha, come quickly!'

From grief to jubilation and back to the cold reality of my mother's perilous condition. She helped me to destroy Katalina, but at what cost? I'm about to leave when I remember something important: Blake has the coin we need to return home. My mother needs urgent medical attention – it's vital that we get her back to

London as quickly as possible, and the only way to do that is through the portal.

I approach Blake cautiously as he kneels sobbing over the body of his son.

'Dexter came here to help us,' I say to him in a soft, sympathetic tone. 'He helped to rescue my mother but now she's dying. I need to get her back through the portal. If I could just—'

'LIAR!' he screams, his head shaking with rage.

I back off as he rises up. A vein is throbbing in his neck. I retreat to the door as he throws out his arms and begins to chant in an ancient language. He is embracing the darker side within himself, the part of him which holds otherworldly powers.

Blake is becoming the Necromancer.

The floor starts to vibrate and it feels like the entire tower is shaking. Blake throws his head back and releases a thunderous roar. At the same time, black ghostly shapes shoot out of the oubliette. They smash against the ceiling, sending chunks of stone crashing down.

I turn and run, scrambling down the spiral staircase two steps at a time. The walls start to crack and bits of masonry showers down from above. I can hear Blake on the stairs behind me but I dare not look back. My only thought is to get to my mother.

A dark shape flies past me and forms a barrier on the stairs. I skid to a halt as the shape takes a menacing form. It becomes a translucent skeleton, with shackles on its ankles and wrists. Blake is summoning the ghost of prisoners and sending them to stop me.

Adrenaline overpowers fear. I point the Athame and focus my emotion. A small blue orb flicks from the blade. It's barely enough to eradicate the skeleton's left arm, allowing me to slide past as its jaws snap at me.

The Athame is losing its power . . . my mother is dying.

I race from the spiral stairs and onto the corridor, gasping for air. A freezing blast of wind follows me as I tear along the passage.

I can hear a destructive rumble behind me, like the sound of floors and ceilings collapsing. When I turn a corner, I can see the torchlight of the courtyard.

Keep running.

Keep breathing.

I sprint out through the tunnel and barely avoid being crushed by a falling keystone in the archway. Aaron stands up as he sees me approaching but his attention quickly moves to the rupturing tower behind me.

'Run, Sash!' He shouts, beckoning me desperately. 'Don't look back!'

He picks up my mother and hurries towards the portcullis. A patch of dark red marks the spot where she's been laid. She looks limp in his arms, her limbs dangling freely. I can hear the crashing of falling stones behind me. If I didn't know otherwise, I'd believe an earthquake was happening.

Aaron gently places my mother on the ground as he starts to pull on the chains to raise the portcullis. I fall to my knees upon reaching her. She looks as pale as a ghost, translucent almost.

'Mum, can you hear me? Mum, please stay with me.'

My emotions can no longer be contained. I grab her by the shoulders and try to rouse her. A dark shape begins to form next to me, its shadow towering over us. My mother half-opens her eyes, places a weak hand on top of mine and lifts the Athame. A thin bolt of blue light disintegrates the malevolent spirit.

'Take me home,' she says, her voice so weak I can barely hear it.

Aaron manages to raise the portcullis just enough for us to slide under.

'Let's go!' he shouts, scooping up my mother in his arms.

I dare to glance back before I follow him and duck under the gateway. A purple haze has engulfed the top of the tower which has now started to crumble. Menzies Blake is standing on the wooden stairs, fearless of the rocks falling down around him. He points at me and screams.

'You can try and run, Sasha, but you'll never leave this place alive!'

He holds up a small, round object; it's the ancient coin we need to pass through the portal. I watch in despair as he places it on his tongue.

Then swallows it.

Chapter 30

Sasha

'Come on, Sasha!' shouts Aaron from the other side of the portcullis. 'Move!'

Every fibre within me wants to turn and run. Dexter is dead. Katalina has been destroyed. My mother desperately needs a hospital. There's not a single reason to dwell a moment longer in this awful place. But Blake has the coin and without it we can't get home.

I stare at the Necromancer as he throws out his arms once more and begins to chant. Despite his misguided fury towards me, I have no desire to kill Blake. If anything, I feel sorry for him. We share the same loss, except that mine has produced sorrow while his has manifested in blind, murderous hatred.

A swirling dark cloud whips around Blake. Demonic figures form as the black mist stretches out like a tornado, extinguishing the torches around the edge of the courtyard.

I feel a strong hand grip me and drag me underneath the portcullis.

'Sash, we have to go,' urges Aaron, raising his voice to compete with the howling wind. 'We're running out of time.'

He thrusts his arm through a gap in the bars and releases the crank to send the portcullis crashing down behind us.

'We can't leave,' I say to him. 'Not yet.'

In the chaos of the storm, my protests are ignored. Aaron gathers my mother in his arms and starts to run away from the gatehouse. I give chase, doing my best to catch up with him. If I can just tell him about Blake swallowing the coin then maybe there's still time to do something. I know Blake won't give it up voluntarily, but if we can somehow make him regurgitate it . . .

A clap of thunder makes me duck instinctively. When I turn around, I'm shocked to see that the gatehouse has been obliterated. A huge hole has been blown in the portcullis, leaving twisted iron bars curled back.

'Sasha!' shouts Aaron, a hundred yards ahead of me. 'Don't stop!'

I try to yell to him but my voice is carried away by the violent wind. It feels like Blake has taken control of nature and is trying to use it to consume us.

My legs burn as I try to make up the distance. Aaron is much further along the track, the weight of my mother not slowing him down. I'm exhausted from my battle against Katalina – drained; emotionally and physically. My body feels cumbersome, like an old machine which is seizing up. I hear a loud crack to my left and see a movement in the trees. Or rather, the movement *of* a tree. I'm forced to dive forwards as a giant trunk comes crashing down, just inches away from crushing me. One of its thick branches slams against my neck and I go dizzy.

When I look ahead, I can see figures in the distance. Has Blake summoned more spirits to block off our escape? No, it's not that. I blink to make sure what I'm seeing isn't a vision. It's Zara and Julietta. I feel so thankful that they made it through. Aaron runs up to them and hands over my mother before turning sharply and sprinting back towards me. His eyes are wide and terrified, fixed on the chaos unfolding beyond the fallen tree trunk. He grabs me by the elbow and pulls me to my feet.

'Aaron, wait. We need Blake.'

I'm unsteady and lightheaded. Aaron senses my condition and picks me up, throwing me over his shoulder.

'Trust me, we don't want anything to do with Blake right now.'

I try to mutter an explanation but my words come out slurred. I'm concussed. It's a struggle just to hang on to consciousness.

Aaron passes me over to Zara and Julietta, who each place an arm underneath my armpits. He picks up my mother once more and leads the way, desperate to flee from our crazed pursuer. As my vision fades in and out, I'm vaguely aware of us crossing the bridge. Voices whisper in my ear.

Keep moving, Sasha.
Hang on, we're nearly there.
You'll never leave this place alive.

That last voice was Menzies Blake, invading my thoughts like a sinister, nightmarish voice.

We come to a stop and I hear Aaron's familiar voice again.

'Look, the portal!' he says, pointing at the black oblong shape which has appeared between two trees. 'Wait here while I check it out.'

He dashes towards it, always the first to throw himself into potential danger. I try to murmur a warning but my words don't form. Maybe Blake was bluffing. Maybe we don't need one of his ancient coins. It wouldn't be the first time he's lied to us or tried to control us with his mind games. I feel a sense of hope as Aaron nears the portal. When he tries to step through it, a long skeletal hand reaches out with an open palm. *It wants the coin.* Aaron stops, unsure what to do. The fingers of the hand close and Aaron is thrust backwards by a powerful blast which sends him tumbling towards us.

Julietta draws her sword, a perplexed look on her face.

'What on God's Earth is that?' she asks.

I muster enough clarity to speak, to tell them all the bad news.

'We need an old coin for the Ferryman. Blake has it but he swallowed it.'

Zara turns around on a stiff leg which has been strapped to a makeshift splint. She is bloody and beaten, in as bad shape as I've ever seen her. In all the dire situations we've faced, Zara has remained resolute. Now, in response to my words, she looks truly defeated.

'Then it's over,' she says.

Her hands rest on her stomach and she dips her head. The air around us seems to drop several degrees in temperature. I crawl next to my mother and cling onto her as the wind becomes louder and stronger. *Blake is coming, and there's nowhere to run.* Aaron crouches next to me and wraps his arms around us. If this is how it ends, then at least we're all together.

'You need an old coin?' asks Julietta. 'Is three hundred years old enough?'

She ruffles inside a small pouch and produces a pale yellow coin, a mixture of silver and copper. It seems incredibly lucky until I remember that Julietta is an immortal who has lived through many ages.

'It's exactly what we need,' I confirm.

Aaron picks up my mother and drags me towards the portal. Zara hobbles alongside us, glancing back nervously over her shoulder. I watch as Julietta tosses the coin into the black doorway. I hold my breath, praying that it will work. The skeletal hand reaches out and catches it, then beckons us in with a long bony finger.

The stern of The Ferryman's boat emerges from the darkness of the portal. We climb aboard hastily and I take a seat at the back.

As the portal begins to close behind us, I stare out into the forest. The black doorway retracts but not before I catch a glimpse of someone in the distance.

A man running through the trees with murderous intent.

Menzies Blake reaches for me, his eyes on fire.

+ + +

Sheer and total darkness. Followed by a light so bright it's impossible to see. When it dies, I'm able to open my eyes and look around. We're back in the Tyburn tunnel.

Aaron and Julietta help each of us to climb out of the boat and onto the stone jetty. I turn just in time to see the bow retract into the portal, disappearing along with the hooded, skeletal Ferryman. The portal dissolves and we're left standing alone. In the seconds that have passed, we've travelled hundreds of miles from the forest in Romania back to the tunnels beneath the streets of London.

'We're home,' says Aaron. 'Now let's get Ashleigh to a Doctor.'

My mother is pale and weak, but she's conscious.

'It's Agent Hunter Senior, to you,' she mumbles.

Her faint smile is all I need to know that she's still with us, still fighting.

Julietta peers across the subterranean river where the portal had just been moments earlier.

'Can Blake follow us?' she asks, one hand poised to draw her sword.

'No, not yet,' I reply. 'He swallowed the coin he needs.'

'Good,' replies Aaron. 'It's a shame he didn't choke on it.'

Zara limps towards my mother, resting her palm on her forehead to check her temperature.

'We can worry about Blake later. Right now, we need a hospital.'

It's so typical of Zara to worry about everyone but herself and I'm touched by her concern for someone she barely knows. I hold my mother's hand as Aaron carries her out of the tunnel. Once at street level, Zara hails a taxi. My mother stares at the buildings and cars around her, taking in the strange sights with wide eyes.

'Hello London,' she says. 'I'm back.'

Chapter 31

Sasha

Zara is kept in the hospital overnight but it's another three days before they release my mother. When I go to pick her up with Aaron, she's being interviewed by the Police. I wait outside her room, pacing the corridor nervously. Since our arrival back in London, my only concern has been for my mother's wellbeing. Every day she looked a little better and every day my worries eased. I never considered the possible complications with the Police.

'Calm down Sasha,' says Aaron, handing me a plastic cup of coffee.

'You think caffeine will help me to do that?'

It's a harsh response, and I apologise as I take the hot drink off him.

'Your mother is resourceful,' he says. 'She'll find a way to explain things.'

He's right about that. In fact, Aaron has spent more time with my mother in the last couple of days than I have in the last six years. Despite his reassurance, I'm still on edge.

'She's been missing and now she turns up at a hospital with a gunshot wound. That's some explaining.'

The door opens and two police officers walk out of my mother's room. One of them gives me a lingering glance before flipping closed an empty notebook and walking off.

'Told you!' says Aaron.

I dash into the room and hug my mother. It's great to finally see her in clean clothes and smell her freshly washed hair. The pain of my father's death will never leave me and it's been compounded by the loss of Dexter and Axel. Maybe, in time, I can learn to accept what happened to them and remember them fondly. Right now, the pain is raw, like an open wound. All I can do is be thankful that my mother is back in my life.

'I hate hospitals,' she says as she strokes my hair. 'Take me home.'

I pull away from her, suddenly remembering that this is one of the many things I haven't told her.

'Home is . . . an old, dingy office in West London,' I say, gingerly.

She laughs, like it's of no particular importance.

'Home is where your loved ones are,' she says.

I couldn't agree more.

I repeat her words as we climb the stairs inside the grim office building. When I open the door, I'm greeted by the smell of a roast dinner. I've never smelled anything so good. To my surprise, Aaron's mother has prepared a meal for us all with the help of Zara and Julietta. Aaron seems more stunned than anyone.

'Mum, I didn't know you had it in you!'

Janet clips him around the head with a dish cloth.

'Make yourself useful and lay the table, Aaron.'

I fix a drink for my mother as Zara carves the meat.

'Have you got a moment?' she asks.

We slip away and into one of the makeshift bedrooms, leaving Janet to play the willing role of host. As soon as we have some privacy, I notice Zara's expression change. I've know her well enough to sense when something is bothering her.

'What's up?' I ask.

'I managed to finish up some research over the last few days. Julietta was a big help – her knowledge is vast and I might not have cracked it without her. I tried to convince her to join us but she told me that it's not the way of an Amaranth. She's leaving us tonight.'

It's sad news but I'm not completely shocked.

'I like Julietta, but I recognise a loner when I see one. Maybe we should make the most of it while she's here. Come on, we'll miss dinner.'

'Wait,' says Zara. 'That's not what I wanted to tell you. There are two things you need to know. The first is about me.'

Her hand moves down and rests on her stomach. I notice the bump on her belly for the first time. Her expression answers my question before I even ask it.

'You're pregnant?'

It seems ridiculous to think she has carried a baby throughout our entire ordeal in Romania.

'It's Lou's.'

Her words stun me and I have no idea how to feel. As my thoughts clear, I realise that a part of my father will now live on – not just in me, but in the sibling I'll soon have. And I couldn't think of a better person to bring my sibling into this world.

'I'm so happy for you,' I say as I hug her. 'I've always wanted a sister . . . or a brother!'

For some reason, Zara is rigid and doesn't reflect my happiness. She takes my hand and grips it tightly.

'Sasha, the next thing you need to know is about you. My research was about your condition – *your eyes*. You might want to sit down for this.'

I take a seat on the edge of the bed alongside her.

'Okay, so you've got my full attention.'

Zara inhales deeply, like what she's about to say requires a lot of breath.

'I've cross-checked everything and ruled out all other possibilities. I'm certain that the crimson in your eyes is indicative of conflicting inherent abilities, good powers warring with bad to cancel each other out.'

'But my mother is a White Witch and my father was a Clairist. Why would those abilities clash?'

'They shouldn't and that's where my research seemed flawed. I almost dismissed it until Julietta explained how she'd seen the same condition once before.'

I move forwards, perching myself on the edge of the bed.

'Really? Who had it, and what happened to them?'

'It was a long time ago but let's just say it didn't work out well.'

'Zara, you've got to tell me more. I need to know!'

She dips her head evasively.

'It can't come from me. There's something else I discovered, something very serious. You need to speak to your mother, Sasha. She should be the one to tell you.'

I want to press Zara further but she stands up and walks out of the room. I'm left poised on the edge of the bed, none the wiser, but a lot more worried.

As we sit around the table and eat dinner, I can't think of anything else. Zara avoids my gaze. The news she shared of her pregnancy has been quickly overshadowed by something that is troubling her. Something about me. Whatever information she's discovered, it's clearly too sensitive to come from anyone other than my mother. I'm so glad to have her home and on the mend but after so long away it feels as though our relationship has been rebooted. She left me as a little girl and she's returned when I'm a young woman.

Aaron places his hand on mine underneath the table.

'Is everything okay, Sash?'

When I nod and smile he knows it isn't, but he also knows enough not to probe any further.

I try to bury my nagging concerns. During the meal, we raise a toast to absent friends. It's a sobering moment which reminds us all of how dangerous our lives are. I close my eyes and picture my father, Dexter and Axel. I hope they're in a better place, looking down on us with pride. Although I never had them for long enough in my life, I'll never forget them or what they did for me.

The mood is lightened when Aaron drops a cake on his way to the table, and then proceeds to pick it up and eat it. We finish the meal with coffees and say our goodbyes to Julietta.

'Do you really have to go?' asks Zara. 'London is a great city to explore if you fancy sticking around for a while.'

'I have been here before,' replies Julietta. 'It was over a century ago and it looked a little different.'

Aaron's mother looks understandably perplexed by her comment.

'Long story,' he says to her. 'I'll explain over what's left of dessert.'

I give Julietta a hug and thank her for all of her help. As I wrap my arm around her, I can feel the sword sheathed underneath her leather jacket.

'Where will you go?' I ask her.

'Wherever evil is lurking,' she replies. 'We'll always be on the same side, Sasha. Keep up the good work. Maybe our paths will cross again one day.'

I hope so.

It's not until later in the evening when I finally get a chance to speak to my mother. She excuses herself to retire to bed and I take the opportunity to follow her. Zara and Aaron watch with serious expressions as I pass by them to leave the room.

I catch up with my mother in the corridor.

'Mum, I need to talk to you.'

'Hey Sasha,' she says with a weak voice and tired eyes. 'I know we've got a lot to catch up on. Can it wait until the morning?'

I'm about to turn away and resign myself to a sleepless night. The younger me would have done that, stewing alone in my self-made anxiety. I'm not that person anymore.

'I'm sorry, Mum, but it's really important.'

She leads me into the small room at the back of the building where a camp bed has been prepared for her. The space feels claustrophobic, with barely enough room to stand and face each other.

'What's on your mind, Sasha?'

I choose my words carefully and try to relate what Zara explained without offloading on my mother.

'Zara has been researching my eye condition for some time. She told me that the crimson glint indicates conflicting abilities – good fighting bad but cancelling each other out. She also told me there was something else she discovered, something I need to talk to you about.'

My mother's expression hardens, like when someone is about to break bad news but doesn't quite know how.

'Sash, there's something you need to know. Something very serious. I planned to tell you one day, as soon as you were old enough to understand. It's about your father.'

I swallow hard. It's made difficult because of the lump in my throat.

'What about him?'

'Lou was the finest man I ever knew. He was the best father anyone could ever wish for.'

I don't need the preamble; I just want the truth.

'I know that, Mum. What are you trying to tell me?'

She takes a deep breath and a prolonged blink.

'He wasn't your biological father.'

The news rocks me to my core. My mother reaches out to steady me, a look of concern on her face.

This should have been about me. Instead, I've been given news about my deceased father that I never expected. Dad and I were always so different, but I never doubted that he was my real father. We had a bond that only a father and daughter can share. I try to remain calm as I work through the shock and denial.

'Then who is my real father?'

My words come out in a grainy whisper. I feel numb, and suddenly empty.

'You need to know that it happened before I met Lou.' My mother looks away, like she's embarrassed. 'Lou understood and accepted you as his own. Your real father doesn't know and I kept it from him to protect you.'

'Mum, if you know, just tell me, please.'

She takes in a long breath and looks nervous, like her words might shatter me.

'Your father is Menzies Blake.'

Epilogue

Menzies Blake

My life, as I know it, is over. I gaze vacantly out of the train window, staring at the snow-glazed mountains of Austria as I pass through the third country in as many days. This traditional means of transport is laborious but necessary. It gives me an unwanted amount of time to reflect, but a much needed amount of time to recover. The pain in my shoulder has been numbed by medication but it can't do anything to ease the pain in my heart.

I hear a knock on the cabin door and turn stiffly as it opens.

'Can I get you any refreshments, Sir?'

I shake my head and wave away the intrusive waiter. The door swings closed, but not fully. When it reopens, the silhouette outline of a large-framed man enters the cabin.

Edgar lowers himself gingerly into the seat opposite.

'We need to change trains in Vienna. From there, it's an overnight route direct to Geneva.' He opens the window and lights a cigar, ignoring the 'no smoking' sign on the wall. 'Do you want to run through the cover story again? It needs to be watertight.'

He blows smoke, which fills the cabin.

'My son is dead,' I reply. 'I don't care about The Agency.'

Edgar nods solemnly but his momentary respect doesn't last long.

'You should. They are your only hope of freedom. Without their protection, you'll be arrested and returned to Cane Hill Asylum. Only this time, you won't have any Agents rushing to break you out.'

His warnings barely register. I'm an empty shell; a used bullet, drained of its explosive power. I've become a different person to the one who travelled to Romania with only the best of intentions. Or maybe that person wasn't the real me; maybe that was just a myth I created to wear as a mask. It leaves me to wonder if that's how all people are: two-sided.

'I have no freedom. I'm a prisoner of grief, and I will be for the rest of this miserable life.'

Edgar leans forward, resting his bearded chin on the balled fist of his one good hand.

'It doesn't have to be that way. The Agency will accept my version of events of what happened in Romania. It was my mistake to recruit Katalina. She was powerful but dangerous and out of control, like a forest wildfire. I've come to learn that you can only trust your oldest of friends. You could have left me to die in Romania but you came back for me. Now it's my turn to help you. Vengeance will set you free, Menzies.'

I turn away from him and lean my head against the cold window. Edgar might be my only friend on the planet but right now I can barely stand his company. Maybe it's because I know he's right. The Necromancer within me is most powerful when my emotions are unleashed. When I relive the surge of power I experienced in the Romanian forest, the tips of my fingers tingle. *It's inside me; I only need let it out.*

My thoughts always return to the same place. While I'm crushed with grief, Sasha Hunter is out there somewhere, reunited with her mother, happy amongst her friends. On the surface, she presents herself as an innocent young girl, struggling to come to terms with herself and the newly discovered underworld around her. But I've seen her other side. The darker side.

She betrayed and killed my son.

I have only one thing left to do with this life.

Sasha Hunter, her mother, and her friends, must die.

A note from the author

Thanks for taking the time to read PORPHYRIA. I hoped you enjoyed this next instalment of the DYSTOPIA series. I have more plans for this series: The next book, MEGALOMANIA, is scheduled for release in 2018. You can get a sneak peek cover reveal on the next page.

I made this book available at no profit to me, set at the lowest possible price on Amazon for my loyal readers who have enjoyed the previous novels in this series. In return, there are a few quick and simple things you can do for me:

Tell me what you liked/disliked – My inbox is always open to feedback (info@anthonyergo.com)

Leave a review on Amazon and Goodreads – Nothing is more important to an author

Tell a friend – A recommendation from you is worth a hundred paid ads from me

I have more plans for 2018 so watch this space! Until then, keep firing that imagination and never give up on enjoying good stories in whatever form they take.

Best wishes,

Anthony Ergo

The next instalment of the DYSTOPIA series . . .

MEGALOMANIA

Anthony Ergo

Printed in Poland
by Amazon Fulfillment
Poland Sp. z o.o., Wrocław